As it is

Omar Zemin

Ukiyoto Publishing

All global publishing rights are held by

Ukiyoto Publishing

Published in 2024

Content Copyright © Ameen Adil

ISBN 9789364948050

All rights reserved.
No part of this publication may be reproduced,
transmitted, or stored in a retrieval system, in any
form by any means, electronic, mechanical,
photocopying, recording or otherwise, without the
prior permission of the publisher.

The moral rights of the author have been asserted.

This is a work of fiction. Names, characters, businesses, places, events, locales, and incidents are either the products of the author's imagination or used in a fictitious manner. Any resemblance to actual persons, living or dead, or actual events is purely coincidental.

This book is sold subject to the condition that it shall not by way of trade or otherwise, be lent, resold, hired out or otherwise circulated, without the publisher's prior consent, in any form of binding or cover other than that in which it is published.

www.ukiyoto.com

Contents

Prologue	1
Chapter 1	5
Chapter 2	12
Chapter 3	89
Chapter 4	137
Chapter 5	165
Chapter 6	201
Chapter 7	251
Chapter 8	270
Chapter 9	303
Chapter 10	317
About the Author	*335*

Prologue

The wisest man is he who can define and comprehend Love in all its totality and purity. We are surrounded by love all over; the world is full of life, and love is the affirmation that keeps it going, for there is no energy greater than love. The amount of love we yield into the universe, the universe rewards us with material and spiritual wealth.

Nothing is free, everything is accounted for.

Love transcends space and time; miracles are the direct result of a great love where the heart has awakened in awe of its creator, or in some people's view, the supreme knowledge or mother nature. It is the heart that loves, because the heart is our connection to our soul whilst we live in this temporary abode.

The word 'Love' itself has many connotations because love gets intrinsically attached to your very being and makes it a very personal experience.

"Yes, but you still haven't explained what love is. Is it just a feeling or an emotion?" Asked Amir.

Love is Magic! It comes out of nothing, born out of nothing. It is not created from anything or any process. Love can exist singularly, on its own. It is not a mixture of emotions or feelings. If in mathematics love is the zero, it nullifies all other emotions and feelings and stands alone.

"Interesting… how about in a religious or spiritual context? What has love to do with spirituality?"

Out of all beings and forms of life on earth, it is the human being who has the highest capacity to love. That is where we stand out and overcome all competition as the dominant species on the earth, or in the universe, for that matter. Of all forms of love, the most enchanting form of love for the human being is the love for his or her creator, because when we love this Great force, it loves us back. Imagine the magnitude of this love. The cognizance that there is a greater force controlling our lives and governing the functioning of the universe leads man into a journey of discovery in thirst of answers to his curiosity and a search for that great force that he has fallen in love with, desires to know, and get as nigh as possible to. The force is present everywhere in nature, even if only in essence.

This is where religion comes into being, for the great prophets and philosophers through all ages of history were magnanimous lovers with beautiful hearts of orectic nature. This flowage of the heart led them in search of answers.

The best example is that of Abraham, who looked into the stars to find answers and laid the foundation of the three dominant religions on earth: Judaism, Christianity, and Islam.

"You have come closer than any explanation I have heard before, but it is taking me close to the concept of nothingness. Nothing is impossible with God. Man cannot comprehend nothingness, so how can he ever fully comprehend His greatness? If God created himself, it has to mean that he did so out of nothing."

Hmm, I see where you are going, my boy.

"Let's think of the first principal. You are saying that God came out of nothing, so this nothingness cannot have any boundaries. It is possible for something to happen inside a bottle or a box because the box was previously there. For example, the big bang can happen within the box or bottle, but the box or bottle literally doesn't exist, or never did, so how can anything be formed inside nothing?"

Exactly, so what's the difference between Nothing and God? If God existed eternally, then nothingness or void was never there. If God created himself, then nothing existed just at the point God decided to create himself.

"Buddhism, especially Zen Buddhism, concentrates on emptiness. They say that if you can still the mind you will achieve great powers," Amir augmented the discussion.

If you can still the mind, you are removing all the intermediaries in between and communicating directly with GOD, a language without words. But is that our purpose here on earth?

"As a kid I learnt that service to mankind is service to God. So, isn't it better to work in fields like science to make the world a better and more marvelous place? Isn't that what true love for the creator is, loving the beings he created? Because you are saying that the wisest are those who love the most profoundly."

I believe that humans as a species need to get our priorities right. I respect and admire your opinion. What is the point of being a monk, priest, or a sheikh, whose only purpose here on earth is to pray and chant mantras and force their beliefs into as many people from the masses as he could? Is this what the all-competent God would like us to achieve on earth?

"Islam says God created Man to be His vicegerent on earth," said Amir.

Every religion says so. Rama lived and struggled to defeat evil. We have not yet found a species more intelligent than humans in the universe, isn't it? Until then, let's assume ourselves as the guardians of the universe for the Almighty King. The lotus Sutra says anyone can attain enlightenment.

"Your point is valid. My explanation of this mysterious thing called love is coming very close to nothingness, which seems to be divine. But then, what is peace?"

This is another nebulous concept we could discuss for hours. Peace and religion go hand in hand. People follow religion for the sake of obtaining peace.

"Yes, and for me that is the ultimate target of life; discovering and realizing this peace, finding this 'elixir of peace'," Amir said.

Chapter 1

1994

The train was speeding away through the mountains and tunnels, grazing the leaves of trees along the way. A young boy of barely eight was sitting by the window seat observing the passing trees and hills across the flangeway. The soothing greenery was the key ingredient that was cooking a wonderful deluge of thoughts in his young mind.

"Beautiful, isn't it?" his mother asked Amir.

He nodded, excitement airing all over his face.

"If you are lucky, you might even see some animals," his uncle told him.

They were travelling from Trivandrum in South India to Bombay in the western state of Maharashtra, which was a three days and two nights passage. He was travelling with his mother, brother, elder sister, and an uncle who had come from Bombay to Trivandrum to travel with them.

Amir's family was from the Republic of Maldives. This was his second trip outside the country. The first was a short trip to the neighboring island nation of Sri Lanka during his school holidays two years ago. This time was different. This meandering journey was not a holiday trip. His family was going to settle down in Bombay or a nearby city. Amir's father had set up his business in Bombay. He was in partnership with a big shot in the city.

Things were changing fast in Amir's life. He grew up as a rich kid in the Maldivian city of Addu. His father was a businessman, trading goods between Maldives and

Singapore and other East Asian countries. He was an intelligent kid who excelled at school and had many friends. Amir particularly liked reading, and he had started reading English novels at a very early age. He also watched Bollywood's Hindi movies with the grownups, most of which were based on stories of the good versus the bad.

He was seven when he started hearing talks about some troubles in the family business. He eagerly eavesdropped when the elders spoke about serious topics, like the family's situation or about philosophies of life. It was just a few weeks before this trip that he learned his father had decided to set up his company elsewhere.

Amir was emotionally distressed when he learned that they would be leaving the country and settling down abroad. He would miss his relatives and school friends, the people he grew up around, with whom he had learned to dream, play, and live.

'Pieces of the wild heart

Attached to a fragment great,

Born from a Love that will create

A promise to meet, but no end in sight.'

His mother tried to make it feel as normal as possible. She initially didn't tell him that they were leaving indefinitely. Nevertheless, she soon realized that he knew, as her daughter told her that Amir had said they were going to go to a different school in another country.

The disappointment Amir had suffered started fading away almost as soon as he arrived in India. He was witnessing fascinating events. He was watching scenes that he had seen in the movies happen in real life, and things he had read in stories were coming alive. Everything excited him; the heterogenous population, sparrows and finches flying across the sky, the touting vendors, the beggars, the stray dogs wagging their tails, the crazy traffic and glut of auto rickshaws, the crowds and the hustle and bustle.

Amir was thrilled when his uncle, who had come to Trivandrum to pick them up, told them they were going to Bombay by train. Amir knew this was going to be a pleasant adventure for two reasons. He had heard about the great and fascinating city called Bombay and, secondly, this was the first time he would be on a train. He also missed his dad. It had been almost two years since his father left Maldives, traveling among countries trying to set up his business operations. His father had very loyal and good friends in different parts of the world.

Amir was soon going to realize that his life was going to be a much greater adventure than he had ever imagined. The hands of destiny were writing a song with him in the heart.

From the first breath
A journey began,
Wonder of destiny,
This child I am,
You know not me,
I know not you,
Come let's play,
The Game of discovery.

The huge train itself was fascinating to Amir. They were travelling in second class berth with couchettes. As the train passed one town after another, one city after another, waving goodbye to one mountain after another, flowerbeds and contiguous farms and houses left to dilapidate disappearing into the past, Amir's mind was flooding with ideas and the great things he would do with his life. The young Amir didn't realize that life would be so uncompromising, causing him to leave behind many a thing he would love in order to move forward, just as the train was leaving behind the rabble, the trees and the mountains, moving forward to reach its destination. Unlike the train, life's journey is just a one-time fantasy from birth to death.

All of a sudden, Amir had the strong realization that he had left behind his previous life and now had to prepare for a totally new one, among entirely different people. Just as the train, he had decided his destination. What was he going to do with life that would help him achieve the prodigiousness he desired? Maybe this was an opportunity given to him by life. By inviting him to a bigger country with so much to experience and things to learn from, maybe he would follow his father's footsteps and become a businessman, or maybe there was some other way to become rich and powerful. The young boy in him knew that he would get there, whatever the cost.

I had a dream,

From where it was born

I know not for certain,

How can that be my fault,

For the dream chose me.

He was lost in these thoughts when the train entered a tunnel. Amir was frightened by the stygian blackness. His mother realized this and put her hand around him and his sister's shoulders comfortingly. Within a few minutes, the train was out of the tunnel and light filled the compartment once again.

Amir's mother told him, "You have to be brave my son. In life there will be times where there is darkness, but if you have courage to face it, it won't last too long, and soon you will see the light. Never give up."

"If the darkness lasts too long, we might get lost," Amir said.

"If there is no way, you have to make a way and keep going," she said.

"Allah helps those who are brave."

Amir nodded in agreement and went back to watching the passing landscapes.

At every station, people entered their compartment selling small cups of tea, coffee, and snacks as the stench of urine and effluvia filled the compartment. The hectic nature of the environment occasionally led to splenetic rants and small skirmishes. Whenever possible, Amir and his brother got out of the train to observe each station. They were scared that the train might leave without them until their uncle told them the train would whistle before leaving.

Initially, their compartment wasn't completely crowded and there was space to move around. However, by the second day, all seats were occupied, and some faces were becoming familiar and friendly. Most people were nice and kind to this foreign family with three kids. Amir's brother was more friendly with the neighbors than he was. Amir was more obsessed with the geography of the country. Looking into the wilderness, he thought of animals living within the jungle and wondered whether people lived there, as he had read in some story books. Curiosity was an inherent quality he would have to live with, leading to the naissance of his dreams.

The second evening just before sunset, a swami wearing saffron robes entered their compartment seeking alms. His forehead was painted with white lines and a tilak. A few passengers gave him some money and he gave them blessings and moved towards the cabin in which Amir's family sat. Amir's uncle pulled a ten rupee note and gave it to him and asked him how he was in Hindi.

The swami looked at the family and started reciting Sanskrit verses. He kept reciting for for few minutes and then placed his hand on Amir's head and gave him a marigold flower he had in his hand.

When he was gone, Amir's uncle asked the elderly Indian man in the next cabin what he told. The gentleman was a professor of Hindi in Mangalore University.

"He recited verses from the Vedas, and then he said."

"Two tusks of dead elephants,

Foxes tooth and cow urine,

Ashes blowing in the wind,

Demons in flight,

Agni and the sacred water of the Ganges,

Darkness engulfing the Navagraha

Asuras and devas,

Conch shell blown,

The battle has begun,

Suffering of the dead,

Cries of the children,

I see a young man,

The end of an age,

Written in his destiny."

Chapter 2

The alarm woke Amir. It was seven in the morning, and he had to be at the office in half an hour. He had missed the first alarm.

Amir was working as a planning officer in the Ministry of Fisheries and Agriculture of the Maldives. He had first returned to Maldives from India when he was sixteen. He was almost twenty years old now.

Amir quickly took a bath, got ready, and left for work on his motorcycle. He skipped breakfast. As usual, he would sign the register and have a coffee with his office mates in the tearoom before going for breakfast at nine a.m.

Amir had returned from India as a teenager after spending his childhood in the Indian city of Pune. After completing his secondary education, he worked briefly as an intern in the State trading Organization before going to Bangalore to complete his pre-university education. He returned in 2004 and almost immediately got his current job at the ministry. However, his prudent mind was always saturated with business ideas. He never envisioned himself working in a job forever. He was looking for the first opportunity to get an investment to start his own venture. Although his family business was going strong, he wanted to start something of his own independently.

Determination is the key,

For discipline is a must,

To destroy the encumbrance,

Faced by one and whole,

Conquered yet

By a few alone.

Amir had worked his plans out again and again in his mind. One thing he realized was that he could not achieve his great dreams solitarily. He needed a strong team of qualified people, not reprobates. So, he started imagining them in his friends. Thus, he was very careful in picking the people he spent his time with. Amir knew he had no time to waste, as he wasn't born with a silver spoon in his mouth. So, all the discussions among his group of friends were all focused on making money and generating business ideas.

In the tearoom, the dudeish Hussain and athletic Shahid joined him. They were having their coffee and cigarettes, zipping up for the work that lay ahead as the day progressed. Amir had been working in the ministry for three months and had built a nascent friendship with these two, Imthiyaz from the accounting department, and the facetious Riyaz, whose gaggery always lightened the mood.

Riyaz joined them and took a sip of his coffee. "Aaah! Thank God every day for the gift of life!" He was a facility inspector, like Shahid.

"So, any good plans after work today?" asked Hussain

Shahid shrugged. "We could try a new place for coffee, in Hulhumalé,"

Hulhumalé was an artificially restored island lying adjacent to the capital, considered part of the Greater Malé Area that was been developed.

"Maybe we can plan a trip for this weekend to an inhabited island," Amir said.

"I have a few new contacts, I'll ring them tomorrow and see if we can get transport," Shahid said.

"Procrastination is fatal, remember that!" Imthiyaz remarked as he entered the tearoom. "If you could speak to the dead, it would be their biggest regret."

"Yet, life is too short to be so disciplined and careful. It's a paradox," Shahid insisted.

They had occasionally made a few such trips on holidays. It was a great escape from city life, and the trips almost always ended too soon for them. In addition to the break from work, it was also rejuvenating and satisfying mentally.

The islands other than Malé, the capital, had seen very little development coming into the new millennium. Nonetheless, with the progress the country was making in tourism, signs of moderate development had started popping up in the islands since the early years of the twenty first century.

Malé, the capital, was at the dawn of becoming a full-fledged Metropolitan city. In the seventies, it was just a town by international standards. However, with the advent of tourism in the Maldives and the subsequent dollar rush, the capital city saw unprecedented development, with land values skyrocketing. By the late 90s and early 2000s, rent in housing and commercial spaces were towering, comparable to cities like Mumbai and New York; this led to congestion, making it one of the most densely populated cities per square km. However, since then, the government has started extensive dredging and land excavation projects, increasing the size of the island manifold and hoping to connect it to other nearby islands through a bridge that was being planned. In addition, a whole new island, much larger than Malé, was being developed in the nearby reef through dredging and accretion, canvassed as the solution to abate the housing problems Malé was facing. Hulhumalé, a landmark project where the government sought to accommodate most of the working population through social housing schemes by building apartment complexes, was almost fully reclaimed and developed.

The only functioning international airport was on an island a stone's throw away from Malé and was the gateway to Maldives for tourists visiting the country from across the globe. From the beginning, the Maldives had adopted a 'one island, one resort' policy. This allowed tourists to enjoy all the freedoms and recreations on the island away from the local population. The Maldives consisted of twelve hundred islands, out of which only two hundred or so were inhabited. The islands were in danger of being inundated by rising sea levels due to global warming. There were many a beautiful island with huge turquoise lagoons, stunning reefs, and flora and fauna ready to be developed into resorts. By the early 2000s, there were a hundred resorts all across the country. The vast majority were close to the capital, Malé, due to ease of access from the airport for tourists who travelled for hours from their hometowns to reach Maldives.

This led to many opportunities for business in the capital. There was an influx of people from islands all across the country who came to find better jobs and business opportunities, as well as to ensure the utility of a good education for their kids, as at the time, quality education was almost nonexistent in the islands except for the two or three larger ones.

During his time in India as a kid, Amir often compared it to his own country. The towering buildings of Bombay and the fortified castles and palaces he saw in Pune always awed and inspired him. These were not sights he had witnessed back home. When he did return to the country at sixteen, he noticed that it was starting to develop much more than he had expected. The roads that were filled with bicycles were now making way for motorcycles and cars. Shops and restaurants mushroomed across Malé, and apartment complexes began to rise in various locations. Quaquaversal structured modern mosques with arabesque designs decorated the landscape. Government buildings and offices were getting bigger and employing the thousands who had to be accommodated in Malé. Thus, real estate was booming.

After having completed his pre-university course in Bangalore, Amir decided to return to Malé to work for a few years before continuing his bachelor's degree. His main aim was to establish a business in Maldives, therefore he needed to research the situation in Malé and explore his options. He wanted to establish an import business, separate from his family enterprise.

Amir knew he would need to get reliable partners, as his plan was to leave to complete his studies once the set up was done. He knew from the experiences that his family had faced that getting a trusted partner was going to be a big challenge. He had realized at a very young age the sway money held and how it could change people completely. However, when he returned from Bangalore, his mother had other ideas. She told him that if he was not going to continue his studies, he needed to get a government job. Although he refused initially and debated the subject with her, he finally agreed, as he knew that it would take time to raise capital and set up a new business venture on his own.

Amir got the job at the Ministry of Fisheries and Agriculture, the first one he applied for. He soon learned the bureaucratic set up and how the civil service worked. He made friends with colleagues who, like him, were newly fledged officers. A budding friendship developed, and they occasionally met for a nook in the tearoom to have a cigarette and a cup of coffee at regular intervals. The office time ended at two thirty in the afternoon, and after going home to have lunch and freshen up, they would again gather for a coffee in one of their favored coffee shops across town. These coffees were the highlight of their days as they discussed everything from art to business prospects, society, culture, and politics.

The times were changing

Yet I stood still,

Wondering, perplexed and unsure,

How can I keep up?

The demands of Time

Born innocent I was,

The world wild and uncompromising,

How shall I trade, with innocence alone.

Although development was generally improving standards of living in the Maldives, there were many social ills the capital city still had to deal with. Drug abuse was one such issue. Marijuana, hash oil, and more worryingly, heroin addiction, were appearing at alarming rates in the streets. Gangs were formed in different parts of the city and ruled their respective areas. There was a rapid increase in inter-gang violence and recidivism. Gangs were also involved in the drug trade, peddling substances through the community. It was soon becoming a Hell's kitchen, as the authorities could not keep up with the pace of the social mess that was building These drug and gang issues stemmed from larger social issues, such as large families living in small living spaces, with parents and multiple kids sharing a room, or number of families living in the small apartment. Situations like this meant that the youth hit the road for an escape from the tense environment at home, finding solace with friends who were in similar circumstances.

Teenage curiosity normally took over these high-strung youths and, starting with a cigarette, they progressed from joints to other hard drugs, compelling them to get involved in crime and deviance with the intention of getting the money needed for the drugs to sustain their highs. Normally, the easiest thing for them to do was join gangs and peddle drugs for them, getting their substance of choice as payment based on the amount they sold in a day or a night.

Being an Islamic country, alcohol was prohibited on all inhabited islands, although it was sold openly and legally to tourists in the resorts. Subsequently, there was a growing black-market trade of alcohol. Bootlegging became a major income source of many trying to earn a few quick bucks. As there was a huge import of various high-quality spirits, some of it was directed to the inhabited islands to be sold to locals and expats at high prices. The gangs were developing various rackets to earn quick money.

The general public of the city were moderate Muslims. Their favorite pastime was enjoying cafés with friends. The various coffee shops across the city were always filled to capacity at night, normally with men enjoying coffee or tea and smoking away their daily worries and tensions at home.

At these times, Amir saw many opportunities for the innovative mind. His experience from his time at the big cities in India gave him a fair understanding on the development stages of the agrarian society and how villages grew into towns, towns into cities, and cities into a metropolis. As an arts student, one of the favorite subjects was sociology. He learned about the gregarious nature of man. Looking through the Maldivian society, he realized that there were worrying reasons for concern. However, these problems could only be addressed by the government taking the necessary steps and employing competent people in positions of power.

Since the beginning of the new millennium, the call for democracy and people's power was gaining momentum, and it looked as if a revolution was on the cards. There were subpoenas issued against all involved in the uprising and many were in jail without a fair trial. The incumbent president had been ruling for nearly thirty years, and his tenure brought with it huge developments, both in infrastructure and human resource development, as it coincided with the rapid development of the tourism industry. There were severe restrictions on human rights, freedom of speech, and other liberties the western world was accustomed to. There were no political parties. A president was elected every five years, when the citizens voted a yes or a no in a referendum to a name sent from Parliament. Unsurprisingly, reigning president Maumoon Abdul Gayoom, billed by some as a dictator, was elected every time with over 90% of the votes. The few of those who dared to criticize his regime and abashed him outrightly dismissed the results and condemned the influence the island chiefs wielded in getting the populace to vote as they dictated. Allegations about tampering with votes were never looked into. Opponents faced ostracism, humiliated, and suppressed. Maumoon's cronies spent heavily to exculpate him. The president himself, who was a good orator gave sententious speeches. Still, a young former journalist called Mohammed Nasheed started leading the call for change and the establishment of multiparty democracy in the Maldives.

Many civilians joined the revolutionary bandwagon. Soon, zealous young Turks took over the movement. It was said that Nasheed enjoyed the support of influential figures from the UK who wished to see a more liberal Maldives. Maumoon's supporters and partisans labeled him as a traitor and a supporter of secularism who was fomenting political unrest. However, the pressure ensured freedom of press, and doggerels and satire boosted the movement for reform.

Despite the hurdles, the revolutionary movement and insurrection gained speed, as there were many who were disgruntled by the growing nepotism in the government and mistreatment of anyone whom the ruling class saw as a threat. There were also serious allegations of inhumane treatment of prisoners in the jails. The widespread odium sowed the seeds of uprising. The regime's opponents had formed an informal political party with its base in Sri Lanka and appointed a shadow cabinet. There were regular gatherings held in different spots in Malé as a show of dissent and defiance. As for Amir, he believed in finding the juste-milieu, so he stayed away from the hype. The roughly four-square kilometers that constituted Malé at that time was becoming a very happening and gruesome center. Cafés and restaurants were open until one a.m., and traffic died out by two. From then until sunrise was the most peaceful time to have a ride on the streets of Malé, as Amir had experienced on many days, especially during weekends when he and his group stayed up at night and slept after dawn. Weekends were special for Amir and his youthful friends, as it was an escape from routine. Therefore, they planned the weekends days in advance and often planned trips to nearby inhabited islands or to a resort. With many members of their families or friends working at resorts, some in very high positions, they were able to arrange a free stay occasionally, helping them experience a luxury their present jobs would never allow.

It was a Tuesday, and they were already discussing plans for the weekend.

"I have a friend who works on a safari yacht. It is anchored near Hulhumalé. I think he may be able to arrange a stay for the weekend. We can pay them something for the food and stuff," Shahid said.

"That's cool," Hussain accepted, "I feel I am getting aged by the minute; we need to make life worthwhile while we still exist."

Amir reflected on the work he had to complete. If he could step it up, his workload would be reduced, and he could have his weekend entirely free. "Talk to him and ask how many of us they can accommodate," he told Shahid.

Shahid had joined the Ministry recently. He was a senior member of a local gang that had a significant presence in the southern area of Malé. Amir had developed a budding friendship with him, and they had started exploring many possibilities for making money. As Amir had the ideas and Shahid had the contacts, they were hopeful of setting up a good venture. They shared an interest in adventure and exploitation of their juvenescence. They would meet every day after lunch for a coffee and plan to try a new thing every day if their finances allowed. Most of the time, they would run out of their salaries by the fifteenth of the month. This meant that Amir had to ask for money from his mother to keep he and his friends' daily routine going. Although he didn't like to ask for money from his family, he was getting accustomed to a lifestyle which demanded it.

Amir and most of his friends were single, and they were on the lookout for a serious relationship and an opportunity to date. Malé being a small place, it was not too difficult to locate and reach out to the beautiful girls who were on their radar. The only dilemma was that the beautiful ones were already taken by the time they completed school. However, many of those relationships didn't last, as by the early twenties they were single again and on the lookout for love. Still, they were likely to be broken inside but tough on the outside. Amir had received advances from many girls, and some had tried to proposition him for sex. Nevertheless, as he had broken up with his first girlfriend just after returning from Bangalore, he was careful to make the next relationship a special one that would result in self-development. His no-nonsense attitude was because he was more interested in making money rather than playing. Most of his friends of the same age were interested in entertainment, zippy cars, sports, and dating. Amir was not averse to the idea of dating, but he had set very high standards for himself. Therefore, he rejected most advances politely. He was soon to realize that the types of girls he liked knew exactly what their beauty was worth, which meant that he had to either shower them with gifts and pleasantries to get them on a date or fight for them with all he had to prove that he seriously loved them. There were two kinds. Amir learned this from his older friends who had had many serious girlfriends previously. He was also warned to be aware of perfidy and arrogance.

That evening, he and his friends met for coffee at a café facing the ocean. It was a spacy and comfortable restaurant that served good coffee and western cuisine. Amir and his friends were regulars there and the staff knew them well and were friendly.

The waiter who normally served them came to them with a smile. "What would you like today?"

"Just the normal, Chooty."

Chooty was the nickname they referred to the waiter by.

"Two black coffees."

"One Lavazza milk for me," said Imthiyaz.

They were joined soon by another colleague, Migdhadh. He had bandy legs and a contagious smile.

Amir sipped his coffee. Looking at the sea and the horizon, he cherished the moment. He was entering his twenties, and he knew that it was now or never to give his best fight to make something out of his life. He knew he had to work hard.

Riyaz's phone range. He spoke on his mobile for a while. "I have a number for you. Nice, innocent looking one," he said to Amir after hanging up.

Imthiyaz gave a chuckle. "In these times, innocence is a wow factor."

"Who is she?" Amir asked.

"My sister's classmate"

"You have a photo?" Shahid asked nonchalantly.

"No. She is eighteen, doing her A levels. I know her address," Riyaz said enthusiastically.

"Well, we can go for a round once the coffee is done. If we're lucky you might get a glance."

It was a zany exercise that usually did work, surprisingly. Whenever they attempted to get a glimpse of the girl they were after, they rode their motorbikes a few times around her area and usually got a glimpse, sometimes her attention, as well.

Amir and his gang were becoming regulars on the streets of Malé as they frequented the cafés across town, taking turns riding endlessly around the island once they'd finished their coffees.

The rides were very refreshing, and Amir felt an instant connection with the land. It took approximately half an hour for one full ride around Malé on the motorbike. Within a few months of having returned from Bangalore, the roads and gullies of Malé had become very familiar. He spent most of the time after leaving the office with his friends and returned home almost by midnight.

It wasn't long before his mother realized that he was going off track. She started calling him every night at exactly eleven p.m. asking him to return home. Amir somehow managed to come back by midnight on weekdays. However, he and his friends stayed up the whole night on weekends.

But what is this life?

A wheel of fortune,

Wake up to a day,

The catch uncertain,

But a reward certain,

And tomorrow strive again.

It was in Bangalore that he had started smoking. Since his friendship with Shahid, Amir had built alliances with many that were part of Shahid's gang, many of whom had just started using marijuana. Unlike other major gangs of Malé where most of the members were addicted to heroin, this gang being largely made up of minors and teenage boys, they were mainly using and trading hash oil.

These youngsters, Amir found out, shared a very brotherly connection. Most were from poor and middle-class families with similar social outlooks. Cramped homes and volatile environments caused by tired and pressured adults made them look for refuge outside the home and on the streets. The gang and their dens provided them with a safe haven. They were young, feeble-minded, and inexperienced. They shared their sorrows and joys with one another. In addition, it gave them confidence, as they knew that they would have the backing of the gang if they were to cross paths in a bad way with members of other established gangs in the city. Slowly, they were inured to violence. Occasionally, there were inter-gang fights happening, most of which were the result of confusion surrounding girls and drug related problems. Due to this fact, the gangs were severely censured by the general public. Those days, the only way the gangs made money was through drugs and getting sponsor money by participating in sports tournaments. It was before democracy took over and politicians splashed their money around to make the gangs work for them and appointed them for their personal security and extortion. However, the gangs had already started gaining prominence, and many had registered security companies while members started working out and body building in gyms.

In addition to his colleagues, Amir maintained good connections with his Maldivian friends with whom he studied in Bangalore. Some of them were continuing their studies, but some had returned to Maldives with him. One of them was Hamdh.

Hamdh was Amir's roommate in his second year in Bangalore. His father was an Indian doctor married to a Maldivian lady with whom he had three children. Hamdh was their second born. He walked with an upright gait and was a very business minded individual. His spontaneous actions, creative attitude, and profligate lifestyle interested Amir very much. Many a day, they bunked college and roamed the metropolitan areas and shopping districts of Bangalore. In coffee shops on Brigade Road, they planned on building a business empire.

As Maldives was a country totally dependent on imports, the main idea was to establish an import-export business with headquarters in Malé and India. Amir soon found out that Hamdh was a staunch friend and a courageous young man. They had a predilection for similar kinds of movies and books, both knowing the dialogues of The Godfather trilogy, watching them multiple times together.

Amir was an avid reader and had read the Mari Puzo novel years back. They imitated the characters in the film and talked of forming their own gang. It was here where the ideas of a La Cosa Nostra of their own was formulated. They spent nights discussing various means by which they could strike it rich. Hamdh's mind was more criminal than Amir's, he was always thinking of making a quick buck through illegal means such as forgery and printing counterfeit notes of Maldivian currency and smuggling it. Unlike Amir, he had grown up in Malé in a middle-class family with kith and kin. Therefore, he had more experience with the realities of the Maldivian society. He explained to Amir the difficulties of building a profitable business and how a select few people controlled everything. According to him, to prove their mettle, they needed to embark on endeavors others would dare not try. Hamdh felt that if they could plan things carefully, they would not get caught, and even if they were caught, the value of goods in hand would be enough to bribe the authorities and walk free without punishment. "They will fear us.' Hamdh used to say.

Amir was not so sanguine.

What Hamdh was suggesting was smuggling and all sorts of criminal activities which would require careful planning and organization. "Make them fear you, they will never underestimate you," he insisted.

Being an ethical person, and one who always tried to be morally right, Amir's initial thoughts were that Hamdh's Machiavellian ideas were lame. He didn't visualize himself as a picaresque hero. Conversely, when he pondered the reality of things, Amir realized that if it was money and power that he wanted, then this was what the people in power were inclined to do and how they became puppet masters. To satisfy his soul's moral characteristics, his mind told him that it was to facilitate the greater good. Once rich and powerful, he could help the needy and effect relief of indigence. Also, he could place people in power who would fill society with justice and equality. He could redeem himself by devoting his wealth to Islam and financing those who propagated the correct version of Islam, because at that time, Amir was a strong critic of extremism and jihadist philosophies, as he had grown up in India and was totally against the jihadist groups backed by hardliners who attacked India and killed innocent civilians. The last thing he would ever be, was a xenophobe. Finally, he thought he could spend the later years of his life in redemption and prayer, seeking forgiveness for his many a venial and mortal sins.

These thoughts formed in his second year in Bangalore fed his idealism and made him ready for a life that could go anywhere, as the roads ahead of him were several, each offering a kaleidoscope of choices. Some came with danger and excitement, others with adventure and pain. Additionally, there was a path that would bring shame and guilt, but he would become untouchable, like Don Vito Corleone. His gang had started taking shape already and all he needed was to make the right connections, get qualified people.

By chance,

Did paths cross,

But to hold the hand,

Decide first,

Loyalty and trust,

A bond Worth,

both the left and right hand.

Since then, Amir made friends only to fill this requirement. During their various coffees and late-night talks, he explained his ideas to Hamdh. Hamdh's interest and eagerness was one of the reasons Amir decided to go back to Malé, before joining a degree program after his pre-university course was completed. He decided that it was important to set up the business in the Maldives and then go to a city from which he could set up an export business as he continued his studies there. That would be killing two birds with one stone, he had told Hamdh, and they couldn't wait to complete their courses and return to Malé to set up the company. Studying was a perfunctory duty he did for his mother, his thoughts would preclude him from living a normal life.

Amir and his new friends in Bangalore were just teenagers, and in addition to business ideas, they were filled with joie de vivre and enjoying the party life. The group of Maldivian students studying with him lived in the same building belonging to a man from Bangalore. It was through his advertisements in the newspaper that Amir contacted him. His name was Rahul, and he was around thirty years of age at that time. He arranged the college admission and the accommodation from his home in Bangalore, along with food and transport. Amir was from his first batch of paying guests, three boys and three girls. The two male students were much older than Amir, but he managed to establish a strong connection with them, one that would define his entire life.

Rahul played the role of guardian at that time. Although he was parsimonious and very business minded, he wasn't shrewd enough, and thus ran into trouble many times. He made rules, but in his jumbled up English vocabulary told them often that 'rules are meant to be broken.' Amir and his group found out that the arrangements Rahul had made for them were not as colorful as he had portrayed to them. Although Amir was admitted to one of the best colleges in town, as he himself had searched the internet and asked to be admitted there, the other students were admitted in middle class or substandard colleges. The accommodation that Rahul provided was homely, but a quaint Indian-style four-story building in a suburb of Bangalore that Rahul had renovated to accommodate the students. At that time, it was one of the biggest houses in the area, built through funds Rahul's austere father earned through his trading company in the Maldives. The building was getting old, and the neighborhood pigeons were nidificated in several nooks and corners.

One of the major problems Amir and his housemates faced was the cagmag food. Being Maldivians, their diet consisted of fish or some kind of meat for every meal. This was something that Indians at that time found hard to believe; for them, having meat once or twice a week was also an excess. They savored different varieties of vegetables every day, cooked in a variety of recipes with flavorful Indian spices, prepared by a kindhearted lady called

Jenniffer ma, who was a Jehovah's witness. Her cooking was against the Maldivians' taste buds, as there always was an ingredient either in excess or too scarce. It took months for the students to adjust to the food prepared by her. Rahul, however, tried his best to make up for it. He would take them for long rides at night and stop at a dhaaba on the highway for some tandoori chicken and naan.

Amir loved these rides, they reminded him of his childhood. He also fell in love with the city. Bangalore's development was to be seen everywhere, from the city to the suburbs and the nearby towns becoming part of the metropolis. Amir's sociology class delved deep into the study of societies and their development, and when he explored the roads and districts of Bangalore, he saw a real-life example of the developmental pyramid. Rahul had taken them to nearby cities of the Karnataka state, of which Bangalore was the capital. The highways connected Bangalore to major towns in Karnataka, Tamil Nadu, and other states where raw materials where supplied, and manufacturing units were established. A new international airport was being built far away from the city and this resulted in a real estate boom. The previously deserted lands that lead to the airport increased in value as a highway and connecting roads were being laid to connect the airport to various parts of the city. It was these roads that Rahul took them for the night rides. There were no buildings or houses, just trees on both sides of the road, although they would come across a solitary restaurant, called dhaaba, on the highway in the dark of the night. These dhaabas mainly served truck drivers and voyagers travelling by bus, providing tasty local cuisine consisting of both vegetarian and nonveg items on the menu. These roads were a treat to the eye even during the day, as Amir and his friends rode their motorcycles to look at the farmlands with lakes and ponds and cows grazing nearby. The endless greenery and the peaceful life of the men and women and grazing animals were a tranquilizer to their minds as they took a break from the city life in Bangalore and their studies.

The following year, things got a lot better for the buoyant Amir. It was a very successful year for Rahul, as he was able to get eight more boys and eight girls for different academic programs, most of whom were Amir's coevals. The new students were to live in the same house, so Rahul allocated the second floor for the girls and the fourth floor for the boys.

Rahul lived in a small room on the terrace adjacent to the dining room and kitchen. The terrace was spacious, had table tennis, and was surrounded with figurine pots of plants. There was also a small seating arrangement of Maldivian style joalis, made of ropes with a steel framework. Rahul tried to lead the boisterous group like a roman centurion and failed miserably at it.

The new boys looked up to the previous batch for guidance. Amir, being younger than the others of that batch, was more adventurous, and easily became the facile princep of the pack. He tried to take a conciliatory approach. It was a friendly and joyful environment at their lodge despite frequent fracases amongst individuals. Amir's intrepidity earned him respect from the crowd. The boys and girls looked forward to every opportunity to get together, despite being on different floors. The boys showed off their machismo and the girls put on a pageant. Soon, pairs started to form. Amir became an advisor to the young, eager boys who couldn't wait to get physically close to their girlfriends.

Hamdh was one of the most experienced in the group, as he had had a serious girlfriend back in Maldives to whom he was affianced, but their relationship ended just a few months before Hamdh came to Bangalore. The couples soon started to get seriously attached and Hamdh too cajoled a girl called Sheereen. Soon Amir had to put up with the numerous stories Hamdh had to tell him when they retired to bed for the night. Some nights, if Rahul forgot to lock the gate of the second floor, Sheereen would sneak into the room, and Amir, whose bed was opposite Hamdh's and just three feet away, had to turn the other side and act as if he was asleep. Soon he got used to it, as sex, mostly oral, became a common habit of the jejune young group. Soon couples started interchanging among themselves. This bemused Amir.

Amir had a girlfriend before coming to Bangalore, but they just spoke over the phone. She was very beautiful and had an innocent face, which captivated Amir from the first moment he saw her.

I see in you

What I first thought was me,

Before I knew guilt,

Before I knew sin,

Before I knew hatred,

Before I knew jealousy,

When I only asked for care,

So, care, I seek from you.

Amir saw her when he was on a stroll with his close friend from school, Haaris. Haaris, like Amir, had an eye for beauty, and this made him a good accomplice for the young Amir who maintained a façade of his dream girl. He saw her coming out of a shop wearing a foulard when they were walking across. Amir immediately stopped Haaris, who automatically realized what was happening. They waited and watched her leave the shop and enter her house. This house now pulled him there like a magnet and, two days later, they saw her again. This time, their eyes met, and Amir was sure she gave a slight smile.

Haaris confirmed it by telling him so. "Beauty is the biggest test; the greatest of the greatest bow down without a second thought to woo this beauty." Haaris told him later.

The girl's feminacy struck Amir's mind like a thunderbolt. He managed to get her home's land line number and started calling her. It didn't take too long for her to realize that it was Amir. They had exchanged cursory glances a couple of times by then. Luckily, her sisters, who picked up the phone, gave it to her when he requested. Before long, Amir mustered the courage to go up to her and introduce himself. Her name was Seema. They met a couple of times in the shop near her house. She was just sixteen by then and her parents had no knowledge of the relationship. She used to tell him a time she would go to the shop to buy some things for home and Amir would wait for her. However, Amir soon had to leave for Bangalore, and the last time before he left, she gave him a kiss. This was his first kiss, one which made him determined to stay loyal to her. The young mind was a zealous advocate of true love.

In spite of this, his determination didn't last too long. One of the girls from the second batch of Rahul's students had her sights on Amir, who proved to be a tough nut for the girls to crack, as he was ambivalent to their overtures. There was also the fact that Rahul used to see Amir as the leader of the group, and whenever there were any arguments or disagreements, he would ask Amir to look into it. This gave Amir some sense of responsibility, and he felt that he needed to care for the wellbeing of the group, both the girls and boys. Amir's nature was not quarrelsome, and his essential idiosyncrasy was to step up whenever there was trouble around him. He made sure that the group eschewed violence. He had a knack for finding solutions and was who the boys turned to when they had a fight with their partner, or potential partners. However, often the rules of the boarding were flouted, and Rahul's cordon was almost non-existent. The gang's rah-rah attitude fascinated Amir, especially how easily the girls changed from one partner to another. It only made him more determined to snub their romantic gestures.

Ayesha, from the first batch, was the closest to Amir among the girls. A few months into the second year of their stay, she was already in her third relationship. However, the strong bond from their first year made them accomplices. Just as Rahul appointed Amir as the head of the boys' group, he let Ayesha manage the girls' department. Ayesha and Amir had many long conversations together, during which she shared with him the stories of what was happening among the girls, how serious they were about their boyfriends and other personal stuff. Ayesha was a bright raconteur. Amir also gave away as much as he could about the boys, although he always thought he defended them more than he should as he had no intention of denigrating anyone. Nevertheless, there was the possibility that Ayesha may share his side with her mates, and he might get into trouble.

It was during one such conversation that Ayesha told him about Nashwa. She was doing her first year of Engineering in the same college as Amir, was two years older than him, and had a zaftig figure. She remained aloof from the boys, and there were many eying her without much success. Ayesha told Amir that Nashwa had told her about her interest in Amir and that she would be ready to get something going, even if it wasn't a serious relationship. Ayesha obviously had told Nashwa and the other girls that he had a girl back home. Amir tried to politely refuse, as he knew Ayesha was close to Nashwa.

However, it was Hamdh who took up the topic with Amir. Hamdh's girlfriend Sheereen was Nashwa's best friend. The boys were at a coffee day outlet close to the boarding house. Sheereen had asked Hamdh to ask Amir to go on a double date with Nashwa and them.

"Does she know that I have a girlfriend?"

"Yes, she says she wants to be good friends…first," Hamdh added.

Amir considered the idea. After all, almost everyone else in the boarding house had become couples except for Amir and the other two boys from the first batch. He thought about Seema. Although he told everyone he was committed to her, they barely spoke once a week. The ISD calls were expensive when he went to a nearby telephone booth operator every Sunday to speak with her for around half an hour. The second year, the calls lessened further, as he was finding it hard to survive on the monthly pocket money that his parents sent him.

His gang had grown and they were always planning one adventure after the other. They frequented the high-end coffee shops in the central, developed areas of the city, sipping espressos, lattes, and cappuccinos one after the other. In addition, they had found out the disco spots of the town that were operated in the evenings, mostly attracting college students on the weekends. This was the only option they had at the time, because Rahul closed the gates of their house by nine p.m.

However, the whole group's first exposure to the disco culture came through Rahul himself, who took them to a birthday party for one of his friends who had a farmhouse on the outskirts of the city. Rahul and his friends played guitar and danced to the music. Slowly Amir and the students joined the Fais do-do. They danced into the wee hours of Saturday night and from then onwards, partying was on the mind of the gang.

Back then, Amir didn't smoke and was a teetotaler. However, he knew that some of his gang were using marijuana and having beers frequently, which was a good arrangement for Amir and others who didn't drink but needed accomplices who did in order to take tables in the discotheques. Soon, the gang found themselves going from spending money in the coffee shops to getting drunk in the discotheques and dance bars. Amir also realized that his forbearance was getting weaker. However, he adjured his group to show restraint.

Rahul found out what was happening long before, however, he tried to overlook their peccadillos. It was then that he started taking them for nights out. Those days there was no curfew, and discos operating at the outskirts ran well into the hours of the morning. The crowd at home used to urge Amir to ask Rahul to take them to try a new disco every weekend. Most of the time he would agree by putting on the condition that they study some extra hours every day and attend class regularly. Little did he know most of the students were going far astray, needing more money because of the new lifestyle.

Amir had to keep constantly adjusting the thoughts of his young mind. He was dealing with very different kinds of individuals, however, he knew that he was the unifying factor and put that responsibility on his own shoulders. The boys he lived with had become close friends who shared every aspect of their life with him. When any of them needed to talk about some issue varying from college to things happening with their girlfriends, they met him privately and asked his opinion or advice.

It was the other two boys from the first batch, the shrewd tactician Aman, and the witty Shareef, who were around ten years older than Amir, whom he turned to when he himself got emotionally drained. "The ordinary shall not suffice a man, who fears not death, because he knows he will conquer his dreams before his last breath." Shareef, who was like an elder brother Amir never had, had told him.

Amir matched them intellectually, although he wasn't as experienced as they were. Amir respected their quaint approach to life and their minds were pugnacious in friendly debate.

The day when Hamdh asked him about the double date, he was awfully mentally tired. He had been bunking many classes at college and the half yearly exams were nearing. He was in a mad rush to complete the topics and catch up with the other students in class. In addition, Rahul had found out about some of the guys in the house smoking weed, which was an illegal substance in India and something Rahul was dead against, meaning he would put restrictions on all of them. It would now be harder for Amir to convince Rahul to take them on rides and night outs.

College was closed for the Navaratri holidays, which was a breather to think things over. Amir needed a strategy to help his friends who were doing illegal activities at home because it would put all of them in trouble. Rahul had spoken to him personally on this issue and had warned him that if they didn't stop, he would have no choice but to castigate them and inform the parents.

Amir finally told Hamdh to fix the date with the girls. They then discussed the various events happening at their boarding and returned home.

Two of the students who were caught smoking ganja where Yameen and Ihusaan, who Amir was fond of. They were fun to be around, mostly because they saw a funny side in everything that happened. Laughter seemed to be the best medicine for them. "Worrying is such a waste of time," they had told Amir.

They usually accompanied Amir and the others to coffee shops while heavily smoked up. Amir and the seniors knew about this and discussed it a few times among themselves, but let it be as a personal matter they would rather not get involved in. Amir felt that Yameen and Ihusaan were letting their talents dissipate, however, with the foul odor of burning grass coming out of their floor every night, Rahul had discovered their secret, and now Amir had to deal with the situation head on.

Amir liked them both personally, but he knew that they were introducing the drugs to others in the pack too. They had started taking tablets and bunked class almost every day. In spite of all of that, Amir didn't mind being around them. Their excessive laughter and interesting, sometimes inane questions made him think.

Since childhood, engaging in his imagination was a pastime and much-loved hobby of his. Every day he would think about a whole new subject and imagine stories about it. Most of the time, he would imagine himself as the hero of these stories. Those stories developed into epics, whose episodes he played in his mind daily. Amir's favorite time was at the end of the day, bidding goodnight to everyone and retiring to bed. He would make sure he did so at least thirty minutes before he actually felt sleepy. During this thirty minutes, he imagined a continuous story of himself, all grown up, and his fight against evil. These thoughts were mostly inspired by the numerous stories he read and the films he saw. Being in India during his childhood, he watched a lot of Bollywood films and sometimes his parents would take him to a theater. Most of these films were about the hardships of life and the triumph of good over evil after many difficulties.

The subjects in school inspired his stories as well. Learning about inventors, discoveries, and the heroes of the past with their rich legacies got him thinking deeply about the realities of the concepts and theories he studied in science and history. He always liked to apply the question of "why?" to most of these, rather than the "how?". Sometimes, his own witticism made him laugh at himself. History was his favorite subject, so unsurprisingly, he was taking a step into the deep and unpenetrated jungle of philosophy and human curiosity. Hence, a new, unexplored topic was added to his bedtime story.

There were two major contributors to the knowledge that Amir fed his young mind during his childhood. One was his elder sister's storybooks. She was four years his senior and her literature class consisted of novels by Charles Dickens, Emily Bronte, and others, in addition to Shakespeare. Amir found this literature astounding, and once he started reading, he found himself in a strange world where everything around him was given a whole new meaning as he attached deeply to the main character in the story. The second contributor was reading the morning newspaper. Every morning at dawn, the newspaper boy delivered the Indian Express newspaper, and Amir made sure he got up early so that he could scan the paper's headlines thoroughly before he went to school. This way, he would wait eagerly all day to get back home and read the complete articles in the paper. There was always something new to learn and a captivating story that formed a deluge in his young mind. In addition, the social issues, business, sports, and entertainment fascinated him, he even read the astrology and zodiac section. Through this information, he could visualize how his life would be as a grown-up. He always made good use of the Longman dictionary at home, as a young man of the twenty first century would use Google. Amir's mind was gearing up for his future, although he didn't realize that technology of the next few decades would see gigantic developments. Although computers, computer programming, and their language were becoming vital subjects of study at all levels, and the use of automated systems was becoming more common, it was the cartoons that he watched on Cartoon Network, like Johnny Quest and The Jetsons, which gave him a vision of the futuristic world that technology would help the human race achieve. In addition to his cartoons, growing up in a multi-cultural and multi-religious society in Pune, Amir was very much an advocate of world peace already.

It is something I feel,

It is something I have known,

It is something I long for,

It is something I was born with,

Yet, it is the one thing I search for,

Maybe it is within me,

It is Peace.

However, it was only once he left the safety of his home and started going out with his friends in Malé that he started getting a realistic insight into the human struggle. He realized it wasn't necessarily good-versus-evil or a fight for peace. It was just a fight for survival, to end the day on a good note, to keep loved ones happy.

Going to Bangalore and living in Rahul's boarding house with the Maldivian housemates was an experience worth its weight in gold for Amir; especially his second year, with the big gang where all the boys shared their stories, and the occasional personal detail, with him, as he was a good listener. He soon learned that credulity was a weakness and intellectual mind games were involved in all of the relationships within the house.

It didn't take Amir long to understand the nature of individual friends. Although there were many common factors, everyone had distinct features, likes, and tastes. Some were religious, others studious, others were vain and bellicose, but most were fun loving and liked to party. However, when the enjoyment factors started going out of hand, Rahul had a private meeting with him. He asked Amir to tell everyone not to forget the reason they were there, to not miss classes and to study regularly. He promised that if they did so, he would take them for a night out every Saturday. However, this was before the ganja bust at home.

Things were more serious now. After the coffee with Hamdh, Amir was determined to meet Ihusaan. When they returned home, Ihusaan was laying on the sofa watching TV. Amir told him he wanted a word with him after dinner. Ihusaan agreed.

The dinner was a solemn occasion, as Rahul was upset with them and gave them all a scolding. He had warned them that if they didn't concentrate on their studies properly, he may need to inform their parents. Although some of them were willing to oblige, others felt that they were paying Rahul for everything and it was none of his business what they did or whether they attended college or not. Amir tried to palliate the situation but knew things weren't going in the right direction. He and the other two seniors needed to discuss the situation, but before that, he decided to meet Ihusaan.

Ihusaan was a year younger than Amir. He had a history of drug abuse even back in Malé. Just after school, he met the wrong crowd. He was from an affluent family that had several business outlets in Malé. When they had spoken before, Ihussan had told Amir about his heartbreak after falling out with his first girlfriend; it was then that he started smoking and gradually fell into drugs. The whimsical Ihusaan was one of the most successful with the girls. He was tall and handsome with hollow cheeks. However, he wasn't serious with any of them. His main objective was getting high, or in his words, "taking a feel of the moment".

Amir often wondered what it would be like to cloud his mind and body with different biochemical reactions, enzymes exploding in his brain, and try to think with his mind in a jumbled state. However, he knew that was a road that would certainly lead to his doom, so he wisely refrained from smoking or drinking, despite being a regular in the partying crowd.

After dinner, Ihusaan met Amir in his room. Hamdh wanted to be there with them too, but Amir knew that there was some bad energy between the boys due to something that had happened with the girls, so he asked Hamdh to give them some time.

"Rahul spoke to me," he told Ihusaan.

"I know. He's a fouter," he remarked angrily.

"I told you guys to be careful; the smell is everywhere, even on the ground floor," Amir said.

Ihusaan laughed slightly. "It's irksome to go out every time. The neighbors will start suspecting. We had no choice but to smoke in the balcony."

"Is this necessary?" Amir inquired. "Rahul doesn't mind you guys having a few drinks and partying, but this is illegal. This could put him in trouble if anybody reports to the police. It's not a trivial matter."

"Yeah, if someone *does* report. I don't think the neighbors would mind, they consider us a wacky lot."

"I heard you guys are taking tabs too. The pharmacist is having good business."

Ihusaan laughed again. "Just experimenting, we have stopped now."

Amir knew he was lying. "Even Anand is sinking into it with you guys."

Anand was the youngest in the group, going to secondary school. He was barely fourteen, with a peculiar schnoz and ambidextrous. He faced the taunts of the older guys bravely but he was foolhardy and didn't hesitate to try out the things the guys gave him. He was already bunking his school, joining the others who were skipping classes and loafing around Brigade Road. They would smoke up at one of Bangalore's numerous parks and then join the rest of the crowd who didn't do drugs in the MG road coffee shop.

Who knows about tomorrow,
This dance of life,
With the hands of fate
I grip tightly,
For you write my joys and sorrows,
But who gave you the right?
This question I ask,
This question I ask.
Nevertheless, I shall love you,
Until my dying breath.

"Look, I'm your friend here. Let's be frank, where will this lead you?" Amir asked. "All of us, except Iqbal and a couple of the girls, are drifting away from studies. I know I've been playing a lead role in it with you guys. I like adventure and exploring new things too, but if we go beyond the limit, everything will come to a standstill, and we will have to face loads of restrictions from our parents, as well as from Rahul."

"I know, dude, we'll try and find a solution," Ihusaan said.

"I am not too worried about the studies yet. The exams are still months away," Amir said.

"Rahul is the problem here," Ihusaan said. He had gone mano e mano with Rahul several times already.

Amir realized it would be futile to argue with him any further; Ihussan wasn't prepared to stop smoking weed.

"The problem is that everyone takes the world too seriously, it's going to fuck us all in the end anyway so might as well enjoy while we can."

"Life isn't easy, I agree with you. But I'm worried about where you'll go from there. It's never going to be enough. Too much more of this and the high from weed won't satisfy you. You're already mixing it with drinks and tabs and it *still* isn't enough." Amir was repeating what Aman had told him about the results of abusing drugs, having previously worked in the police department. "And in addition, the whole situation in the house has become tense, which adds to your stress. So, what's so cool about this? I don't understand the kicks you get from it, and I would rather not."

"Well, bro, you gotta try it," Ihusaan said. "The music will feel absolutely out of this world. crazy man, it will be crazy."

"Thanks, but no thanks. Life is hard, but I don't share your philosophy that it will drown us all. There are success stories, albeit a few, but I intend to be on that list, whatever the outcome."

"I know," Ihusaan nodded. "You are a good leader; you can achieve many things. You're able to unite people with different personalities and characteristics, and it's because of you that things are the way it is at home."

"My philosophy is simple; good thoughts, good words, and good deeds," Amir said.

"Thus spoke the Zarathustra." Ihusaan laughed.

"I cannot do anything alone." Amir's tone was serious, "I need intelligent guys like you to help me. You see, I don't believe in coincidences. I think God places people in our life for a reason, to either learn a lesson or to build something together, great or small, it depends, but who we choose as friends certainly effects every one of us. Friends define us," he continued. "I want to tell you today, I have big dreams. I don't intend to become famous, but I want to be powerful. Powerful enough to control, or at least have a say in, the way the world functions. Our country is small but significant. If we are able to get a stronghold there, we can influence the world. I want to change it for the better. For that, the first requirement is money, and that we must get by hook or crook, so, let's build this together. We need to get our priorities right. Please complete the course you are doing. I will convince Rahul. He will take us for outings and picnics. But you've got to keep the illegal activities down, or at least control it enough to be insignificant."

"I understand" replied Ihusaan. "But I daresay I am skeptical. I do not have so much hope for this world as you do."

"Why is that?"

"Look at everything that's happening. It's not right. Evil is taking over the world. Religion is becoming a lost cause. People believe it's all science. Man is a selfish animal, destroying nature in the name of development. The beautiful philosophy of simplicity has lost significance. How long can we go on like this? When all the earth's resources are depleted, we feel nature's wrath with environmental calamities and catastrophes. Isn't this where we are heading?"

Amir realized there was no real reason to confute the argument. "Quite right, society is becoming increasingly foolhardy," Amir nodded. "Isn't it more reason for us to do something about it?"

"How can we? First of all, we will need to join hands with the evil people who are already in power. It would be naïve to think the puppet masters will give up the juggernaut of globalization and capitalism without a fight."

"True. As the Chinese say, we will need a mandate from heaven" Amir said.

"In Xanadu, did Kublai Khan."

They both laughed.

Amir let his thoughts wander. It was indeed true that the world was making rapid progress materialistically, but spirituality was in a decline. The human understanding of happiness seemed to be changing. It was like filling a bottomless bucket.

Drained are my hopes

When I look at you with closed eyes,

With love in my heart,

But despair I feel,

For I know not for certain

The road to you.

The lack of interest in spirituality was not without reason. In the name of religion, even spirituality and magic, for that matter, several conmen, quacks, and institutes have been duping the common man just to get their money. Religious practices based on personal beliefs were becoming weaker, and the notion of working harder to achieve success was becoming more of a philosophy than blind belief in systems preached by ancestors and priests of old. Science was doing wonders and giving explanations to many a thing never imagined centuries ago. Who could have thought an invention like the television could exist, where a scene played back in time is telecast to boxes of electrical devices at several homes through signals that were invisible to the human eye? The internet and artificial intelligence aren't even questioned now by the kids of this generation, as they are born into it, and it's something that works and should work. Why it works isn't even asked, and schools have started to teach students how it works through coding and computer language. Things the paleolithic man could never have conceived in his mind.

The idea now was to graduate and get a 9-5 job and work as a drone, buy a house or a luxurious apartment, drive a modern car, marry a wife who earns as much as you, and have children with her, who in turn would follow the same principle.

In time, humans would be so alike they forget to try and be different.

Amir remembered George Orwell's thoughts in his book 1984. The Society wasn't so Dystopian yet, or maybe it was. It was just the priorities of man going through a paradigm shift with aggravated egotism. So, what was dystopian, or perceived as dystopian, decades or a century back may be the ideal society humans envisioned today.

His own country had a president who was in his third decade in power. Although the democratic process was gaining strength, the old guard was still strong. The opposition were gaining strength through western media support and had labeled the incumbent as a tyrant, a dictator, who manipulated the votes to be elected by a margin of over 90%.

Amir was a keen follower of Indian politics. India was the world's largest democracy and had a well-planned structure that started from the grassroot level in the villages with village panchayats. He had studied the system in depth and very much enjoyed his civics class at school He had read about and knew the leading figures in Indian politics and all the parties, including regional ones, and the volatile inter- and ultra-party fights. Democracy was seen as a mechanism for a liberal society. What liberalism was, exactly, was a matter of opinion based on whom you asked. At least, that was how it was at the start of the new millennium. To be free from control and able to do as they liked, as long as they didn't harm anyone else may have been the western concept of liberalism, but live and let live philosophy was a challenge to all religious dogma, including Christianity, despite a propitiatory approach. In a few decades, the winner would have to be chosen, Amir had imagined.

However, there were rebels. Rebels who challenged the control the rich and elite had on them by creating this class-based society to batter poor workers. How can you do whatever you like if you didn't have enough money in the first place to fulfill the basic necessities of life? The fulfillment of desires and its surges had made civilizations collapse in the past, which may have been why religious or sacred laws were followed by the faithful and fearful despite pungent criticism.

Every society has its artists and experimenters. To Amir, people like Ihusaan were in this category. They liked to enjoy the moments of life to the fullest and were artistic in their outlook. They liked to combine a good view, good music, good friends and occasionally add a high to the mix. The problem was that they were doing so at the expense of what tomorrow might bring. In other words, they were purchasing tomorrow to enjoy today, which was a scary situation for someone ambitious like Amir. He had decided to learn from the experiences of these friends, to be close to them and be a part of their journey. In fact, he found most of them kindhearted and caring, which he desired in all his friends, as he abhorred people who intended evil on others. What he had learned growing up in India was not to trust the unkind and evil natured.

"I want you to know, we are all in this together. We need each other's support to successfully complete what we came here to do and keep our parents happy. Your actions will have an effect on others. I know you are intelligent enough to understand these things, but just be careful."

"I understand," Ihusaan nodded.

Amir glared at him quizzically.

"It won't happen in the house again," he added.

Amir knew that it wasn't going to last for too long, but he appreciated that Ilhussan was ready to try. "So, any new good music?" he asked, changing the topic.

"I've downloaded a few on LimeWire, I'll share with you."

It was Ihusaan who introduced him to trance music. As a kid, Amir enjoyed Bollywood's Hindhi music. During his early teenage days, he fell in love with slow rock. Metallica and Megadeath filled his playlist until they started going to discos and enjoying hip hop and rap. However, trance was something completely different for him. He developed a penchant for it, and since then, Ihusaan had become his music guru.

They spoke for another ten minutes or so and Ihusaan left. Hamdh came back to the room almost immediately and asked how it went. Amir gave him a short brief.

"I spoke to the girls about the date," Hamdh seemed excited. "They said this weekend."

"That will be fine," Amir concluded. He thought about Nashwa. Friends with benefits may be the furthest he was willing to go with her. An expedient relationship it would be.

The excitement of an adventure,

So funny how it ignites

A spark in the brain,

For a fulfillment of a desire,

To adore the danger.

That night, Amir was wakeful and debated the matter in his mind, countervailing the negative thought with positives. He could keep the matter under wraps and his girlfriend back home may never find out. However, he was wise enough to realize that he would need to crack the moral mindset he had developed since childhood of honoring the trust others placed on him. As he grew older, he learnt that this was not an easy thing for even the bravest to stick to. He was learning through friends how exactly things were so very similar to the books he read and the movies he watched.

Amir decided to have a go anyway, as he needed a partner for the discos they were attending almost every weekend. Plus, it would be good to have a close friend to share things with, because now it was him to whom all the boys came to when they needed someone to lend them an ear. However, he was still debating when sleep took over.

The following Sunday, the two girls, Hamdh, and Amir went to Brigade Road Pizza Corner. They spoke about random matters and ordered their food. Amir was trying to be as normal as he could, although his raffish nature was evident. Hamdh's girlfriend passed teasing comments occasionally about them.

Amir knew he had to man up yet be careful to not act in a manner that would repel Nashwa. So, he asked a few questions and used the connection he had with Hamdh to keep the environment joyful. After eating, Hamdh suggested they meet in MG road barista for coffee. He told Amir that he and Sheereen had some shopping to do and would meet them in half an hour. Amir understood then that the plan was to leave him and Nashwa alone together. When they were alone, Amir smiled and asked, "So, what do we do?" He immediately realized it was a stupid question. He had not yet had such personal relationships with girls, he realized.

Nashwa shrugged coyly.

"Let's stroll for a while, we can check out some shops if you want," he said. "So, how is college going?" They walked in the opposite direction of MG road. The sidewalks were small and the road was full of traffic, so they had to go slowly. Amir's idea was to walk to the end of the road and then turn around, walking back up to MG road and the Barista outlet there, where they would meet Hamdh and Sheereen.

The crowd got thicker. Amir moved closer to Nashwa, trying to protect her from the crowd. Her perfume smelled like frangipani and she suddenly held his hand lightly. In return, he welcomed her hand by holding on more tightly. To the young, inexperienced Amir, this situation was testing him. He could either act like a gentleman or adopt the bad-boy attitude that many girls seemed to like. If he rushed things, he knew that she would know that it was just sex on his mind, but if he didn't, she might think he was weak.

These thoughts crossed his mind and he felt his body become stiff. However, within a few minutes, his fears subsided and he actually felt very confident. It was very manly to be protecting a young girl, leading the way. He felt a kind of happiness he hadn't experienced before. He looked at Nashwa, their eyes met, and she grasped his arm with both hands, gripping it higher than before with a blush on her cheeks.

Amir realized that there was no need to seek each other's approval, their bodies and minds were giving all the right signals. It was just good chemistry, he thought, like an experienced scientist mixing two chemicals, bringing wonderful results. In their excitement, they reached the end of the street without saying a word. At that point, they looked into each other's eyes and smiled. The jubilation was evident on her face too. He had carried out the task with aplomb.

"Maybe they have gone to Barista," Nashwa said shyly.

"Well, they can wait," Amir told her, trying to sound confident. He realized that he actually was doing better than he had anticipated, so he decided to take control from there on. "Let's go into the mall."

As they went in looking around the shops, they stopped at a stall selling wristbands, necklaces, and tawdry artifacts that were on trend at the time. When he realized that Nashwa was keen on a penannular wristband, he asked her whether she liked it. It was a green leather band with silver-colored ends and resembled two serpent's heads side by side. Nashwa nodded in agreement and asked the salesperson for the price.

"Two hundred."

"We'll take it," Amir said before she could answer.

She flinched and thanked him politely.

Amir immediately felt better. He didn't like the idea of her making the first move. So, he was inventing ideas in his mind for ways he could make up for his rigidity. They started walking back to MG road Barista.

"You didn't have to do that," Nashwa said.

"It's a gift, cheers to our friendship."

"We were friends already, all these months," She reminded him.

"Well, then for more than friendship," he added. "Let's get to know each other better. You can be my dance partner. New Year's Eve is around the corner and DJ Ivan and some other foreign DJs will be performing."

"Yeah, everyone is talking about it."

"You don't have a boyfriend back home?" he asked her.

"Would I be alone with you like this if I did?" She replied.

"Hmm, that depends. I have a girlfriend, but I am here with you."

She laughed. "You guys are like that. We're girls, we are more delicate but more dangerous, so be aware," she teased.

Amir shrugged. "Dangerous is exciting."

"Is there anything else you guys think about other than excitement, adventure, and partying? According to the girls at home, that's all you discuss."

"Well, I think the culprit is me. I have a philosophy. What if there is no tomorrow? We need to live life to the fullest, with zest."

"Living life to the fullest means enjoying?" Nashwa challenged

"No, making everyone around you happy, making them feel special, spreading a positive vibe and energy."

"Ok, so if it pays to make people laugh and smile, you will be a millionaire soon," she laughed. "But not all agree with you."

"Oh, is that so?"

"Yes, few of the girls are really religious. I won't name names, but they think that all these discos are spoiling the good ones among you guys."

"Well, that's new, but religious zealotry is not welcome here," Amir added peremptorily.

They reached the Barista outlet. Hamdh and Sheereen were not there yet, so they took a table and sat down without placing the order. It was a spacious, open-air café with four benches and a number of tables and chairs under the franchise's trademark orange umbrellas.

It was one of Amir's favorite places on earth, where his dreams took shape as he sat there chatting with friends, developing ideas, even crass ones, to pass the time. Being the young, inexperienced, innocent youth that Amir was, he was making plans and dreaming dreams few would dare to. He somehow knew he would triumph, although he had no idea what the world would make out of him.

That day, for the first time, he was sitting alone on a date with a girl. Amir already realized that the next chapters of life would be different. First, he was going to cheat. Second, the environment they were living in was inviting and free, therefore, the chances of getting physically close to Nashwa were high. It would only be a matter of time.

Time, the vindicator,

No beginning no end,

Infinite wisdom,

An endless sea,

But I shall swim,

Here there and everywhere,

Until I taste,

Sweetness of your secret.

They spoke about events at home and college.

"Shall we meet again, next Sunday?" Amir asked.

"The four of us again?"

"No, just you and me," Amir said, looking directly into her eyes.

She immediately looked down and muttered, "Yes."

At that point, they saw Hamdh and Sheereen coming. "Sorry, found a few interesting things to send back home," Hamdh said.

"So, how is it going for you two?" Sheereen teased Nashwa. Nashwa gave her a thumbs-up and chuckled. "Romance is light for the mind but heavy for the heart," Shereen smiled.

Four weeks after that evening, Amir had sex for the first time. It all started with a kiss on the staircase of the boarding lodge, wild and insatiable. He pressed Nashwa's body against the railing, holding her face and waist forcefully. Along with his youthful exuberance and energy, the magnetic attraction to her grew day by day.

Since their first time together, Amir's mind was preoccupied with thoughts of sex; the moans and the ecstasy, the unimaginable attraction, a force so strong and visceral it made him realize that a relationship between two souls and two bodies created a magical adventure, that longing was sacred and indescribable.

Everything he had read or heard about sex fell short of explaining this feeling, leading Amir to think deeply about the institution of marriage and the attraction married people felt for others. He thought that it was naïve to think that extramarital affairs wouldn't happen. He also thought about it in a religious context, the concept of it as a major sin. Sex was something that was so essential to human survival, both biologically and psychologically. There were so many rules and conventions regulating it in different ways across cultures at all times of human civilization and existence. This certainly was something that created a powerful energy, a force that the human species as a group used to break down all veils that separated them from the spiritual.

He didn't disagree with the religious doctrine of performing a ritual of marriage in order to get permission for man and wife to use each other's bodies as their own. In fact, he found it quite a charming tradition that should survive the test of time. However, looking all around him, he knew that these traditions were vieux jeu and dying out slowly. Liberalism was a raising wave sweeping across countries like a huge Tsunami and impiety was a norm.

The thirst,

The salacious hunger,

For every sweat that breaks,

From your thought of me,

And my thought of you,

Entangling your mind,
While the heart beats,
Asking for more…

Despite the physical relationship and strong affection Amir shared with Nashwa, he was not ready to give up his first love, Seema, as he was her first love as well. Nashwa had already been seriously involved with other boys, so the issue of being serious with Nashwa never crossed Amir's mind. He was just getting closer to her as a friend with benefits while they happily lollygagged around the city.

However, despite the fact that Nashwa initially tried to show that she was okay with this arrangement, she started becoming more serious as time passed, unbeknownst to Amir. He always waived any of her questions regarding Seema. *He* knew that this relationship with Nashwa was a transient one.

It was December, and the students in the boarding house were preparing to celebrate New Year's Eve. The boys were finalizing their partners, as there were strict "couples only" entry rules for the infamous parties of the night. Amir wasn't bothered about it, as he knew Nashwa would go with him.

That was until Ayesha called him the night before and told him she needed to talk to him. Amir agreed, and they met that night outside the kitchen. Ayesha told him that Nashwa was very upset and had told her that she would not go to the New Year's party. Surprised, Amir asked why. He had everything planned, and now there was no time left to change things.

Ayesha sighed and said, "She's getting serious. She wants you to make her your only girl."

Amir looked stunned. "But she never told me anything like that. We have been enjoying our time together very much."

"You need more experience with girls, I guess," Ayesha told him sarcastically. "No one wants to be someone's fling, maybe for a short period, but they will either get bored, underwhelmed, and leave, or they will become dead serious."

"But I can't! I have a girl back home to whom I am committed."

"Well, I can see how committed you are, cheating on her with Nashwa. So, Nash has a point," Ayesha said firmly.

"Look, I will tell Seema about this arrangement with Nashwa if I ever have to and then she can leave me if she wants to. I will not extenuate, but I am not letting go of her," He was not pusillanimous, nor was he scared of aspersions.

"Alright. Is it ok with you if I told Nashwa about this? She is also my friend. I need to tell her not to waste her time."

Ayesha was asking if this was his final decision, which also meant his plan was foiled and he would be without a partner on New Year's Eve. However, he didn't like the foofaraw, neither did he want to be impudent. Amir remained silent for a few minutes. The mafioso in him took over from the emotional gentle friend and he decided he needed to pull the axe. "Alright, inform her of what I told you, and tell her I am grateful for all the beautiful times we had together."

You make an offer,
A trade, was it?

I understand not why,
An indelible ink,
Is written with pain,
Sung with joy,
the story of life.

The news spread around the house that night like wildfire.

Amir came to know, because Hamdh hurried into the room while he was reading and told him that Sheereen told him that he and Nashwa had broken up. Hamdh was worried because Amir would not be able to go to the party without a partner.

It was Ihusaan who came to Amir's rescue. He had learned of the breakup through his own fling in the girls' floor.

"I know a group of Maldivians who came last month for some medical issues. I have known them from few years back and they have some girls in the group. They also party a lot. In fact, they asked me for guidance for New year's. Let's meet them."

"Alright. Let's get coffee tomorrow evening then," Amir said.

The next day, the last day of the year, Amir was to meet someone who would influence his life's journey in ways he had not imagined.

Ihusaan and Amir took an auto rickshaw to the Barista on MG road. When they arrived, there was a group of three girls and two boys. By the look of it, Amir assumed Ihussan's friends were marijuana smokers too.

One guy immediately caught Amir's attention. He had a piercing look and a slim athletic body like that of a surfer. Ihusaan introduced him to Amir and said that he was one of his closest friends, Khalid. They ordered their coffees and discussed the party plans. One girl named Shaaz took particular interest in Amir. She was short haired and very stylish and modern, the type Amir liked to hang out with. Amir always had a keen interest in fashion and the latest trends. He and his gang hung out in these hot spots of the city for what they called "bird watching", to catch glimpses of trendy, beautiful girls for which they had developed a fixation.

Shaaz, who was a very bold character, gave a flick on Amir's arm and struck up a conversation. Amir was jazzed. She accepted the invitation to go with Amir for the New Year's party with alacrity. However, Amir was more interested in what Khalid, who appeared to be the coolest man at the table, had to say. He uttered a few words now and then and Amir realized that he and Ihusaan where buddies back in Malé. Amir observed Khalid silently. He was smoking one cigarette after another. Had a friendly smile on his face but looked both street-smart and affable.

Little did Amir know that Khalid was going to be his right-hand man for the rest of his life.

Man searches for wealth

Without recognizing the gems by his side,

A brother who brings a smile,

A stranger that touches

The deepest veins of the heart,

To share life here,

And rejoice hereafter.

The next day at the New year's bash, Khalid and Amir bonded well. Shaaz was Khalid's cousin, so they were close the whole night. It was evident to Amir that Khalid too was keen to pursue the friendship. Amir guessed it was because of the recommendation from the very selective Ihusaan, who wasn't too friendly with just anyone.

One hour past midnight, when the whole crowd was in a dreamy haze due to the intoxicants and powerful trance music, Ihusaan looked at Khalid and Shaaz who found a good corner and waved them all over. Khalid pulled out a joint from his cigarette pack and lit it. Yameen came from nowhere and joined them. There were five of them in the circle, and when Shaaz passed it to Amir, Ihusaan quickly interjected, "He doesn't."

Not knowing what had come over him, Amir took the joint and had three puffs. Ihusaan and Yameen looked at him, surprised. Amir looked back and said, "It's a New Year's party," and shrugged. The smoke clouded his mind, and he felt a euphoric rush in his brain as the music grew louder and stronger. He surprisingly felt a sense of security among this group. They kept passing the joint, and once they were done, Shaaz led him back to the dance floor. They danced the night away as Amir lost touch of time. He felt he was flying. He was having the night of his life.

By the end of the night, Amir and Khalid had talked and shared and laughed their heart out. The laughter was what Amir could recall the next day when he woke up. From then until Khalid left Bangalore, they met every day and smoked the occasional joint before going for a coffee.

Amir returned back to Malé three months later and started working in the Ministry.

After having coffee Amir, Imthiyaz, Shahid and Riyaz left on two motor bikes in the direction of the house Riyaz had mentioned. They circled the area for some time but were not lucky enough to get a glimpse of the girl. They gave up and went for a ride around the city, then stopped at one of their favorite places, known as the wave spot, where the surfers surfed, and undulating waves splashed on the bank. A wall was built around the city of Malé, in addition to the seawall, preventing the waves from spreading into it except in rough weather. Amir had lost count of the times he and his friends sat there looking at the waves during high and low tides.

When each wave hits the land

Will the sea remain the same sea?

Is it the destination?

The waves in the sea

Playing a game of chance,

Moments of time

Never to return,

A fader I am not,

Fragile, Fragile, Fragile life.

After spending some time there, they decided to go home and reunite that evening. Amir decided to call Ayesha and ask her to get some girls to have coffee with them. They occasionally had such get togethers, often leading to interesting conversations and games like truth or dare, creating opportunities for the boys.

Ayesha said that she would be free by five o'clock. They agreed to meet at seven thirty. Amir asked who would be coming with her.

"It's a surprise," she said.

"Ok, see you at seven thirty."

That night, Amir called Riyaz and they went to Lilly's on Amir's motorbike. Most of the time, Amir enjoyed sitting in the back and letting his friends ride.

When they arrived, Ayesha and another girl were seated at a table close to the sea. Amir and Riyaz sat down, and Ayesha introduced the girl as Dheena. She was extremely good looking, with a dark complexion and nice figure. She had strong eyes and a long nose, and as Amir observed her, he noticed a mischievous smile on her face. She was wearing a white top, a black skirt with a red flounce of gossamer fabric, and a tassel around her neck. They ordered their coffees and spoke about general stuff like office work and things happening in society. Shahid too joined them after a while.

Amir was enthralled by Dheena's beauty. Ayesha told them that Dheena was half Sri lankan from her mother's side. Before long, Amir started putting on his best charm and took the normal, forceful front he put on when he was ready to go for a girl he liked. Ayesha, who by now knew his nature and taste in girls, was happy with what was cooking.

The girls finished their coffee, and they exchanged numbers before the girls left. All of them were ready to have a go at the lithe Dheena, who undoubtedly was among the most beautiful girls of their generation in the city. Amir said he would call her later in the night and the others understood his intentions.

Amir had been single ever since he broke up with Seema, despite a few short-term flings every now and then. When he returned from Bangalore, he was very committed to his relationship with Seema. He met her every night at her home, and when her family finally approved of their relationship, he was allowed inside the house, later getting permission to take her out for rides and to dinner.

Her purity was her biggest asset for Amir, and he believed he would marry her and build a life with her. For this reason, they had refrained from sexual intercourse, despite intense foreplay leading to oral sex, orgasms, and detumescence. But things started to change once he started working at the Ministry. He was earning his own money, and the city of Malé was throwing hundreds of opportunities his way. His friends were becoming experienced with all kinds of endeavors and enjoying their youth, and according to some of his close friends, the ambitious Amir was too serious about everything. They urged him to enjoy life when he still could, for when married with responsibilities, he might be overwhelmed with obligations and may rue the way he spent his youth. To Amir, it was just their opinion. He had other ideas to achieve greatness.

Amir's friends' influence on him was getting stronger by the day. In the occasional café, chain smoking cigarettes, he formed a strong bond with people from different backgrounds and characters. Out of these, he enjoyed Khalid's company the most. Amir had a knack for knowing people's hearts, and Khalid was one of the kindest human beings he knew. He had the gravitas of a true comrade whom Amir could rely on, one who would knuckle down and get the job done. Despite this, Khalid had a resentment for the system and the elite and their machinations and guile. Amir had on occasions, to bear the excoriation of the lot by Khalid. His nature was rebellious, Amir had decided. Over the past months, Khalid had become the friend he would call for an isolated coffee to discuss personal matters tiring his mind. He knew the stolid Khalid was a friend he could trust to keep his secrets. In return Khalid too shared his personal matters with Amir.

Khalid was from a middle-class family from Malé. His father was an expert piscator who loved the sea. Kahlid inherited this love and was a powerful swimmer and expert surfer. Growing up in the city, he was an influential member of a large group of his generation. These guys, according to Amir, were the coolest people in the city. They had artists, DJs, entertainers, and organizers among them. Amir had been fascinated by the work done by them, and Khalid too was well involved in these works, as he was the among the heads of the group of nonconformists. From Khalid, Amir got insight into how these guys worked, their ideologies and temerity. Most of them were of Khalid's age and thus almost a decade older than Amir.

Most of the time when he was on rides around the city with Seema, Amir would come across this gang sitting on the wall dividing the city and the sea. He would occasionally stop for a chat with Khalid, who very much approved of Seema. The artist he was, Khalid was always fascinated by natural beauty.

The problems with Seema started a few months after Amir returned from Bangalore. He started realizing that although Seema was good natured and beautiful, she could not match him intellectually, and Amir found himself testy with her on occasion.

Amir was a big dreamer while Seema was a school dropout. She was a very homely girl, taking care of household chores. She had ten siblings, five of whom were younger than her. Amir had to put up with her childish tantrums often, which were becoming increasingly annoying.

When he started working in the government and mingled with the female staff, making more friends, he started to realize that he needed more adventure in his life. He was becoming more sapiosexual by the day and was always in search of intelligence. Vacuity of mind and gossip bored him. His search for intelligence involved not only girls, but those male acquaintances whom he took as friends. With a keen interest for knowledge and wisdom, Amir could lead any conversation, and he could instantly grasp those who could match his intellect or thoughts, although in conversations he was humble and always deprecated the acknowledgment of his intelligence by others.

The time in Malé was allowing him to evolve. He decided that he didn't want to live circumspectly. It was then that he started to try to change Seema to the modem and active female he believed his girlfriend should be. It wasn't that she was shallow, she was just not interested in the modern way of life. Amir's pressure started making her morose and the thought of marrying early slipped from his mind.

However, Seema was not weak-kneed. She noticed these changes in him, and quibbles started to lead to dustups over insignificant things. She was surprisingly stubborn. Her ultimatum was that she was who she was, and it was for Amir to accept her or not. She was not going to force him.

Amir took this negatively. He felt that if she valued him, she wouldn't have said that. Amir started reflecting on the fact that he had the world at his feet. He was just twenty. The world was his oyster. Then one fine day, he decided to call it quits.

They had dinner in a small restaurant, and Amir was asking her to agree to a trip on a nearby safari yacht, which belonged to his friend Alika's uncle. Amir needed a partner on the trip, or he would feel left out, as all his friends were paired up.

Seema flatly refused, saying her parents wouldn't agree. Amir argued that they were already spending late nights together and what would 'just one overnight in the weekend do?'. She was enraged at his presumption. She blandly repudiated it and said that they should get married before any such thing happened. This irritated Amir, for whom marriage wasn't a close reality.

He lost his cool and said some harsh words, which were met with equally harsh replies from Seema. Amir finally decided to end their relationship and said so. She gaped at him, not saying a word. He dropped her home and decided that he will not call her again.

Surprisingly, for the whole night and two days after the incident, he kept checking his phone. Seema did not call him. On the third day it dawned on him that the relationship was really over.

That night, he sat with his close friend Haaris on the beach, looking into the ocean covered in darkness. With a heavy heart, he thought of the time spent with Seema, the dreams they shared and the fallacious peace. Tears flooded his eyes and he let it flow.

This defeasance was a big decision, but his dreams were more important. He would conquer the world one day. He knew that he had lost his first love, but he had to be imperious.

Over the years, life would teach him that this was a big mistake, as he would have to struggle to redeem himself. A poignant reminder of what could have been.

Shattered, destroyed, lost,

If I could define my status,

Then I am alright,

I will find my way back.

Amir, being a believer in destiny, knew that he was yet to meet his soul mate. With this thought he carried on with his life and dreams.

Will always live in your heart,

If the flame of my soul extinguishes,

I know I will live,

In your heart,

So may you live on,

Now and forever.

After returning home from the coffee shop, Amir had dinner and went to his room. He debated whether to call Dheena or to send a text first. As he could not make up his mind, he flipped a coin three times. It was heads twice, which meant he had to call.

Amir instantly picked up the phone and dialed her. She didn't answer. So, he went to the washroom and got ready for bed. It was almost midnight when Dheena rang him back.

She said she missed the call, as the phone was in the room, and she was outside chatting with her family. They spoke about how the evening went and about how they each had become friends with Ayesha. Amir made an impetuous decision and asked Dheena if she had a boyfriend. She said that it was just a week since she had broken up with her only serious boyfriend. She was completely heartbroken, as she had spent three years with him and was ready to get married. But it seemed that the guy was not faithful to her, and she discovered it just few weeks ago, deciding to end the relationship. Clearly, she was devastated.

Amir thought about the opportunity that lay before him. Dheena was not a girl for just a short fling, she was girlfriend material. Added to that, she was too beautiful and sexy to not have a go for it. Amir changed the topic and spoke of the safari trip with Alika and friends, which still had not materialized, as he was without a partner. He asked Dheena if she could be his partner on the trip. Surprisingly, she agreed. Although she said that she would have to tell her mom that she would be spending the night at Ayesha's home. She inquired whether Ayesha could come as well. Amir told her that he would need to ask Alika if there would be room and would let her know.

They said good night and Amir tried to sleep. It was obvious that Ayesha had given Dheena a good recommendation about him. He had tried his best to make a good impression as he had read many times that the first impression is the strongest.

Two days later, they met alone for a coffee at Amir's suggestion. He said that they should meet and discuss things before going on the trip. Amir went to pick her up and they went to a chic coffee shop that had opened recently in the center of Malé. It was a cozy upscale restaurant with tables laid a comfortable distance from each other. Soft music playing in the background with friendly waiters moving about taking care of the few customers who were there just after sunset. This was just before the peak hours and Amir and Dheena found the atmosphere perfect for their first proper date.

The conversation for the most part was about her previous relationship and her sorrow, which she recollected with a glout on her face. Amir was reverent. He consoled her and tried to upraise her, saying she would get over it soon and that he would be there for her in this time of need.

Despite the coddling, they both knew that there was a strong physical attraction to each other growing by the minute. The need to grovel was disappearing. They kissed and played with each other on the beach that night. Everything was let loose between them, physically and mentally. They started sharing their life stories, struggles, work, and family life, but it paled in comparison to the attraction they felt for one another. It was insatiable, addictive.

It shames me,

How can I tell anyone

A beast you turn me into,

The smell of your skin,

And the fresh blood boiling,

Come release the smell of your thoughts,

Are they as crazy as mine?

I want to know,

The limit of my insanity.

On the yacht with Alika and friends, they spent almost all the time in their room, coming out only for lunch and dinner and a coffee with the others. As the days progressed their attachment grew, but rifts also started appearing because their personalities were different. Although they tolerated each other's whims and fancies, they realized they had underestimated each other.

Dheena's previous relationship had made her afraid to commit and she was presently focused on her career ambition and helping her family. She was the only sibling who was earning and the only breadwinner after her father. The family wasn't very well off, so there was a lot of responsibility on her shoulders. Amir, on the other hand, had less to worry about and was carefree, enjoying his youth.

They found themselves disagreeing frequently, even over petty things. Questions were met with turbid responses. However, despite the war of nerves, they would make up easily, progressing to cuddling and sex. They did it everywhere possible, without a worry about getting caught, and Amir wondered why he was so lucky to get away, as his friends had told him about many a situation where they were ticked off by the police for immoral practices in public places and public lewdity.

Amir and Dheena were licentious. It was everywhere, at home, on the beaches, in dark galleys, in cars, and in rooms borrowed from Amir's friends for nights of ecstasy. Amir's desire was savage. It was as if all they had on their mind was their fervor for sex. When they finished, their bodies were marked with scratches and love bites. They had no fear of being sullied. This was the most physical relationship Amir had had in his life. Dheena, on the other hand, was already more experienced than him.

This thought troubled Amir. He was losing his innocence. The city was making him grow into a rough, street smart, aggressive young man. Most of his energy was now been consumed by the relationship and he needed an occasional coffee break with his friends. He couldn't let his mind be vitiated by infatuation.

The friend he enjoyed most, who gave him much needed peace of mind, was Khalid. Although he preferred large gatherings of friends in his normal coffee meetings, he met Khalid alone, most of the time in a café that was different from the ones he hung out in with his gang. Khalid himself was not a regular member of his gang and hung out with his own group of friends, but he gave importance to Amir's call and would immediately free himself.

Amir discussed essential topics and worries with Khalid. Khalid told him the stuff that was happening in his crowd. Amir liked Khalid's attitude. He shared the dreams of his businesses and ideas to conquer the high standards he had set for himself. Khalid listened interestedly and praised Amir's intelligence, encouraging him to go ahead with his plans. Khalid, on the other hand, said that he did not have any intention of going for great things himself, but would be happy to be led by someone with a great vision and mission.

Amir introduced Khalid to Dheena, who also instantly liked him, just like everyone else. Despite his good nature and heart of gold, Amir knew that Khalid was what would be in Mafia terms called a "qualified man." This was only because Khalid had shared with him so much of his inner character. If not, it would have been almost impossible to read his true nature, as he brooked no interference into his very private life, Amir had realized.

One weekend, Amir, after having spent time with Dheena in her home, called Khalid and met him in a crowded and dimly lit café serving tasty coffee and delicacies. Amir looked flustered and told Khalid that the relationship was going through a rough patch, that he needed some advice. He said that Dheena got a scholarship for a three-year program in Kuala Lumpur and would leave in September, just a month away. Amir had spent six months with her, and from what he had experienced, he knew that a long-distance relationship would not be a very good idea.

Khalid was pensive for a while. "If she is ready to leave you and go, well, there is the answer. If she is not as serious as you are, there is no point going on, although I agree she is going to study, which will benefit you both in the future. but I know that's not what's important for you."

"Yes, and it's a group of boys and girls. They would be staying in a boarding house, and we both have experience of how things work in such an environment. It would be a test of fidelity for both of us."

"Correct," replied Khalid with a smile, knowing what was going through Amir's mind. "But be tactful, if you are asking my advice. From all that that has happened between you both, I believe there is no need to hold on too strong."

"Yes," replied Amir. "If she values this and trusts me implicitly, time will tell soon. This relationship has actually been an obstacle to achieving my dreams," he said brashly. "I cannot concentrate on my business, the only thing I can do is work on my job and the rest of the day is spent with her."

"I know," replied Khalid. "Maybe, have a joint and think about this."

Amir smiled and thought about it. Since coming from Bangalore, he had refrained from smoking marijuana except once on his birthday. He had tried to adhere to this principle, being extra careful, as he knew that if his mom realized he was doing drugs, he would be financially cut off and would have a hard time, losing most of the freedoms he was enjoying. Khalid also never asked him to smoke, and this was the first time he was offering. He must have realized that the news of Dheena leaving, the almost certain end of something he had worked so hard on for the past months, was mentally disturbing for Amir.

"Alright, I have reached my yield stress point," he said.

The coffee was done, and Khalid signaled to the waiter to bring the bill. "Give me fifteen minutes, I will meet you in the fisherman's park." He told Amir.

Amir rushed home on his bike, changed clothes, and got ready for the evening. He was at the fisherman's park by seven thirty. The park was dark, with most of the streetlamps not working. Khalid was sitting on a bench. When he saw Amir parking his bike, he got up and signaled to follow him. Beside the park was the harbor, where boats carrying passengers from the nearby airport travelled back and forth, and there was a path leading to the opening of the harbor they could walk up to an isolated place.

They sat there and Khalid pulled out a cigarette, instructing Amir to light it, and took the joint from his cigarette pack, smiling. They were the only ones sitting there, and the only people that were visible were too far to get the pungent smell of the smoke. Amir was a bit concerned, but through experience had learned to trust the smooth operator Khalid was.

"The guys in the boats can see us," Amir said, watching the vessels come in and out of the harbor.

"There is always a risk, that's the adventure in this. If there's any trouble, just drop the shit."

That was all they worried about, as after a few puffs their minds cooled down, sharing the joint and two cigarettes before they left the spot. Amir went to the regular den and called Shahid and their other colleagues. Khalid waited with him till Shahid arrived and then left. The weed had Amir consumed in his thoughts, saying little as he kept sipping coffee and smoking cigarettes.

In a second

relationships change,

It's the human condition.

Dreams of yesterday

Pierced and killed,

By the dagger of Today.

Amir shared what had happened with Dheena with Shahid and Riyaz, who joined later.

The two listened carefully, but did not give any judgement, even though Amir tried to elicit a response. Their blandness was because they obviously liked Dheena, who was pleasant company in several of their outings and trips over the past months. However, it was the conversation with Khalid that mattered, and Amir decided that he would go with the flow. With this thought, he was of the notion that it was not going to last too long. Amir always had the conviction that in addition to tenacity, knowing when to stop something or end something was going to be his strongest asset in the journey of life.

Amir was reminded of the character of Estella from Charles Dickens's Great Expectations. He read the book as a child, and it had a deep impact on him. Since then, he had been careful of his interactions with the opposite sex. Amir cared for his heart and was not ready to let anyone lacerate it.

However, Amir discovered that this was not as easy as he had thought. Dheena's decision had jeopardized the very foundations of the relationship. The following days, the quarrels got more intense, and along with it, heated arguments took place. After a few days, they both realized that they were growing apart. Maybe it was time to say goodbye. Their vanity was getting in the way of any protraction.

Amir finally came up with the ultimatum. If she was serious about the relationship, she should give up the idea of going to Malaysia and rather travel with him to India where they would enroll into a graduate program, and he would set up his business. They would settle down there.

Amir was already doing business between Bangalore and Maldives through an arrangement made through his college friend Rayan. Amir earned a share of the profit from the Indian side by getting orders from Maldives for the Indian company they had set up.

Amir was forthright and proposed this idea to Dheena in the room he had rented with his friends. After an intense period of sex, intimacy, and fulfilling haptic sensations, Amir made a coffee and looked at Dheena, lying naked on the floor. She was beautiful and intelligent. They had shared so much together, mentally and physically. However, he knew that what he was going to ask from her would be faced with stiff resistance and a strong test to his non-aggressive nature.

Amir lit a cigarette and asked her to sit beside him. He told her his plan, that it was the only way to continue the relationship. She was shocked, saying that it would force her to quit her job, and settling down abroad wasn't going to aid her as she had a family to look after. Amir agreed with her spurious reasoning, but he decided that he would stick to his plan to test how much she was ready to sacrifice for the relationship. Afterall, he was going to let her study, and if he was earning well, he could assist her family too, but he refrained from suggesting this, knowing that Dheena was a fiercely independent woman and would remonstrate.

The look on her face said it all. She wasn't ready for marriage. The scars of her past had not left her. Amir read the situation inside out. She was doing her best to subdue her anger. He knew it was over. Not because he couldn't convince her, but because he knew she wasn't ready yet to be his for life, even though she was giving everything to keep the relationship going. In simple terms, she didn't trust him, didn't believe in him. All these thoughts brought out the aggressiveness in him. He told her that if she didn't agree, there was no point in continuing the relationship. Dheena was taken aback at how firm he was.

She balked and her voice quavered, "It looks like you have already decided to let me go, how can this be so easy for you?"

"Yeah, right, aren't you the one who planned to leave and go for three years without giving a thought to how I would feel?" Amir repined.

"Come on, it's my career, it will help both of us. Besides, even when we started this, I kept telling you I am not ready for marriage, but I am fully committed to you."

Amir looked away. "Okay, we are both young and we don't need commitments either, but this relationship is nagging my head, and I can't concentrate on achieving the things I want to."

"Well, yes, I can see that! So why don't you find someone who will do everything the way you want and not disturb your peace?" She blurted. "It certainly looks like I am not the one!" The tension in the room was palpable.

Amir looked at her, amazed. He had actually almost proposed to her, and she was acting like the victim. Dheena glanced at him and immediately understood the rage in it. The energy was repulsive. She looked away, took her clothes, and started putting them on.

The relationship was dead meat and Amir was no scavenger.

He controlled the urge to vituperate and lit another cigarette. All was said and done. He was going to drop her home and call Khalid and release the stress over a coffee.

That was the last he saw of her. He learned from Riyaz later that she had to go to Singapore for the interview just a week later and her program had been preponed, so she went to Malaysia directly from there.

The winds of fate,

Carries you far away from me,

I cannot hate you,

Neither love you the same,

I blame the wind,

For it didn't take me with you.

But let the feints fade.

The relationship had lasted eight months. When Amir reflected back, it was the most serious relationship he had had after Seema, and the most physically intimate one. Their bodies had almost become one, and now his body demanded sex so badly that he needed to get occupied in other things just to get the thoughts of Dheena out of his mind. There was no need to feel animosity for something that was bound to happen. Nevertheless, the beginning of the relationship was an idyllic period of his life.

He sought refuge in work and doubled his efforts in developing his existing business. He discussed with his dad the idea of operating the company in India, with him being stationed there, so that he could source goods locally. He knew that this idea would get approval from his mom, as he told his parents that he would enroll into a college and complete his bachelor's degree in Bangalore. He decided to quit the job in the ministry and started preparing an escape route. He was also smoking weed habitually.

Amir also started dating some girls but did not find a flame with any of them. He had casual sex with a former colleague, but she wasn't girlfriend material, so he avoided her after a few meetings.

Amir knew that his world was going to change. His time in Malé was going to come to an end, and he was returning to India once again. India was his playground, and as he could read and write Hindi, he felt very much at home there. Amir had decided to be there by the start of the next academic semester, which was three months away. He was determined to enjoy these last few months in Malé. He also had the idea in his mind to persuade Khalid to come to Bangalore with him. The obdurate Khalid had become his best friend. He was like the stick around which Amir fought. Together they had become a formidable team. They were respected by every crowd they were amongst.

One day, after he finished his work in the ministry and was going home when someone yelled his name. When he turned and looked back it was Ihusaan. He had returned from India some days back. They exchanged mobile numbers and agreed to meet at night.

They met for coffee at Lilly's that night with Khalid and Ameen, another close friend of Amir's, who was a heavy marijuana smoker and had become Amir's potner, along with Khalid. He was taciturn, but flashed ideas and jokes at regular intervals. He was also a dawdler who kept everyone waiting.

It was such a comfortable environment, with tables laid by the sea with waves coming and crashing against the seawall and the atmosphere was humid and salty and the cool breezes filled the surroundings at night. They ordered coffees and all of them lit cigarettes, along with a joint, and passed it around.

They reminisced about their time in Bangalore and the fun they had. Ihusaan had ordered a coke, and after drinking half of the glass, he pulled out a bottle from his pocket and topped himself up with its content. "Whiskey. My brother from another mother working in the resort brought this gift for me in the evening, when I met you."

After a few sips he passed it to Khalid, who also drank some, and passed it on. Amir and Ameen refused, initially. If he did drink, Amir would have to be very careful when going home. It was almost certain that the smell would get him caught, as his prim mother waited until he returned home to open the door every night.

"Let's have an overnight party in Hulhumalé, Shahid and others in my gang will also join. We can get a few bottles and joints and spend the night on the island. I can get a few rooms in my friend's building, but we can party by the beach all night long."

The others liked the idea and joined in on planning the trip.

Amir learned that Ihusaan had tried heroin and got into trouble twice, escaping addiction by a thread. Now, he was dead against heroin, but was getting deeper and deeper into psychedelics. "Young, courageous and shameless we are, with no happy future, so what's there to fear?" Ihusaan always kept repeating.

Khalid and his gang too were experimenting with LSD, meth, and tablets, such as ecstasy.

The overnight trip in Hulhumalé was arranged. They partied all night long and went to their rooms at dawn, everyone sloshed. When Amir woke up, Khalid and Ameen were having a coffee. The rest of the gang, which numbered up to eight, were still sleeping on the mattresses laid on the floor. The house belonged to Imthiyaz's uncle and was not in use yet.

"So, how was the party last night?" Khalid asked, smiling.

"I still have a hangover."

"Me too," replied Ameen.

"Have a coffee."

"Some lime juice might help," Khalid said.

"Too tired to go out," Amir said, constricting his eyes.

He made a coffee and went to sit beside Khalid and Ameen on the balcony overlooking the lagoon and sea. It was a gorgeous landscape. The beach, the lagoon, the reef, and the wild sea lay across from them. Birds fluttering around and welcoming breezes from the ocean mixed with the strong rays of the scorching sun made a delightful atmosphere. Amir felt he could stay like this, in this moment, forever. After a long time, his mind was free, and the hangover also seemed to have gone away.

Amir reflected on the natural beauty of the country. They were certainly blessed to get this experience free of cost, whereas tourists spend thousands of dollars a day to just get the same feeling they were enjoying.

This amazing perfection,

Simply sit and gaze,

Nature laid down

In perfect order

For you and for me,

From a force

Knowing all,

The true essence,

Witnessed by all.

When the others woke up and got ready, it was past evening, and the starving gang went to a nearby café for food, finishing their lunch and having a coffee until it was dusk. The group opted to stay another day as it was the weekend, and the first working day of the week, which in Maldives is Sunday, was a public holiday.

Amir called his mom and fudged a story, telling her that he would be staying another night and would be home by the evening of the next day. She questioned him about many things before agreeing. Amir knew she wasn't pleased with the way he had been behaving lately. She had also found out that he had broken up with Dheena. Amir knew he had to slow down with his hash intake and reduce the partying, but ever since meeting Ihusaan there was no way out of it, as he was continuously calling and asking if there was "a program", which usually meant a joint or some other stuff and a get together. The old coffee gatherings had become insipid, and a new infusion was needed to make it lively.

Before he realized it, Amir had become addicted to Hash oil and was smoking it regularly in the mornings, afternoons, and evenings.

One day when he returned home and rang the bell, his dad opened the day and was taken aback at how red his eyes were, immediately inquiring about it. Amir said he was feeling a bit sick and when to his room immediately. He knew that his parents realized he was feigning sickness and he would have to face their ire. They didn't say anything but seemed worried ever since and Amir had to play it very carefully. The last thing he wanted was to face was their reproach.

As usual, it was Khalid whom he shared this experience with. Khalid told him that the way they were smoking and partying, it was no longer safe, that they would be caught by their families and, in the worst case, the police, if they continued this way. They were smoking hash oil all over the city, in parks, cafés, beaches, and every kink and corner of the streets. They knew that the police were conducting sting operations. Taking this into consideration, they called Ihusaan and the other close members, which had now become rather small, as not everyone could keep up with Amir, Khalid, and Ihusaan's intake. So, the others kept drifting away, and now other than the three of them, only Ameen and Riyaz were in Amir's core group.

The five of them met and Amir proposed to them to go to Bangalore, where they would study and party. Amir had already spoken with Khalid and made him agree to join him and told him about his business venture from Bangalore. Khalid believed in him and said that he would give his full support.

The other three were also in on the prospect, but they said that they would need to speak to their parents, as they would need financing.

In the end, Amir, Ihusaan, Khalid, and Riyaz were in on the plan. They would be staying at Rahul's boarding lodge initially, and Amir told them that once the business took off, he would rent a place in Mosque Road, near where his business partners lived. Staying with Rahul was convenient, as both Amir and Ihusaan were familiar with the place. Khalid too was acquainted with the area, as he had visited it many times to meet Amir and his gang during their previous time in Bangalore.

With Amir's foray into the drug scene, he slowly started befriending others in Khalid's gang and Ihusaan's group, who were hardcore smokers of hash oil. They were now experimenting with chemicals, methamphetamine or crystal meth and LSD. These people recounted their stories of their travels, mainly in India, along the hippie trials, and Amir noted the names and places so that he could visit them if time allowed when they resided in Bangalore.

Initially Amir refrained from using chemicals but was seriously growing interested in a variety of herbs. He began researching the different varieties of marijuana, or ganja, as it was called in India. He also learned about other psychedelics such as magic mushrooms and datura.

Before long, his parents had learned that he was going astray. Family friends, relatives, and people close to Amir's mom started reporting to her that he was hanging around with the wrong people and that they were concerned for him. Amir acted innocent but realized he had to exercise control if his plan to escape to Bangalore was to come true.

However, by now they were almost addicted to the substances, and the days would be occupied waiting for every opportunity to have a joint, just as they used to smoke cigarettes.

Getting deep into the dark side of the city enlightened Amir on the huge market for drugs in the city. It was almost as if no house was spared, and the stock was always low. Amir and his gang discussed the business prospect, mainly as Amir was into imports and was getting goods from India, which was the main source of the hash oil and heroin. Amir was cautious and knew that he had to build a strong, legal, business empire before he ever tried his luck smuggling drugs or any illegal goods.

He knew that he could make such a strong set up that no one would suspect him of any wrongdoings. He had to employ the correct people in the right places, conjoining theory and method. Knowing he had good comrades like Khalid and Ameen in Maldives gave Amir the confidence that his task wouldn't be too difficult. He just needed to build his business empire and set up his buying offices in different parts of the world. The business knowledge and the salutary lessons he drew from his father when he was a kid were being utilized very thoroughly, and he had a knack for identifying hinky situations.

The days left until Amir's departure were closing in and he was spending time with the friends he had made, belonging to all sectors and classes of Maldivian society. The country was being washed by a wave of democracy, and the populace was deeply divided among the left-wing and right-wing ideologies. Politicians maligned each other openly and haughtily on podiums and the citizens were unified only by the idea of economic development. Nevertheless, along with the wealth, society was in shambles. Social ills and issues had reached alarming levels, and despite adhering to one religion, the ideologies of individuals were very diverse. Thus, the authorities had to condone several activities. Now, the democratic process was giving a voice to all, including the minorities, and with the developments and fame it was achieving internationally, human rights groups, watchdogs, and media freedom organizations' attention fell on the island nation.

Amir planned farewell trips to a local inhabited islands with Shahid, Alika, and other friends whom he would be leaving behind. However, he never got time to plan it properly as he, Khalid, Ihusaan, and the smoking gang were too preoccupied with their daily doses and coffee meetings.

Finally, the day to depart arrived. Amir had gotten used to this scenario. He always made great friends and started building things based on his dreams, only to have to leave the place and start all over again in a new place with new people. He had to be like an agama lizard and blend into the new society. He had grown to love Malé, the days he spent with his friends, circling the town on lonely roads past midnight and before dawn, time spent in various coffee shops and labyrinthine streets and galleys and comfortable spots facing the sea for a chat with dear friends.

All this was coming to an end. He would be away for at least three years, although he would visit occasionally on holidays. The only solace was that his best friends would accompany him on this new adventure.

Oh, my city,

how kind you were to me,

your walls gave me
a safe refuge.
Like a comfortable bed,
I slept and dreamed in you,
I bid you farewell,
Forget me not, I, your valiant soldier.

Chapter 3

At the airport, Amir met Rahul and the new batch of students he was bringing to Bangalore. In addition to Amir and his friends, there were three girls and two boys. Amir looked at the girls. They were all much younger than him and had just completed high school. Amir particularly liked a girl who was wearing a floral top and had a wonderfully endearing smile. As he was observing her, Rahul approached him.

"So, all set, Amir?" Rahul asked him.

"Are these all the student going this time?"

"Yes, students from the previous batch left two days back. There are five or six guys there at home," Rahul said.

Soon, they checked in and were on the flight to Bangalore. Amir looked out of the window as the plane took off, leaving Malé. He thought of the days he spent there, a bit grieved because he had spent some of the best days of his youth in the city below.

But he was going to start a new adventure again. If he stayed in Bangalore for a couple of years, he would be in his late twenties, and if he were to achieve his dreams, he would need to work very hard and without a break. All this meant that his carefree days were over. He would work ultra hard day and night to fulfill his dreams, but with his friends, he would smoke and party during the weekends. That was his plan.

However, it was only the first few weeks of the beginning of the semester that Amir, Ihusaan, Khalid, and Riyaz attended classes regularly. Their brittle determination to party only on the weekends fizzled out terribly. Amir and Ihusaan's room was the party den, facilitating the beginning of their festivities at sunset with all sorts of cocktails, weed, and techno music, partying on until dawn. When they finally retired to bed, the sun would have already risen. The others in the building also started joining Amir and his friends and the crowd grew bigger.

It was the wonderful conversations they had when they were high and garrulous that were exceptionally pleasurable to Amir's young mind. They could talk for hours about several topics impacting society and the human condition. It was not normal conversation of ordinary folks. Amir wondered whether it was just the like-mindedness of his friends or the drugs that were making them imagine these incongruous things, bolstering ideas to quench the inappeasable thirst for wisdom.

Despite the foray into drugs, all four of them in the core group were staunch believers in God, although they never were able to practice religion as prescribed.

A few months into the academic year, Amir realized that he should at least do enough to pass the exams and started attending the college at least once a week, getting notes from his classmates. He would wake up by one o'clock in the afternoon, and after getting ready, had a coffee and smoked a joint. He would then go to Mosque Road to meet Rayan and his other Indian business partner.

The business was pulling in regular orders and they were making a small, regular profit. However, the money Amir earned was spent on his group's entertainment. Thus, it was never sufficient. Amir, even when soaring high at night, was preoccupied in business thoughts, calculating profits. He would dream of making bigger profits and the methods that would make it possible. As the night progressed, he would think of how he could build his business empire. He would call his friends in Malé and persuade them to order from him. The drinks normally did the talking, and he was always able to get a few orders every week. However, nothing had become permanent, and Amir knew he needed to get investments in order to get a steady, profitable business going. Profits had to at least quadruple for things to become stable.

Business and partying with friends kept him occupied. His studies were always in the back of his mind, as he knew how disappointed his mother would be if he didn't complete his degree, having to face her platitudes. Therefore, Amir was too busy to think of any other form of entertainment.

That was until one night, when one of the girls asked him if he could drop her at a friend's place. She was the girl with the amazing smile, Hawa. Amir agreed and dropped her off, asking her to call if she needed him to pick her up. She said she would if she couldn't get a ride. When he returned to the house, the other guys started teasing him, saying that she never asked any of *them* to drop her, despite many of them having approached her multiple times.

It was common knowledge to everyone in the house that Amir was Rahul's favorite and thus the leader of the pack, deciding how things were done in the house. The vivacious Hawa was leading the things in the girl's dormitory.

They had gone on some group outings and picnics. However, Amir, Khalid, and Ihusaan were too occupied with smoking ganja and waffling about to bother about the things happening around them. After a few joints they were stoned, observing the surrounding nature and listening to Bob Marley during the afternoons.

Amir gave the prospect some thought. Hawa was three years younger than him. She wasn't exactly what Amir would call beautiful, but she was very cute and seemed kind. Amir reflected on her delightful smile. He made a mental note to ask her if she would care to go for a coffee with him. He then immediately returned to his room looking for Khalid, who was on the balcony in deep conversation with Ihusaan.

"It's simplicity, that's what we need," Ihusaan was saying. He was turning into a naturalist. Herbs, nature, and simplicity was what he was advocating, and Amir and Khalid had to listen to his diatribe against materialism.

This was a different concept to what Amir believed, having been a typical materialist since childhood. He had big dreams of achieving material success and power. However, when he got into the smoker's gang, he found a group of people whose outlook on life was very different. They were happy just enjoying the moment and the good things in life, deferring important tasks without worry. They had a fatalistic attitude. The paradox was that they liked the quality things in life like good brands, cool gadgets, and technology. At first, Amir was bewildered. However, as he got into further conversations, he realized they were the way they were due to past experiences in life, mostly bad incidents and heartbreaks. They were emotional beings. What he liked most about them was that they did not discuss people, but indulged in creative thinking, imagination, and developing ideas. They were oblivious of other people's opinions. However, they were extremely lazy, and the indolence was contagious. It was affecting Amir's business activities, and his Indian partners had to call him numerous times before he would meet them every day to discuss business.

While Amir was chilling with them in the balcony, he got a call from Hawa. She asked him if he could pick her up. Amir, having just smoked a joint, was feeling too relaxed to move. However, the prospect of new sex gave him an energy boost.

"Good luck," Khalid told him as he picked up the keys and left.

Amir's idea was to ask her out for coffee, however, when he picked her up, he asked her if she wanted to go for a ride. She agreed, and he took the newly opened highway, which didn't have much traffic, filled with trees decorating the sides. It was a wonderful ride, and they were chatting about things at home. Amir tried flirting and asked her if she would care to go out with him. She agreed. On the way back, she hugged him from behind. Amir was taken aback but knew that it was an act of approbation and that the cat was in the bag. He held her hand, driving the bike with one hand.

That night they were on the phone for a few hours, talking about life. She was quite interesting and intelligent for her age, Amir thought. More interestingly for him, she was a virgin, and had not had much sexual experience, although she had had some causal relationships.

Two nights later it was *fait accompli*. She agreed to come to Amir's room, and they French kissed as Amir opened the buttons of her blouse, kissing and licking her cleavage as she felt his scrotum tenderly. They were mesmerized by casual sex and lost count of time. Her breasts were enormous and sensitive, making Amir feel euphoric. She showed some reluctance when he tried to penetrate her, but the resistance didn't last long, and soon she was urging him on.

Amir, who was smoked up and had a few shots of vodka, was having an ebullience of total bliss. This combination was going to be an inseparable addiction for the next couple of years.

In the following days, he found that the sex with Hawa was fantastic. She could last the whole night. What's more, she was slowly becoming a best friend, as they talked for hours together as they lay next to each other after sex. Her kind heart reminded him of Khalid. In fact, the two of them were very much alike. They were nice to everyone, always ready to help and featly in all their endeavors. Amir could not believe his luck.

As time went on, the drugs were losing their effect and the dosage of consumption kept increasing so fast that it was affecting Amir's friend group's finances.

To resolve this issue, Amir was to increase the income from his business activities. He was receiving pocket money from his parents, so he couldn't ask for more. The profits he earned from the business were all drained off to fund the clubbing life.

The group began to think of ways to make a quick buck, discussing ways to smuggle hash oil to Maldives. If they could get the goods past customs, they wouldn't have much of a problem selling it off in Malé. However, a lot of arrangements had to be made before anything could be made realistic.

They decided to find the source of the pure refined hash oil and a trustworthy contact who could deliver the goods as per their demand. From their talks in Malé, they knew that the goods were coming from Thekkady forest of Kerala. Most of the shipments coming into the Maldives were arranged through Maldivians staying in Trivandrum, now known as Thiruvananthapuram, which was the capital of the state of Kerala. They had also researched methods of extracting hash oil from the marijuana plant. The viscous hash oil was the quintessential form of the plant and had the highest potency of THC.

One day, during their coffee gatherings, Khalid told them about how some guys from his gang had visited Vattakanal, a town near Kodaikanal in the neighboring Tamil Nadu state. There, in surrounding areas of the town, were edible magic mushrooms giving a psychedelic experience. Amir and the others were enthusiastic about trying them and they planned a trip to Kodaikanal. Amir recommended they take public transport so that they would have enough money to rent good rooms and spend on good stuff. Amir, Khalid, and Ihusaan made the trip.

As it turned out, this was a marvelous trip. Amir realized that with the beauty of the place, which was green, yet very cold, was a wonderful mixture. One need not have any substances to have a wondrous experience. They got rooms and immediately asked around for weed, finding it easily. However, getting the magic mushrooms was a bit hard, although with some persistence they managed to get some.

That night they tried one full packet of mushrooms, however the mastication did not give a kick like what they saw on the internet. The next day they decided to go to Vattakanal with the hope that they would get better stuff.

The trip to Vattakanal by car was a magical trip. Amazing greenery kept their imaginations colorful. They were lucky to spot an Indian Gaur grazing in the woods. Vattakanal was the epitome of natural beauty. It was a very small town with few huts laid across the mountain top amongst the spellbinding scenery. Luckily, the driver who drove them there talked to the locals and managed to get them a hut atop the hill. Amir was wonderstruck. It was a priceless experience, he thought.

Sitting on the knoll outside the hut, looking at the horizon and the numerous hills across with loyal comrades was captivating. He was also excited, as they would be trying the shrooms again. Amir felt maybe there was a slight buzz, especially when he smoked a cigarette. Their pupils were dilated. That night, they lit a bonfire outside the hut and had another packet of shrooms. Although none of them got a very intense psychedelic trip, they all felt different, and the conversations were deep and strange. Mixed with the spellbinding environment, this was a night they would all remember forever. They were awake until the campfire smoldered and then lit another.

They spent two nights in Vattakanal and then returned to Bangalore.

Amir was feeling relaxed and fresh after the trip. He decided that he would cut down on partying and concentrate on business. If he could make such trips once in a while, he would have the motivation to work hard the rest of the days. They had realized that they could make such trips to different parts of India on a very small budget if they used public transport. During the weekends that followed, they took the bus from the city's main bus station and travelled to nearby cities and towns, a couple of hours away, and returned after spending a night there. Towns like Chicmagalur and Gokarna were memorable trips. However, in most towns they had to be careful with the ganja, as these were not mainstream holiday towns which foreigners visited.

Amir enjoyed discovering the way of life of the locals. Sometimes they enjoyed food and drinks in a beanery with some farmers and workers. Although they could not speak the language, Amir was able to communicate with them through signs and the bits of Hindi that they knew. After a while they spoke in Kannada or Tamil as if Amir understood every word they said. He kept nodding his head as his mind tried to grasp their feelings that they were expressing.

During these trips, he missed Hawa. She had become an important part of his life. However, he didn't want to destroy her innocence. He kept her away from the drugs and his other indulgences except for sex. Amir firmly believed that whoever was her partner would be a very lucky person, despite the fact that he wasn't sure yet if he could go all the way with her and tie the knot. Nothing in his life seemed certain, as he saw himself as a soldier fighting a battle that could change course anytime. However, knowing that there was a woman who would stand by his side was comforting. During much of the time he spent in these beautiful towns across the states, he had been lost in thoughts of her, as if she was beside him, watching the hills as the sun sets.

A relationship so honored,

I feel you with me

Wherever I am,

A constant companion.

That, my friend,

Is unconditional love, philia.

As far as he was concerned, Amir was finally building the foundation that would help him achieve his dreams. He had established his own business in India, he had loyal and capable friends whom he could entrust with work as well as have a terrific time with, and he had found a wonderful companion in Hawa.

She was able to satisfy him physically as well as mentally. However, as their time together progressed, Amir started liking her more as a friend than as a life partner. She was quickly becoming his best friend. He could share everything with her, and she would listen eagerly. She also shared her every emotion with him. She believed in his dreams and encouraged him to achieve them. She was like a gem that Amir was growing to treasure.

However, they never spoke about marriage. They were both going with the flow as friends, giving the most they could to each other. Nonetheless, Amir knew from experience it was only a matter of time before they made the relationship formal. He was afraid. Afraid of losing this excellent human being, who was kind to everyone and cared so much for everyone around her. He felt special because she chose him to be part of her life.

Amir discussed the propitious situation with Khalid. "She is such a lovely girl," Amir said.

"And you can make her more beautiful, too," Khalid added.

Hawa wasn't actually fashionable, and since his days with Shaaz, who was herself a fashion designer who flaunted her ultra-modern styles, Khalid knew about Amir's tastes.

"Yes, I know," Amir replied thoughtfully. "Everything's great about this city, and now that the business had kickstarted with regular shipments, I want to settle down here. Of course, I would need you here. I think Ihussan and Riyaz will leave once their courses are done. You can get work visa through our company," he told Khalid.

"So, you want to settle down with Hawa?" Khalid asked eagerly.

It was obvious that Khalid liked her and had asked Amir to take care of her many times previously.

"I think so, we are already living as if we are husband and wife, just need to sign some papers and go through a ritual ceremony to make it official," said Amir, chuckling.

They completed the first year and went back home for the holidays. It was refreshing to meet family and old friends. Amir also met his business contacts who were giving him orders for export. However, it was the gangs that approached him asking if he could source heroin and hash oil in kilograms that got him thinking. According to them, all he had to do was source the good quality stuff and hand over in the port cities to the gang's personnel, who was a staff member in the cargo boats.

Amir was entrusted with this perilous task because he was friends with Shahid, who was by now a senior member of the gang. Shahid knew that he would not be a recreant.

Khalid's gang also approached him. He got a call from Khalid one evening asking him to join him for a coffee with one of his closest friends, who was a leader of their gang. Amir had occasionally met the man for coffees and exchanged greetings. When Amir arrived, Khalid and Niyaz were waiting for him in a familiar café on the seaside. When they had settled down, a joint was lit. Niyaz asked Amir, "Let's get a shipment?"

"Yes, I have been getting offers, but we will need to get direct to the source".

"I think it's available in Munnar, Thekaddy, and one other point, which I don't remember."

"We can go there and ask around and try and get deeper into it. Right, Khalid?" Amir said.

"Yes, you will need to find the right contacts and try and win their trust. That's the difficult part. It's not easy to penetrate the inner core of these groups. Specially they keep foreigners out. That's why those who do this business get it in Trivandrum from Indians who have connection with the Mafia guys running things in the forests."

"But the profit is less because the middlemen ask for high prices and the quality is bad," Khalid said.

"The quality is low. They mix all kinds of stuff like engine oil into it. You would know, we pay frequently for bad shit," Niyaz said. "You have your own business as well, right? Exporting stuff."

"Yes, but it's just getting regularized and it's still not on such a large scale. For now, we can only source and hand over to the guys who can ship it and arrange it through customs. Later, we can plan the whole thing risk free and include within some shipments," Amir said.

The other two agreed with the arrangements. Amir knew that he needed to find what really was happening in Thekkaddy forest, in God's own country.

A few weeks later, they returned to Bangalore. Hawa had gone a week earlier with her parents, so they weren't able to meet much during the holiday in Malé. She told Amir that she needed to consult a doctor and do some checkups. She was complaining of shortness of breath and discomfort in the chest.

Amir called her as soon as he reached Bangalore. She was at home, and when he inquired about her health, she tried to downplay it. Yet, when he persisted, she told him that she was having heart issues and was on medication. Amir was very grieved to learn about this and told her he wanted to meet her as soon as possible. She told him that it was difficult with her parents still in Bangalore. She had obviously not told her parents about their relationship, which was understandable, as they never discussed going all the way together.

Such a beautiful heart was suffering. Was this the way of the world? Suffering was everywhere. Life was a hard test.

The man struggles on,

Suffering, a companion

teaching him

to love others

as they struggle on.

Amir wondered where all the things he was assiduously planning would lead to. He was getting deeper into Mafia activities. If he ever got involved properly, there would be no way out. The offers he received back in Malé were because he had proved his mettle and become qualified enough to be able to pull off deals. Amir, however, was cautious, and he decided not to plan anything unless he got full assurance and confidence that things would go smoothly from all sides.

Things did not go as he planned.

Khalid had to go back to Malé because his brother, who was the family's bread winner, fell ill and he had to look after their shop as the other siblings were occupied with their jobs. Riyaz did not join them this time either as he was not able to pass his first year of his pre-university course.

Amir decided to shift from Rahul's house and found a home close to Mosque Road where his business partners stayed to save time and travel costs. It was also because Hawa's parents had rented a house near the college for her, and she had moved there with three of her friends.

Amir shared the new flat with Ihusaan, who was doing his second year of his course. However, after the housewarming party, Amir was alone most nights, as Ihusaan went to stay over at his girlfriend's house. Ihusaan also had to get treatment for his insomnia and was on flurazepam.

Amir worked hard during the day and smoked weed only for morning coffee and after sunset with drinks. He favored whiskey but tried a different spirit every night. Without Khalid, his best drinking partner, he was starting to feel lonely, and his consumption increased by the day.

He started going out for coffees with other Maldivians living in Bangalore. He made friends with Shujaa, who lived with his family and had a brother of about the same age. Amir started visiting their house to play chess. The games with Shujaa were extremely competitive, despite Amir being a rather good chess player.

It was during one of these visits that he met Yunus, who had come to smoke weed with Shujaa and his brother. He had got some good stuff and was rolling a joint when Shujaa escorted Amir into his room. Yunus and Shujaa's brother were sitting in an alcove in the room with a small window. Yunus was a rough looking short guy with a French beard and stylish hair. He was wearing a garish T-shirt and long shorts. During that day, Amir learned that Yunus had been to rehab, as he was addicted to heroin, but had now recovered. Amir observed that he was finicky and developed an instant liking for the guy. A good friendship developed as they laughed away the hours.

In a later meeting, Shujaa told Amir that Yunus was not comfortable with the room he was staying in currently and was looking for a new place to stay. Amir considered it, as he had one empty room in the house, and some extra money would be of help, combined with the company he would have. Ihusaan now spent most of the time in his girlfriend's house. He visited often to share drinks with Amir but left again soon and didn't stay the night unless he was jaded.

Amir met Yunus for a coffee to discuss Yunus shifting to Amir's rented flat. However, Amir's mind was occupied that day from what he had searched on the internet the previous night about a Union territory in the neighboring Tamil Nadu state. The town was Pondicherry, which was previously a French colony. He read that there still were French families living there in an ashram called Auroville. In addition, there was a popular beach, and the main town was laden with restaurants and guest houses with vestiges of French colonialism.

He wanted to explore the city and planned to go there the following week. He would normally have gone alone, as he was getting accustomed to solo travelling ever since Khalid left, but the week coincided with his birthday, and he decided to take some friends along. In the end he decided to ask Yunus if he could join him, to which he agreed eagerly.

They took the bus from Bangalore's Majestic bus stand. The trip took longer than expected, as they reached Pondi after more than nine hours. It was dawn when they reached the city's bus stand.

They took a rickshaw and looked at some rooms in some cheap guest houses but did not like any, so when they spotted a nice café overlooking the Bay of Bengal, which was situated near the heart of the city, they stopped and went in for a coffee. It was a very French café offering varieties of coffees and delicacies.

The tired Amir sat there looking at the sea. In the distance, he could see some cargo boats. He wondered whether shipments were arriving at Pondicherry's port. He had read about the beach, so he decided that he would look for a guest house nearby so that he could have a dip in the ocean. As they sat there sipping coffee and smoking a cigarette, they spoke about plans for the two nights they would spend in Pondicherry.

"So, where is this Auroville?" Yunus asked Amir.

"I think it's an ashram, we can just go through the main city and take a rickshaw and get a guest house near the beach."

"I want to take the feel of the ocean."

"It's very inviting, isn't it?" Yunus said.

After the coffee, they strolled around the main city and checked the port, which had fallen into desuetude. The main town was filled with European style architecture and restaurants and was pretty clean by Indian standards, with a sizable number of foreign travelers walking around.

As they had not yet found a room, they were walking with backpacks. Amir decided to get a rickshaw and ask for a room close to the public beach. They were taken to a big guest house situated a stone's throw away from the shore. The rooms were not in a very good condition, but they decided to take it, as it was cheap and clean enough. Anyway, they would be partying hard, as it was Amir's birthday night. They threw their belongings into the dooket and went out immediately.

That night they had an epicurean feast and drank like horses, sitting on the beach afterwards. There were strong waves pounding the beach and when it retreated, it took with it a forceful energy from the land. They sat a bit far from the water and chatted about life in their intoxicated state.

It was the first time they had indulged in strong drinks together and the conversation was interesting. Yunus told Amir about his time in the rehab and his days of addiction back in Malé. He also spoke about the only girlfriend he had, telling Amir about their relationship and how they broke up. Amir, as usual, spoke of business and his ideas to achieve his big dreams.

"The world is a funny place," Yunus said after a while of silence. "Everyone is running after something. It's a wild goose chase. For instance, you have your dreams and I have mine. Both very different. You want material success. I want to be healthy again and live a peaceful life."

"Maybe you should resort to spirituality to elicit the truth," Amir told him.

"You mean religion?" he asked.

"Yes," replied Amir, pondering. "But I believe any form of spirituality has to do with God. I think. However, without guidance it could lead us to Maya or illusions. Otherwise, its energy you are after. Energy is present everywhere on this planet and in the universe. Like gravity. You can unlock and use its powers through various methods."

"You mean like the sun's energy?

"Exactly, look at the moon and how it impacts this sea in front of us. Those who know how to use these energies also call themselves spiritualists. But I don't agree," Amir said.

"And what do you think?"

"I think spirituality is just between myself and the creator. The creator of the universe. This desire leads me to rarefy myself, for I don't believe that all this which we see as we sit here, and the order of things can happen just out of nothing. There is a primordial being, or force, or the fontal light. Getting closer to that force must mean freeing oneself from attachment to everything in this world, or the universe, for that matter, and use your inner spirit to communicate with God," Amir said, trying to put up a cogent argument.

"You didn't seem religious," Yunus said. "But I agree with you."

"Oh, I am more religious than you can imagine," Amir got up and walked towards the sea.

The tequila was having its effect and the dancing sea was inviting him. He sat down where the waves hit the sandy beach. Slowly, with the tide rising, the strength of the waves was pulling him back into the ocean along with the salubrious air. Yunus ran fast and got hold of him as he was almost swept away. They both fell on the beach, drenched and covered in sand. They laughed out loud, and it reverberated in the eerie silence.

It was past midnight, and the beach was deserted. It was dark and haunting. Amir was enjoying the whole experience. They walked zigzag in the sand and stayed for more than an hour, Amir continuing to play with the waves. He sat there and wondered what lay across the horizon. If the waves took him with such force he may end up in Indonesia, he thought to himself amusingly.

Inspiration, I seek thee,

Wake me up from this dream,

Give me the cup
Of my soul's desire
That shall light
My body, like the moon above.

They went back to the room, smoked a doobie and he called Hawa. Her parents were staying for a couple of weeks, which was why she was not be able to go out with him like the previous year, when they went to a disco and partied on his birthday.

Amir and Yunus had a good time exploring Pondicherry the next day and left for Bangalore in the night.

The next morning, he was awoken by Hawa's call. It was afternoon, and she said she was skipping class for an hour and coming to visit him. Amir freshened up and waited for her with a coffee.

When she arrived, she seemed worried. Amir urged her to tell him what was wrong. She declined and started kissing him and they soon made love. As they lay on the bed after the intimacy, Hawa told him that she might not recover fully as the doctors had told that her heart was palpitating and very weak. According to them she had had cardiac arrests before.

Amir was taken aback. "But you are so young!" he blurted.

"Yes, but it's possible. Not everyone has a healthy heart," she said, looking away from his eyes.

"You will be just fine," he told her, holding her palm in his.

Her parents had come because she was sick and were trying to diagnose her in one of the best hospitals in the country. However, she told him that her chest pain was becoming unbearable and the medications made her weak.

She was also his best friend now, Amir realized. Ever since the day he dropped her at her friend's place, they had become each other's shoulder to cry on, to share all the worries and joys of life with. They didn't burden each other with unnecessary commitments, but always made time and space for each other when needed.

The following week Amir had to write his exams, but he hardly attended class and had to get notes from classmates, occupied the whole month preparing for one exam after the other. Amir was busy studying for his last exam when he got a call from Khalid.

"It's time," he said.

Amir understood what he meant. So, he said that he would travel the next week and get the job done. They exchanged routine questions and Khalid hung up.

Amir had researched on the hippie trail of India. He knew the spots in Kerala where he could get contacts. The fluency in Hindi made it easy to get around the country. However, in south India, people rarely spoke Hindi. From previous experiences he knew he could get around through with some Hindi and body language.

Amir decided to finally do the trip to the Thekaddy forest once he was done with the exams.

Some trips are written by the hands of destiny for people from different places to meet that changes the trajectory of human civilization through the sheer force of the energy generated when these meetings take place.

The young Amir's life and dreams was about to take a turn in a direction where he would have to tread the road few had walked. An extemporaneous journey awaited him.

Amir started sensing strange events around him in Bangalore. When he looked up in the sky he saw shooting stars, galactic halos, and familiar majestic constellations above his head. He also had black cats crossing his path and strange looking locusts visited his flat when he was smoking alone in his flat.

He started getting spam emails from various psychics who said they could perform magic and healing. They offered to perform rituals which would bring in wealth and power. These wise guys normally tried to sell pentagram pendants, wrist bands, gems, and necklaces which would attract wealth, health and power. Amir used to read these emails and visit their websites because of the stories they associated with their merchandise, which, according to them, derived their powers from Hellenistic mythical forces and Angels. In the recent weeks, he saw an increase in the number of such emails. Some said that his life was about to change, others informed him that he was about to meet someone very special, someone who would change his life forever. Unsurprisingly, they asked for some fees to perform rituals for him to attract positive planetary energies. As usual, Amir didn't pay much heed to these emails, as he knew from experience that these were just ordinary folks trying to make some money through their knowledge of astrology and mythology.

One week after the exam, he called Yunus for a coffee meeting and told him that he was about to make this trip and that he needed to find a good source who can get the quantity required to smuggle the drugs to Maldives. Over the previous meetings, Yunus had gained Amir's trust and was a candidate to become his handlanger.

Yunus thought for a while. "We have to be careful, it's very likely that these places will be carefully watched by intelligence agencies in India."

"I know but trust me. We will act as tourists. Backpackers trying to get high. Once we gain the trust of the peddlers there, they can lead us to the source."

"But then we might be required to stay there for a while."

"Yeah, that's what worries me too. I have limited finance, so we must complete the project before we run out of money. Of course, I can call home and get some money, but I wouldn't want to use the ATM in Kumily," Amir said.

Amir had done his research. Kumily town was the gateway into the Thekkady forest. He had planned the trip very carefully. He would not tell anyone where he was going, except Hawa, to whom he said that he was going to get products for a shipment in a city close to Bangalore. He also told her that he might not be able to call frequently, as they would be extremely busy. They would travel by public bus, so there would be no records of them going, as a conductor issued tickets on the bus and they gave him paper currency or coins, and they planned to change buses at major cities.

On the night of their trip, Amir and Yunus had a couple of beers and smoked a joint before leaving for the Majestic Bus station. They took a local bus from Bangalore to Coimbatore and from there planned to change bus to a bus going to Madurai. The sordid buses were filled with poor and middle-class passengers and were quite noisy when the buses halted, but as it drove on the highway, the cool breeze of air satiated everyone, and they could fall asleep on the chairs with their heads on the backpacks. Despite the pitfalls, the ever-high Amir preferred this mode of transportation to save money for experiences on the rest of their trip. From Madurai, their target destination was just around four hours away.

However, they were misguided in Coimbatore by some locals to whom they spoke who said that it was better that they go to Kottayam and travel to Idukki from there. This lengthened their trip by five hours, and they started developing the fantods. When they reached Kottayam, in Kerala, it was almost evening. If they had taken the Madurai route, they would be almost in Kumily by then, Amir told Yunus.

With no other choice but to continue their journey, they had a hearty meal in Kottayam before taking the bus to Kumily. The conductor, talking in Malayalam and showing his watch, informed them that it would take about five hours to reach Kumily. However, the wonderful geography and the astounding hills reminded Amir of the trip to Kodaikanal. They were going higher and higher after every town.

When they reached the hill top station of Kumily, it was around eight pm, and the town center was bustling with people. They spotted several white tourists wandering about as well.

As soon as they got off the bus they talked to the taxi drivers about a guest house. The first one took them to a place just across from the bus station. It was pennyworth with very few amenities. However, Amir agreed to take it, as they would just need the place to crash. They had work to do that night. As soon as they settled down, Amir befriended the driver and asked him for ganja. When he got them the stuff, Amir took his number and told him that they would call him to go to a good place for dinner.

After dinner, they shared a beer with the taxi driver and asked him about hash oil. He initially told them that he could get it but later acted strangely, as if he did not properly understand what they were talking about.

They asked him the price, and he asked them to give five hundred rupees, telling them that he would be back within half an hour and asked them to wait in the guest house.

He returned and gave them more weed and said it was for the five hundred rupees.

Irritated, Yunus reminded him that he said he would get hash oil.

The taxi driver looked timid, and his speech flurried. He told them that he could not get it and that it was a very high-class drug and not readily available. He left them soon.

"Well, at least we have enough weed now to last the trip," Yunus said.

"He didn't say it's not available, he said it's not for everyone." Amir's mind was focused on the mission, despite the dismal performance of the night.

"Well, we look like Indians, maybe they give it only to foreigners."

"Yes, we should stop speaking in Hindi and look more lost," Amir said, knowing that they had to be vigilant.

That night, they went out to explore the town and tried to make acquaintances if they found anyone who looked capable of helping them but had to be careful of those trying to swindle them. They had no luck; everyone was vacillant when they said they wanted to buy oil. After more than an hour, they had roamed the city center, and Amir realized they would have been noticed by the locals and guides who fossick for tourists. They had tea in one of the stalls and went back to the hotel around ten pm. At that time, most of the shops were closing, and the hustle and bustle had ended.

When they woke up the next morning and went out, the weather was cold and pleasant. Immediately after having some snacks and tea, they returned to the room for coffee and cigarettes, as they were not able to get strong black coffee at any of the stalls and the restaurants were not yet open. Amir's legs were quaking from the cold. It took an hour for them to have a joint and the coffee along with cigarettes. After gathering enough energy and mental preparedness, they set out again in search of hash oil.

They were approached by some guides and Amir started conversations with them about places to visit nearby. His idea was to find a good guide to explore the town and the nearby hills with. They took a taxi for sightseeing and the driver, who was also the guide, told them that it would take around two to three hours for the trip for two thousand rupees. Although it was a big amount, Amir agreed, as he felt he could befriend the driver. After chatting and exploring places, they stopped by spots with good views of the beautiful nature surrounding the rich hills and Amir asked him about hash oil.

The driver said it was available but that he did not know anyone who could get it. Amir knew that he was lying and was just being careful, as it was clear by now to him that they didn't give it to just anyone but offered the dried plant instead. However, as the day progressed, the guide was realizing that they were not Indians and were actually proper tourists as Amir and Yunus spoke in their native language.

They told the driver that they had checked out of the hotel they spent the previous night at and asked him to get a good room in a good place outside the town with a good backdrop, encompassing natural beauty. He agreed and took them to a beautiful area. Both Amir and Yunus liked the surroundings and asked him to get a room there. He stopped near an elegant-looking building and asked them to wait. He phoned someone, and an elderly man wearing white shirt and a sarong came out.

The driver spoke with him for around fifteen minutes before the man came up to them and spoke in English. "How are you?"

"Fine, thanks, how are you?" Amir said.

"I am good," he said. "Where you from?"

"From the Maldives," Amir told him.

"Ok, enjoy your stay," he said waving his hand.

The driver got in. "We are going back to the city," he said.

"Why?" Amir asked.

"You want hash oil, right?"

They had hit the jackpot.

"Yes."

"You will get it there," said the driver.

Amir and Yunus looked at each other eagerly. They were on track, but they still needed to be cautious until they got the stuff in hand.

The driver brought them to the spot where they had met him, the taxi stand just outside the bus station. He got out and asked them to wait till he came back.

After a few minutes, the car door was opened by a man who, according to Amir's first impression, was in his late forties. A thin rugged figure with bewitching eyes. He was wearing a shirt, jeans, and Reebok shoes. "Good evening," he said as he opened the door to let them out. "I am Abdul Samad, tourist guide."

"I am Amir, and this is my friend Yunus, we are from the Maldives."

"Maldives, yes, I know. You want oil?" He asked directly.

Amir was delighted, and before answering, observed the man. He looked like a tough and qualified warrior, but he smelled of rum. *Have to be careful*, Amir thought, but there was something intriguing about this man from the hills. "Yes."

"How much" Samad asked. "Grams?"

"What is the price?"

Before answering, the guide asked, "Where are you staying?" It was evident that he was a bit drunk and wasn't observing them too well, but he was doing his duty as a tourist guide.

"Need to find a guest house," Yunus said.

"Come with me. I have good rooms," he said. "Safe places, you don't have to worry." He immediately started walking and asked them to follow him. He had nimble feet and a characteristic flair.

He took them to a guest house which wasn't far away. He spoke to the owner and led them to a comfortable-looking room, which was clean and tidy, but the floors and furnishing were old and out of style. It was more like a homestay room. Amir asked him whether they could get a more modern room.

He understood Amir's taste but said, "No need to stay in hotels. Stay with locals, you give them some money, it is good for them. Earn bread and butter, understand?"

Amir nodded. He didn't need any luxuries, his only concern was dirty, fetid toilets.

"Okay, you wait here, I get you oil." he said. "How much you want?"

"Ten grams first," Amir said.

"You want ganja also?"

"We have enough for now."

"Okay," he said and left.

Yunus sighed. "Finally."

"Yeah, I had almost given up, but let's see if he gets some good stuff, or if he tries to fool us."

"Doesn't look like the kind to do that. He seems like a big smoker himself," Yunus said.

Amir realized that this man would know everything that was going on in the city and, hopefully, in the mysterious Thekkady forests, which he desired to explore.

The Call of the Wild. The name of the book he read as a kid echoed in his mind.

He had met a man of the Jungle. The key maker who would have the password for his entry into the deep, magical, and dangerous forest, with its numerous varieties of maroon and black trunked trees, trailing vines and creepers, and dense wilderness teeming with arboreal animals.

Samad came back after around twenty minutes. He gave them *stuff* wrapped in cellophane paper. The oil inside was a greenish, gold colored stuff. Amir opened it, relishing the smell. He passed it to Yunus, who immediately took out cigarettes, mixed the tobacco and the hash oil, and tamped it down to begin rolling a joint.

Samad stayed with them, and they shared the joint. It was extremely good stuff, the best that Amir had smoked up until then. Maybe this was reserved for the tourists. If he talked of buying in bulk for business, he might not get this kind, Amir thought as he sat there knowing that he had reached his target. Now the only thing needed was to get closer to this character.

When they finished the joint, Amir asked Samad if he would care for a coffee. He declined and said he had to look after some tourists but would be back in the evening.

"You wait in the room," he said, "I will come pick you up. I will take you sightseeing and meet some friends." Maybe he guessed that they were tired.

When he left, Amir and Yunus exchanged knowing glances. "This stuff is fantastic," Yunus said. "Must have a dab." He looked for foil to heat the stuff on.

"Yeah, the best I've had. Job done, let's kill the fatted cow."

"Tonight. Now let's have a coffee and relax till he comes."

They heated a drop on the foil and sniffed the vapor before it could congeal. Amir had the crazy sensation of becoming the plant itself.

They put on music and enjoyed the moments on the balcony with a view of the jungle in the distance.

I see myself
Reaching the end,
Yet I am here,
Afraid to take the first step.
A frightful path, a snare,
With no returning back,
It is innocence
I am selling,
So, I ask from thee
A high price.

Samad came back exactly two hours later. He asked them if they had lunch, and when they said no, he was surprised. "The oil doesn't make you hungry?"

"We didn't have much stuff yet, and you asked us to wait in the room until you came."

"Okay, okay," he said, as if he just remembered.

Amir asked him, "Shall we have some beer before sightseeing?"

Samad agreed instantly and headed in the direction of the bar.

Amir ordered three Kingfisher, but Samad told the waiter, "No, Two Kingfisher and one Old Monk rum quarter."

Amir laughed slightly, "Okay".

"After this, we will go for lunch," Samad said.

They had lunch and Samad took them for a walk through the jungle embracing the psithurism of the trees with wilderness occluding some paths. On the way, he showed them his humble home, which was basically a hut abutting the jungle. According to him, the municipality had started giving land from what was the jungle, thus extending the town premises, but no one else had yet built any dwellings there.

Amir could guess why, as just a few steps away was the wild jungle itself. He wondered what animals and creatures would be there.

Samad was a fast walker, and he didn't look back when leading them except to show some fascinating birds or giant squirrels and at every nice spot they stopped and smoked a cigarette. Despite his uninterested outlook, Amir began to realize that Samad was actually observing them very intently.

During one stop, where they were surrounded all types of greenery and a scenic view of what looked like a barranca, Samad looked at Yunus. "You please shave your beard."

Yunus was taken aback.

Samad also noticed their nails. "You must cut them short."

Amir tried to downplay the comments with a laugh but realized that Yunus was indeed pretty irritated by Samad's pedantic observations. He wasn't the type who would kowtow to anyone.

This man was the best chance they had to get deeper into the enchanting forest, and therefore the drug business. However, Amir knew instantly that this was not a man who could be coaxed. He quickly changed the topic and told Samad that there was a huge market for hash oil in Maldives.

The guide asked them how much it was sold for, and Amir calculated the rate for a gram and told him. He looked shocked. "It's good business. Here, one lakh rupees you can get one kg."

Amir applauded himself silently as he had gotten straight to the point. Yunus smiled at him knowingly. At that instant, Amir realized Samad was observing the two of them, not only through body language, but was keenly interested in the comments they exchanged with each other in Dhivehi. Since meeting Samad, everything was going full throttle.

Amir gauged the situation and wondered if Samad could indeed be a cop. He assessed the unfolding sequence of events. The man in the white shirt and sarong, after meeting whom things had changed, and now they were getting whatever they asked for. In fact, they were in the middle of the jungle. Anything could happen to them here and no one would ever uncover what happened if things went wrong. He had to have an egress plan.

Contemplating all these events, as a wasp purred above his head, he knew he had to be very conscientious. He wasn't so naïve as to not know that these kinds of operations were done in partnership with the authorities and the country's mafia. India's mafia was associated with caporegimes operating within the country for the Dons sitting in Dubai, who would cater to the rich Arab sheikhs and to the rest of the world.

Things were shipped in containers, including drugs, gold and products banned from export and even women. Everything was carefully planned, and the authorities were bribed to comply with the operations. The logic was there would be money operating within the country through the sale of these goods. But this was at the expense of the common man. Amir knew about the way of the mafia as a child, as he had listened to talks of his Uncle Mufeed and his father, who had interacted with big shots of the day in Bombay.

Samad, if he was able to get good stuff for them, was very likely a henchman for the local mafia.

"I have friends in Malé, they want to buy kgs."

"I can get them. But first, you have to give money," he said.

Amir cautiously asked if he knew the correct source of the goods.

He came up with a good recital about a local who produced and sold the goods. It seemed that he was caught and now was in jail. However, the business was now carried out by his wife and son. She was known by the epithet "rani", meaning queen in Hindi.

"I can talk to her directly," Samad told them.

"Ok, let me know the price of heroin too," Amir tried to sound as normal as possible.

Samad had a grin on his face as he tried to dissemble his emotions. "If you buy big quantity, I get commission," he said.

Amir realized he wasn't acting under false pretenses. They plodded for a while and before Amir realized, they were back in front of Samad's house. They had walked in a circle. It was almost dusk, and they parted with Samad, who said he would meet them for dinner.

Amir could not wait as his mind was filled with business ideas. If he could get some shipments done, they would also help him get access to the legal, natural resources of the land, which would make him a Don of sorts. That night, he needed to make the deal so that all the travel did not amount to nothing.

Samad turned up a little late. He was outside when he called them on the mobile. It was eight. The moment Samad saw Amir, his eyes lit up, surprised and taken aback. He shook Amir's hand "Amir, I am so lucky to meet you!" His body language expressed excessive groveling.

Amir didn't understand what was happening and looked at Yunus, who looked equally startled. Amir decided that maybe it was the business he was offering. Maybe his commission might be very high.

They went to the same restaurant to have dinner. Samad seemed to be in another world. He kept calling someone and speaking in Malayali. Amir wanted to talk business, but Samad somehow was not much interested and told them that a very 'loving' friend of his would be joining them.

A young man in his early thirties with piercing eyes and a friendly smile soon showed up. He introduced himself as Johnny and told them that he was also a tourist guide and a very close friend of Samad.

After the introduction, Johnny and Samad spoke in Malayali. Amir knew they were talking about him. He tried to look uninterested and kept a conversation going with Yunus. Soon, Johnny's interest was diverted to him. He spoke fluent English, telling them that he had completed his Bachelor of Arts and was interested in applying for IAF, but family responsibilities didn't allow him to, yet. He proudly told them that his brother was an SP in the local police force.

Amir and Yunus exchanged knowing glances. The last thing they wanted was a police officer following their trail.

As if reading their minds, Samad said, "Don't worry, he is like you. Crazy, man."

Johnny laughed. "Samad told me you want kgs," he said laughing.

As usual, Samad was having his rum and sharing it with Johnny.

"Yes, if the offer is good, we could do something. I have good contacts in Maldives."

"Risky business," Johnny said, "But possible. Money matters."

They discussed the drugs scene in Maldives.

Johnny pulled out a thick hash piece "It's a gift. For special person. Charas."

Amir and Yunus couldn't hide their excitement. They were eager to finish dinner and go back to the room to try it out. Amir told them that they would leave Kumily the next night. Samad told them that the next day they would go on a jeep ride and that he would show them the most spectacular places and the Thekkady forest. Amir agreed enthusiastically, but he knew he had to keep check on his finances, so, he decided concretely to leave the next day.

On the way back from the restaurant, Amir went into the bar and bought a bottle of whiskey for the night. Samad asked him if he could have half of rum and Amir bought it for him. As they walked to the room, Samad told Amir that there was a friend he should meet. Amir tried to tell him to delay it until the next day but realized that since he met Samad, all the planning was done by him. He had an aura that made everyone around him tractable. That was the first where Amir, who was a natural leader, was concerned, so he agreed.

They reached a cottage and climbed to a terrace of sorts, which was decorated by pots of variety of plants surrounding a table and a few chairs. The background areas were covered by a variety of trees and was a comfortable looking space for a drink and apropos for intense conversations. There were two people engaged in deep conversation.

"Hello Mr. Flint," Samad waved to an elderly physically infirm man sitting on a folding chair holding an artistic knife with a long scabbard. A lazy looking dog adoze by a tree nearby. Mr. Flint was expostulating with someone much younger, who Samad told Amir was Mr. Flint's nephew. They were discussing eclecticism. Amir, Samad, and Johnny took seats forming a circle around the table.

"Think of death. When it all will end. The taste to be felt by one and all. A similitude is when you were in your mother's womb when you knew nothing of the outside world. In the darkness finding solace, content. Created with love, a life lived trying to find true love, ends one day, where the next stage awaits you. No one alive on this earth knows what will occur next. It could be we return to dust or live as spirits of the dead, bodyless and powerless, or it may be that we step into a world from another dimension of time. Whatever it is, your next tier will be a continuation of the journey of your soul. The soul, which is with the creator, yearning to be one with the spirit self, undergoing the journey of life in stages until one day when the soul, spirit-self, and body are one. An invincible super being in the kingdom of God.

"All the great saints, sages, teachers, and philosophers try to dwell into the secrets of the universe to find a solution to end human suffering. If human beings are born into love, it can also be stated they are born into suffering, for crying we come and when we go, we make our loved ones cry. Everything in between is a story of struggle. A struggle in which we fail to remember our true purpose on earth. The use of the human intellect to make the earth a more livable and human-friendly place has been the main objective of august scholars and kings of the past generations. In this case, we may seem to be succeeding but one may ask, at what cost? The creation of a materialistic society, centering on money and wealth has given rise to a workforce that is enslaved by a system run by a privileged few who have taken into their hands all the powers of both the materialistic as well as the spiritual realm. In this process, there is a vile agenda to make the common society less spiritual and confirm them to scientific theories and their scope of work making the weak-minded individuals merely robots, programmed to obey the commands of the owners, who control virtually everything that is in front of their eyes from the media to banks to all places of worship. Religion, if at all is surviving because it fills the coffers of the royals through the holy sites visited by millions of followers and churches, mosques synagogues, and temples receiving millions in donations.

"The fact is that all the books of magic, occult, numerology, astrology, astronomy, and all the Holy Scriptures have been sabotaged by the ruling class. Having come to know of their powers, these ruling families have come together centuries ago to use these Hermetic tools to form a system that would one day control the rest of the human species and render them powerless against the authority of the ruling class who have all the wealth and spiritual secrets passed just amongst their families and partners. Even Jerusalem had one of them as a titular or figurehead king. The witch hunt of the medieval period the destruction of the Sufi mystic culture of Islam and the

Templars of Christianity centuries ago and vandalic acts against heresy, tradition, and cultures of the East, are well-planned atrocities to make sure the spiritual powers remained within the elite alone. It can, however, be said that the wisdom of the universe is greater than what we humans can plan. The crafty ideologies set by the elitists have given rise to an age of reason, wisdom, and logic. Where scientific progress is met with curiosity to know the depth of secrets of the universe, where did existence come into being from? Questions with answers beyond the comprehension of the greatest scholars are being raised by youngsters and laymen."

It was enriching for the curious mind of Amir to hear such a complex, yet ostensible idea of the order of things in the world. According to his guide, here was a man old enough to be Amir's grandfather, an architect by profession, who had long retired and lived a solitary life in the hill station. He received his monthly paychecks from a daughter and son living in their native Australia, spending it on celebrating what seems to be the last episode of his life with friends he made in the village. Everybody in the town knew him, and whenever the tourist guides met a person who shared a philosophical view of life, they introduced him to Mr. Flint.

Amir was curious to know of his past life, but felt it impolite to ask him, as this was just their first meeting. However, Amir was keen to return one day to explore the woods and tea plantations, so he had a good chance of running into him as the guides were always keen to have a drinking party with the old man with stories to tell.

"Interesting," was all Amir said,

"What?" He responded.

"Your point of view, your ideology," said Amir.

"Well, my boy, it's far more dangerous than that. As precious as life may be, it is very very fragile. You must know to choose which battles to fight and which to give up."

"What about you? Are you still a warrior, battling it out?" Amir couldn't help but ask the thin, balding, long-haired man, with a youthful glint still in his eyes.

Before answering, he lit up another cigarette. Amir noticed he was smoking Marlboro, which was not locally available. He offered him one and said, "Gift from a nice French lady," as if reading Amir's mind.

As Amir lit up the cigarette, Flint asked him, "How old are you?"

"Twenty-four."

"Well, my boy, I am seventy-three. I have lived long enough to accept the world as it is. When you are young you have a point of view. You feel you can change the world. You are ambitious. The world is your playground. I can see that in you, and it's a great thing, but be warned, there are forces controlling everything that's happening, some of them you can feel, some you can't. But if all of humanity gets together there is nothing they can't change or achieve. It is only once in a very, very long time that such a man comes with a philosophy that reveals the secrets of the universe, changing us all, and the universe, for good."

Johnny refilled Amir's empty glass and told Flint, "Maybe people like Gandhi and the Buddha reached the zenith, but we just live our life fulfilling our purpose."

"What is our purpose of life?" Amir quickly injected.

"The purpose of life is to build a home, get married, have children, earn bread and butter" said Samad.

Samad was a father of two, married to Priya, living in their humble home near the woods. As a guide, and a truly good one at that, with a good command of English, he was able to earn enough every day to keep his home happy. From the past few hours Amir had spent with him, he realized that Samad was a very intelligent man, a very quick learner, and to define him properly– a qualified man. He told Amir that he would show him his hometown, surrounding villages and hills, and reveal the wonderful scenery and photographic views which, according to Mr. Flint, would be worth much more than every penny spent.

"Amir is a businessman," Johnny put in.

This interested Mr. Flint and he asked Amir about his background. "It's my dream to visit Maldives," he said.

"I can arrange it for you. Just let me know," Amir put in.

They smoked a joint, which Mr. Flint told Amir was bosker stuff, along with the drinks as the night progressed. They listened to some music, chatted about various aspects of life, and had a joyful time. Mr. Flint told him that although they agreed with Samad on the purpose of life, all of them were noncompliant and adventurous.

It was one of the best times Amir had had in a while, especially since Khalid left. Here, he felt he had found people who were genuine and worthy candidates to be his comrades in life's journey. The ceilidh ended too soon for him, as he was getting addicted to Mr.Flint's philosophies of life and Samad's intelligent comments. Johnny told Amir that Mr. Flint was a Kabbalist and that Samadh and Mr. Flint had a great solidarity due to their knowledge of the esoteric.

Samad reminded Amir that the next day was his last day there and they would need to leave early for the jeep ride. Samad and Johnny dropped them at their guest house and left soon.

Amir and Yunus went into the room and immediately started observing the piece of Charas. Yunus heated it with his lighter and Amir asked him to smash it into pieces. They were about to light the joint when there was a knock on the door. It was Johnny. He had bought another quarter bottle of whiskey with him.

Amir invited him inside. "Good timing."

"Yes, Samad wanted you to sleep to get up in the morning. That's why I dropped him off and came back quickly. I knew you were planning on smoking," he laughed. They shared the whiskey and lit the joint. "You need to come back," Johnny said.

Amir didn't properly understand. "Why?"

"Samad spoke to me about you. You have some lines on your head. Like the Nazarene lines"

"Really? Samad told you?"

"Yes, Samad is not normal. He has connections with the spirit world. Listen to him carefully, he will guide you."

"Oh okay, alright," Amir said. "But he is drunk most of the time."

"Yes, he is stigmatized as a drunkard around here, but he doesn't care. It's not easy to get things here, Amir. We have to be very careful of whom we let in, and you are lucky because we already feel you are one of us. Nature has endowed you with great power. You know, we belong to these lands, some of us still live deep in the jungles. The tribals, you would call them, are our blood brothers, but it has all been taken over. We have just become slaves to a system," Johnny said. "We need to be saved. Someone like you can save us."

Amir didn't say anything but just smiled. He didn't know why the people from this place were being so kind to him. However, he felt a deep connection with the place, as if he had known it from eternity. Maybe it was the business he may give them by buying the drugs, or maybe it was something else.

"I am a sinner," Amir said.

"So am I. Maybe we need to bath in the hallowed Ganges for decades to wash our sins."

They laughed.

The effect of the Charas mixed with the drinks was too high and they all agreed they needed to sleep. Johnny lay down on the sofa and they said goodnight to each other. Amir sat by the window looking at the moon until a haze of clouds covered it and all of them fell asleep.

They were all still asleep when Samad came the next day and knocked on their door. They used the bathroom one by one and were ready soon. After drinking the morning coffee, they went to the taxi stand next to the bus station. Samad's friend Murugan was waiting for them in his Jeep.

For the next few hours, they traveled the outskirts of Kumily. The town had an equable, pleasant climate. It was a magical and enchanting journey.

"Sometimes, just sometimes it feels like we are in a film," Yunus said.

It made Amir realize that these adventures could spin a good yarn.

Johnny and Samad were interested in Amir's life story and asked him about his family.

"You must get married," Samad said.

"Well, I have a girlfriend," Amir said.

"You have photo?"

Amir took out his wallet and showed the passport size photo of Hawa he had in his wallet.

Both Johnny and Samad looked, and Johnny said, "Nice girl."

"Yes, she is kind girl, but I don't know, maybe not your wife." Samad said.

Amir contemplated what he just heard. This strange man was talking about him as if he knew Amir better than he himself did.

"Maybe, but we have a very unencumbered relationship," Amir explained.

"Samad is a true shaman. He understands nature and the signs. He can help you activate your kundalini," Johnny told him.

"How do we become one with nature? I mean, how do we talk to it or communicate with it?" Amir asked.

He had read so much on Alchemy, the philosopher's stone, and all the mystical doctrines. Moreover, he considered himself a quasi-student of the great teachers of the Islamic golden age. He studied their discourses about creation in detail. There were Sufi saints who practiced Islam as a form of love for the creator. Thus, if they didn't love the creation, they cannot love the creator. These erudite scholars became the founders of various disciplines of study that are shaping the modern human world and technology.

However, it was their spiritual side that interested Amir. They traveled through the lands in search of the elixir of life and the Saint Al Khidr, whom prophet Moses met in search of knowledge.

"Sit in the jungle and observe nature deeply. It's very simple, but it depends on the person. Some people have good minds," Johnny said.

"Deep consciousness," Yunus put in.

These were topics they discussed frequently, but these people and the jungle were giving it a whole new meaning. The connection with nature was incredibly possible, the only factor was that they needed good guides.

Holding your hand,

O, the true divine one,

I am climbing down

Into the abyss,

Beneath which lies

The secrets of your heart

So that I may get wings

To reach your highness,

Exalted is thee,

I ask naught

But your hand, to guide.

Amir was always fascinated by the way of the universe. The great developed cities always fascinated him as well. It was like as if there was a terrific energy in the land, guiding the people fighting for survival and bestowing greatness on those who worked hard. Here in these misty hills, it was a totally different and unifying energy. He was now attuned to the forest. He revered it.

They got back around three in the evening after a highly satisfying trip. Finally, they had their lunch, kulfi in a roadside stall, and went back to the room and made coffee. Samad and Johnny stayed with them.

"So, what about your business," Samad asked.

"I will call when I reach Bangalore."

"Maybe we will visit you once, in Bangalore. We want to see the city," Johnny said.

"Have you been there?" Amir asked.

"Not yet."

"Amir, I want to tell you, many things are going to happen in your life. You have a great future, but also many difficulties, because of malediction. You must be strong to achieve success, either spiritual or monetary," Samad said.

Amir nodded, agreeingly. He knew it was an unfeigned expression. "Thanks for the advice."

"Please, you come back here again. We are loving friends now."

"Yes, it's so good to have met you both," Amir said, and Yunus agreed.

They had had a fantastic time and were leaving reluctantly. Amir knew that he would be back again soon someday, even if there was no business, just to have a good time with these newfound friends who seemed to have a deep connection with nature's magic.

When they returned to Bangalore, Amir called Hawa but got no response. The last two days he was so preoccupied in Kumily that he had not gotten in touch with her. Later in the day, he got a call from her friend Fathimath, saying that she was in the hospital as she was complaining of chest pain and was undergoing high-flow oxygen therapy through a nasal cannula. Her parents were with her. Amir told her to accompany him to the hospital.

When they reached the hospital, Hawa's father was waiting outside while her mother was in her room. Her father told them that the doctor said things were stable, but they kept her under investigation, as she had had a minor cardiac arrest. The doctor said that this was a very rare case, as there was abnormal blood clotting.

After a while, her mother came out and Amir and Fathimath went inside. Fathimath sat down on the chair and Amir sat beside Hawa on the bed, holding her hand.

"I am fine," she said, looking ghastful, before Amir could say anything.

He nodded his head. It was awful to see her in this weak, corporeal state. She had become his closest friend, and closest relationship. He held her hand tighter. "This is a good hospital. You will get good treatment and will be back to your normal self soon."

Hawa looked away and tears flooded her eyes.

Amir couldn't control his tears and kept winking fast to hide his grief. They spoke for an hour or so, and Amir left.

Hawa was discharged the next day. By now, her parents knew of their relationship, and he was allowed to visit her home. Although they had to meet in the living room, they were left alone when he visited.

It was their escapades, facilitated by skipping class, that became more and more frequent. They had intense sex and spent time at the best restaurants and cafés in town as Amir tried his best to please and comfort her.

Their relationship and the city were becoming entwined. Amir would always remember Bangalore and Hawa together. He loved them both. They were like two true friends who would be there guiding his heart wherever he went and whom he could air hug from any distance, anytime.

Frozen moments

Cherished forever,

Blessings and abundance,

A union so pure,

No conditions,

No promises,

Just grateful

That you passed by.

Three months later, Hawa died. Her heart stopped functioning during midnight, and she didn't wake up from her sleep.

Amir was shocked. This was the closest experience of death for him. No one who was so close to him as Hawa was had died before. He had attended the funerals of some distant relatives, but not anyone whom he really loved or couldn't do without. He had not believed that Hawa's condition was incorrigible.

He was left regretting not having spent more time with Hawa, blaming himself for not doing more to cure her and her ailing heart. It was an immutable fact. He was devastated. The keening of his heart terrified him. He was unnerved.

It took months for him to come out of depression. He couldn't concentrate on studies and the business was also starting to suffer. He would fainaigue, and even thought of going back to Maldives and be with his parents for a while, but decided against it, as his parents wanted him to complete the degree. He tried everything possible to console himself. His mind composed elegies and delved deeper into epistemology, what reality was, and the nature of death.

Death is not an end,

How can it be?

When I have known

the ultimate realm

Through which I,

Wise, become.

Chapter 4

The second year was coming to an end. Amir's productivity was at an all-time low. He was just smoking up with Yunus and other friends occasionally and spent most of his time alone, in torment. He kept thinking about how fragile life was and how he could end up losing the people closest to him. He was thinking of amending his way, leading a religious life, and praying to God to give his parents a long life.

During these days, Yunus was the only close friend he had. Samad and Johnny called him frequently, but Amir wasn't in the mood to travel or discuss the business. Additionally, Khalid had told him that now that he had the contacts, they would plan the project when he visited Maldives in his summer holidays after the exams. They had to be cautious and evasive as their mobiles were tracked as Khalid's gang was already famous as stoners and were on the red list.

Amir's room, where he spent the majority of the day was untidy and a total mess with stinking odor of cigarette smoke and old buts scattered around. In addition, the scent of cannabis wafted from his apartment to the neighboring houses. He had never been that careless.

Amir had slept late and woke up by the afternoon since the days after Hawa's death. One day he received a call which woke him up. It was Samad calling. He didn't respond and tried to sleep thinking that he could call back once he woke up, but Samad did not stop and rang continuously. Amir picked the phone up on the eighth ring.

"Hello Amir"

"Yes?" Amir said sleepily.

"We are coming to Bangalore. Me and Johnny," he said.

Amir tried to digest the news.

"We are taking changing buses. Now passed Coimbatore." Which meant that they would be in Bangalore before nightfall.

"Please, you arrange a room."

"How many days are you going to stay," Amir asked.

"Two days, maximum," Samad replied.

'You speak Johnny,"

"Hello Amir, we are coming to Bangalore."

"Yes Johnny, call me when you are nearby, I will go to the station to pick you up."

Amir kept the call and immediately called Yunus and told him the news.

He said he would come to Amir's flat in the evening.

Amir debated the idea of keeping them in his flat or booking a room in a hotel. When Yunus came, they discussed the matter and decided that they would book a room for them in the hotel near Brigade Road. It was a cheap but comfortable hotel that constituted the top three floors of an office building, just a few meters away from the bustling Brigade Road, the city's main shopping area for branded goods and delicacies and all sorts of flavors. Amir and Yunus decided that they would show Samad and Johnny the areas around Brigade Road and MG Road because they knew every nook and corner of the streets and all the hip restaurants, pubs, and shops. It would be good to show them the city life. Amir called home and asked his father to send him some money. He explained that some business partners were coming from Tamil Nadu to meet him.

Amir and Yunus picked them up from the Majestic bus stand and took a rickshaw, with the four of them cramped inside, to the hotel. When they reached the hotel, it was around seven in the evening. Amir asked them to freshen up and they went to a nearby restaurant to have dinner. The travelers were edacious.

After ordering the food, Amir asked them why they came suddenly. They didn't give a direct answer but said they wanted to meet him before he went to Maldives.

After dinner, Amir took them to a zappy dance bar that he had visited a few times before. It was simply a pub with young girls dancing to Bollywood songs. The customers gave them some money and the waiters also demanded money.

This was a good experience for Johnny although Samad didn't much appreciate the circumstances as he had an aversion to modern ways. However, after a beer, his interest was also in one particular girl with very long hair dancing rhythmically to a good tune and looking like she was in a trance.

After a while, Johnny and Yunus were a bit high. Their conversation was becoming increasingly slur. Amir was engaged in talks with Samad when the two of them left. Amir too was feeling intoxicated. Maybe it was the environment having its effects. Soon a waiter came up to them and gave them the bill and asked them to leave. Amir didn't know what happened and Samad spoke to the waiter in Tamil. At last, Samad told him that they had to leave.

"But where are Yunus and Johnny," Amir asked.

"They are outside," Samad told him. When they went out of the building Johnny and Yunus were there. It seemed that the guards had thrown them out. When Amir asked Yunus, he told them that Johnny asked the manager about taking the girls home for sex. Yunus was speaking louder than normal, and Amir realized that they were all intoxicated and high. This surprised Amir a bit because they were all strong drinkers and had not had much liquor compared to other nights. But the ever-watchful Amir was realizing something amiss. Things were different in the dance bar compared to other days. Their room was filled with young beautiful, fashionable girls and seductresses whereas normally there were rotund, old fashioned or over-made-up girls dancing in a desultory manner.

The energy within the bar was also different. On the road, too Amir started experiencing a rather awkward scene. It was as if everyone was watching him. These streets that he had walked hundreds of times, seemed strange.

Yunus too noticed what was happening and looked surprised. "Somethings not right," he told Amir looking indistinct.

"I know," Amir replied.

"It's Samad, I think we are being followed. Maybe it's the cops," Yunus put in.

Amir wondered whether they were getting paranoid. Samad's antics were making him look like a devil incarnate.

His instincts told him the best idea was to get to the hotel room. After all, they had had dinner and drinks. There was a wine store close to the pub. They bought a bottle of whiskey and a half bottle of rum and went to the room.

Johnny, however, was complaining saying he needed to see the city. His mind was in a flashover by seeing the stylish girls walking to and fro in the high-end trendy shopping area.

But it was Samad calling the shots.

"This crazy man," he told Amir pointing at Johnny.

Samad was looking different and was a stranger to the kindhearted but ruthless, intelligent man they met in Kumily. The light in those eyes which Amir had recognized so well in Kumily had gone off. He was also speaking in an eldritch voice.

They went back to the room, and everyone crashed into comfortable spots. Samad and Johnny were quarreling about something. Amir tried to talk to Yunus. But he looked stoned, at last, Amir asked him to roll a joint which he began doing immediately. Amir thought the weed would cool them down. However, things didn't go as he planned. He asked Samad what was going on and he started speaking to Amir in Malayalam or Tamil, which Amir could not understand.

However, Johnny responded.

"Samad has gone crazy Amir."

"what's going on?"

"It's you, Amir, you are the problem," Johnny said.

"What did I do?" Amir said, trying to make sense of their boorish behavior.

"You don't know Amir; the energy is so powerful and indomitable."

At that point the minatory Samad again interjected, and Johnny started arguing with him again.

Yunus just sat there saying nothing. He looked lost.

Amir decided that they should leave. However, Samad and Johnny who were belaboring verbally at first were having a fistfight. Samad gave a stentorian roar and threw a ceramic plate on the ground, breaking it into shards. There were cuts on Johnny's face and blood was trickling down. A chair lay fallen on the ground with the rivets popping out amid the clamor. Sensing the danger, Amir recited some verses he knew in Arabic for protection.

Suddenly there was a strong breeze and an influx of energy within the room. Johnny laid down immediately on the bed and Samad came and sat down near Amir. Yunus too lay down on the armchair in the room.

"Hello Amir," Spoke Samad in a different accent to his normal tone.

"Yes, what's going on, the party isn't going according to plan."

"You need to get serious in life. Great things are awaiting you."

"Who are you?" Amir couldn't resist and asked.

'We are from the order. Order of Om"

This certainly wasn't Samad speaking. The person was speaking fluent English in what appeared to Amir as a very British accent. It looked to Amir as though he was possessed. Maybe they were trying to becharm him.

Amir started reading the verses from the Quran in his mind silently.

"You are thinking right," said Samad. "We can read minds."

'You know, we are everywhere. Some of us are always with you. To protect you."

"Why? And who are you?" Amir asked.

"Let's say we are the guardians of the human universe. You have to perform certain rituals to see us. However, it can only be done when you are chosen."

"Oh, so if I am not chosen why are you revealing yourself to me?" Amir asked.

"Because you are the one that can make the change. The one who can unite both worlds."

"Which both? As far as I am concerned you are Samad."

"There are two of each of us. The physical and the spirit forms. The parallel universe as laymen would call it."

"You are different. Your spirit form does not leave your body. We have tried all methods known. Methods that have worked for centuries and through which orders and sects have developed. Samad and Johnny are important members of our order. I mean in their spirit form although they may seem pretty useless in the physical dimension of yours."

"Well, I think very highly of them."

"We know that. You can sense the people with powerful souls, and you are befriending them and building a team."

"Samad and Johnny won't remember anything that we are talking about now tomorrow." said the one speaking through Samad.

"But we have our methods of seeing into the future. It was known that Samad would meet 'the one' in the jungle someday. Maybe it's you but we can't be certain. So many possible candidates have come and gone in centuries and millenniums."

"So, what do I need to do."

"Be yourself. Don't be timid. Luck isn't on your side yet. But when it does, you are going to gain unmatched status and power. Not by fluke but because of your skill. Use it to gain knowledge for the human race. It all depends on the choices you make."

"Well, why don't you expose yourselves? I mean none of this is in any textbooks we learn in school."

"How can we make people believe in things they cannot see? We aren't the only dimension. There are forces stronger than us. We are not independent; in fact, we are slaves to this race of higher beings from a different dimension. Just a part of the admix of the jiva and the ajiva."

That was all he narrated and Samad went into an erratic trance-like state, uttering nonsense sounds. When he came back, after more than nine minutes, it was the normal Samad.

He immediately looked around and asked, "Where is Johnny?"

Johnny had removed his jacket and put the blanket on him and was asleep or acting so.

Samad asked Amir for a cigarette.

"Where were you?" Amir asked.

"Here, maybe. I don't know," said Samad.

You spoke differently just now, many things. What's going on?

Samad looked at him. The eyes were back. This was the real Samad whom he had met in Kumily and who earned his trust so easily.

"Amir, who controls the world?" he asked.

Amir thought for a second and said "God."

"Well, then something like that," Samad said.

"I think you need to come to Kumily again. Maybe you will understand then."

Amir knew he had to get to the bottom of things and understand what was happening to get inner peace. That would be pivotal to slake his thirst for wisdom. It would be almost impossible to come out of the mysterious jungle unscathed once you enter it.

Slowly Yunus woke up and Samad called Johnny who also got up. It was past midnight. They shared a drink smoked a joint and acted as if nothing untoward happened. Everything was back to normal. Amir decided not to discuss the events and just observe. The others didn't talk much either and after a while, they were overcome by lassitude and slept.

The next day they woke up in the afternoon and Amir and Yunus went to their houses to freshen up. When they met Johnny and Samad again it was evening. They had a coffee in the café' coffee day outlet near Brigade Road.

After that, they went exploring the city on foot and by dusk, they went into a trendy pub. Samad and Johnny liked the place very much. However, Samad was disturbed to see young girls drinking and smoking and condemned it. It wasn't that he was illiberal, but he had his prejudices.

"This is not good," he said.

"Women should not be like this."

"Samad is old-fashioned Amir," said Johnny who was enthusiastically enjoying the experience.

Amir took them for dinner at his favorite restaurant, which served the best Hyderabadi biryani that he had ever tasted. The restaurant was close to his house, and he decided to take them to his house to have a last drinking party as they were to leave the next morning.

At the house, he asked Samad about the parallel universe.

"Amir, why you are worried? They cannot harm you."

"But I want to know, these are not anything written in any book and I read a lot."

"That is because only some people know these things. Powerful people," Johnny said.

"That is too dangerous, you better live in this world. pray and have a family and earn bread and butter," Samad said.

"Amir, if you cross dimensions you have to pay a high price," Johnny said.

"But it will come to you one day and then you will realize how helpless we humans are, slaves."

None of these made proper sense to Amir but he knew he wasn't going to get a direct answer to his many queries. Amir guessed it was better to keep his mind intact and not worry about these peculiar events. He thought of Multiple Personality Syndrome. Maybe all the weed was playing tricks with their minds. Amir shrugged off these thoughts gushing from his brain. He was wise enough to know that these were not ordinary events unfolding ever since he met Samad.

After they left, Amir felt much better than he had felt in a long time since Hawa's death. He decided to refine his ways and work vigorously on his studies, reorganize the business structure, and concentrate on reality for the time being. Although he was not prone to forget the peculiar events of the rendezvous in Bangalore.

After the exams, Amir returned to Malé.

He met Khalid and his friends to discuss the drug nexus. He told them that he could get the supply and guarantee the quality and he would deliver the goods to Tuticorin or Trivandrum or any port in South India. His role in the deal would end from there. Although he had the export business going, he didn't want to take a risk just yet as the business was legal and had only just started expanding. They told him that they would arrange the process to ship and told him that they were having some difficulties as none of their personnel were on the ships. Amir told them to let him know when they were ready and that the cash should come in advance.

He had decided to go with Khalid's gang despite having offers ready from the other gangs such as Shahid's, but Khalid was his trusted caporegime.

Amir had met Khalid for a coffee on the day he arrived. He told him all about the events that had happened in Bangalore, except about the parallel world as he could not describe it properly because he barely understood what had happened.

He spent the rest of the days meeting old friends like Aman. It was also mentally rewarding to spend time with family and friends.

Amir recalled one piece of advice Samad had given him. "Amir, you love your mother very much but love your dad also." Amir loved his father a lot, but it was his mother who had the most influence on him and whose discountenance he was most afraid of. He wondered how Samad knew all these things. Many such incidents made him trust Samad so easily.

When Amir returned to Bangalore for the final year of his degree, he realized that his circle of friends was growing smaller by the day. Though he knew a lot of people in Bangalore, both Maldivian and his Indian business partners and their crowd, Yunus was his only true confidant. Ihusaan too had left the previous year after completing his course. Amir visited a few others to smoke a joint with, but it was only when with Yunus or when he was alone in his flat that he left himself loose.

Despite the promises from the Maldivian gangsters, they were not able to arrange a way to ship the drugs safely from India and import them into Maldives. Amir half expected it as he knew about their lazy lifestyle and how preoccupied they were with smoking and getting high.

Amir and Khalid discussed these matters by chatting online. Khalid's advice was to grow his export business to a large scale and then they could make an arrangement themselves. Amir occupied his mind with business activities during the day. He took two days off from work to concentrate on his studies as this was his final year and he had to re-sit a few exams which he had not passed or attended during the previous two years.

The months went by and Amir had completed his fifth semester exams when Khalid called him to tell him that he was traveling to Bangalore with an uncle of his who was paralyzed and needed treatment. Amir immediately worked in his mind a plan to introduce Khalid to Samad. Either he would ask them to come to Bangalore or if Khalid could get some time out, they would travel to Kumily.

Khalid told him that his cousins were with him, and he could take about three days' holiday and go with him to Kumily. Amir was thrilled.

They left a week later. When they arrived in Kumily it was after sunset. Samad greeted them at the bus stand. Amir was excited as he would after a long time be with the people he was closest to. Especially to be with Khalid and Samad gave him a sense of security and confidence. He believed that his dreams were coming true. He always knew he had to build a team. A team of close people that will form the 'Cosa nostra.'

In the room, Amir introduced Khalid to Samad as his best friend. Samad told them to freshen up and told them that he and Johnny would join them for dinner.

Amir asked Khalid how the town was. "It's cold and nice. The trip was also mesmerizing, don't know how the time went by."

They had smoked joints at regular intervals when the bus stopped in the bus stations of towns where some passengers got out and others got on. The weed made the surrounding nature more inspiring. Especially the road from Madurai to Kumily at the top of the hill was fantastic. The greenery, occasional waterfalls, and misty mountains refreshed the soul, mind, and body. Despite sitting on uncomfortable chairs in the public transport buses, they enjoyed the ride as a child enjoys a joy ride.

Amir was looking forward to the house party that night. He had decided they would do another jeep trip to show Khalid the surroundings, during the day. Samad, the guide would be a perfect planner, Amir thought.

Samad called at eight o'clock and asked them to come to the Kumily Gate Hotel restaurant.

Samad and Johnny were seated in one of the huts. They ordered a couple of beers; A friendly exchange took place before they ordered food.

"Amir, you want to see the jungle?" Johnny asked.

"Live in the jungle, among the gorges and lakes. With the tribals. Forest bathing"

"Yes, that would be wonderful," Amir said.

"It's illegal, but we can take you," Johnny said.

"Please give five thousand rupees," Samad said.

"For everything?' Amir asked.

"Yes, Food and everything," Samad said.

"That's cheap."

"Yes, but maybe you stay three days, better," he said.

"Will it be alright?" Amir asked Khalid.

"No problem, I think they will manage it at the hospital. I will tell them we have some business matters," said Khalid enthusiastically.

"Deep jungle?" Amir inquired curiously from Johnny who was zapping away mosquitoes.

"Yes. Tomorrow morning, we take the bus to a village called Arsadee. From there will have to walk into the jungle. It will be a long walk."

Amir reflected. This trip was going to be better than he had anticipated.

Life is but a stroll,

Why take it so seriously?

Befriend the strangers,

They will be called companions,
To each his journey,
You are in his story,
He is in yours.

The next morning, Samad was at the door by seven thirty, and Amir and Khalid were fast asleep. They slept after midnight after having a long chat with Samad and Johnny over drinks.

Amir woke up reluctantly opened the door and made coffee for all.

What time do we leave?" he asked Samad.

"Nine o'clock, when the hotel bar opens, we have to buy two bottles of rum. One for the tribal chief and one for us. "

"Just one will do?"

"Three nights?" Amir asked.

"We have the ganja," Samad said.

"Better enjoy nature. I think," he suggested.

"Can we get cigarettes there?" Khalid asked Samad.

"No, nothing is there," Samad said.

"But if it is urgent, one tribal man will go to the village and he can get cigarettes and maybe some brandy if lucky, sometimes. But not sure."

"Okay, did you call Johnny?" Amir asked.

"Yes, he is getting ready."

"Amir please give me some money, and three days of food for my family," Samad said.

"How much?"

"Thousand enough."

Amir gave him the money and he left asking them to get ready before eight-thirty to go for breakfast.

"Why are they taking us to the jungle?" Khalid asked.

"Who knows? These are strange people."

"With Samad around, there is always the possibility of adventure," said Amir laughing.

"We can discuss business in the jungle," Khalid said.

Johnny and Samad came to the room at eight-thirty. They had backpacks and Samad was carrying an additional bag which had an axe covered in a sheath. They did their shopping in Kumily town, and they left for the village in a local bus that was crowded in the beginning, but as towns passed by it was getting empty. The final destination of the bus was the village they were going to. The village wasn't big enough to get the status of a village and was an outlandish settlement. There was just a shop with some chairs. It was serving tea. There were a few huts in the distance. Amir guessed that maybe people living or working in different parts of the jungle came there to shop.

He asked, "How far is the place we are going to stay from here?"

"Not too far, maybe we will reach before evening." Five hours of walking was what he was suggesting.

"Good thing we bought enough cigarettes," Khalid remarked thoughtfully.

It was a long and fascinating walk. The geography and landscape were changing every few meters they walked.

They stopped for a joint when they walked long enough and found a nice-looking resting place. Normally a shady tree within the savanna grasslands and a picturesque spot within the evergreen dense wilderness with good scenery to ponder on. It was all chains of mountains, trees, and marshes, though some terrains looked wild and ustulate. As they got deeper in the jungle the greenery was getting thicker and dense and the walk was becoming a bit difficult as they crossed one mountain after the other. The indefatigable Samad was very agile and an expert in walking the mountains. He knew the road and routes extremely well and kept leading from the front. When he started walking, he didn't look back and Amir, Khalid, and Johnny followed obediently. Some paths were a bit dangerous as Amir looked into the abysmal depths he could fall if he got his steps wrong and tripped.

It took seven hours for them to reach the spot in the jungle where they would be staying. Their jeans were smudged in mud and water. On top of a hill, there was a small hut. Wisps of mist and tenuous clouds were hovering and moving about as winds gusted through the branches of the trees. Around the hut, there were a few middle-aged men. These were the tribals. They were shirtless and wearing lungis or sarongs. Amir realized that they were not uncouth and were welcoming. They knew Samad and greeted him. Amir looked around. This was going to be a million-dollar experience, but he wondered how safe it would be.

"They will take us to our spot," Samad said.

"Oh, I thought this is where we are staying," Amir said.

"No, we are staying in a tent, inside the deep jungle.'

"Yes Amir, there is a nice lake," Johnny said.

Maybe some animals will come to drink water." Johnny said and Khalid laughed at the thought.

The spot was like a piece of heaven. Situated within the deep jungle with trees forming an umbra was where they laid the makeshift tent. There was a lake originating from a small waterfall sliding through striated rocks. As they were parched, they drank water from the lake and its purity satiated them.

Samad hacked off some branches, pruned some trees, and tied a large piece of leather cloth between the trees, forming what would be their shed or tent.

Three tribals guided them there. Samad had given their chief the rum bottle and the delight was visible on his face.

"Where do the tribals live," Amir asked.

"Nearby," said Samad.

"I will take you there in the evening. They have family there. Women and children"

"Samad brought you here to meet them, Amir. Some of them can understand and see what we can't," Johnny said.

Amir and Khalid immediately went on an excursion exploring the trees, rock formations, and surrounding majestic hills. The lake had pure water but was weedy and had a lot of life beneath it. Amir spent some time playing with the tadpoles and tiny fishes

Amir felt an intense connection to the place. Sometimes he wondered whether he had seen the place before. Sitting there, he thanked the timeless God for the gift of life. Whatever may happen in the future, these moments will be treasured and become priceless memories.

Tears of gratefulness,

Sighs of excitement,
Spellbound by the beauty.
I want to know you,
For how can this
Natural splendor be
But by your divine decree,
Standing still.
I want to ask this tree,
Do you know your Lord?

They had brought rice and cooked it in an alloy pot on a small bonfire and ate it with a vindaloo-like curry made by the tribals. That night they lit a bonfire and smoked joints around it. Amir was fascinated by the simple life of the tribals. Samad asked to keep the rum bottle for the next night and enjoy the surroundings and nature in the dark of the night. Amir reluctantly agreed but later realized it was a good idea as they had a good time bonding with each other with candid conversations under the myriad stars. By the end of the night, Khalid too had become very friendly with Samad and Johnny. They discussed their past, future, and relationships in addition to the acausal phenomena they were witnessing in their surroundings.

"Won't any animals come?" Amir asked.

"Possible," said Samad.

"Tiger also there in the forest."

Johnny laughed and said, "Don't worry, they won't come here, but sometimes deer with fawns and elephants come to the lake to drink water but the tribals know all the spots well, they will know in advance if there is any danger lurking."

As an aliform bug flew past him, and with the synchronized sounds of the forest in the background, Amir gave a thought to the fact that when they were all asleep under the makeshift tent they would not realize until any predators came and had them for dinner.

However, many dogs were guarding their spot and one of the locals kept vigil. Amir thought maybe the guides did bring special people to the spot, so things would have to be safe and taken care of. Samad knew the route so well, which meant that he must have been there many times.

With these thoughts, Amir was lulled to sleep as he was very tired due to the travel and excessive walking done to reach the spot within the dense and isolated jungle.

The next day when he woke up, he had a kink in the neck. The incessant cawing of the crows was the first thing he heard. Samad and Johnny were bathing in the river. Amir got up and called Khalid and they boiled some water with the help of the tribal escorting them and prepared coffee and had it with a joint. They sat there sipping coffee and smoking cigarettes when Samad returned fresh and ready for the day.

"Go toilet and have a bath and get ready. We have to make lunch."

"Where is the toilet?" Amir asked.

Khalid laughed with Samad and said, "Open air toilet."

"You can choose your spot."

When Amir finished bathing and returned, Samad was busy making some sort of soup they would be having along with rice."

"Today the tribals have function. They invite you," Samad said.

"Oh good. I like to talk to them," Amir said.

"They don't know English, but they understand you," Samad said.

That night the tribals had lit a large bonfire and they all sat there in a circle chanting some words and clapping their hands. It was the celebration of an auspicious occasion. The priest with long hair and paint on his face officiated the process and put caustic material and coconut husks into the fire. Amir was given a chair in the center and was asked to sit there while the others sat on the ground forming a circle around the fire.

"They know you are the chief," Samad said smiling.

After the procession, dinner was served in their lodging which resembled a casern. It was a buffet with vegetables and other victuals served with flatbread. The utensils were made of earthenware. The tribals were facultative hunter-gatherers. After dinner the tribals gathered around a tree and one of them stood near the tree as the others poured water on his head through buckets one by one. Amir thought of it as some kind of initiation ceremony or a levee.

"Why are they worshipping the tree?" Amir asked Johnny.

"It's not the tree, they are not worshipping the tree," He said that much and looked away and spoke in Tamil to one of the tribals. Amir learned that these people spoke a dialect of Tamil although with a unique accent where the words were uttered very slowly. Amir and Khalid looked at each other knowingly when they spoke. It was as if they were genuinely stoned as the words came out in a drawl.

After the ceremony, they went back to their spot and Amir opened the rum bottle. The drinks in this perfect environment filled his mind with an infinite number of ideas. Khalid was busy chatting with Johnny and Samad was beside the bonfire with their guard.

Amir went and sat next to Samad.

"This is a wonderful trip. Thank you so much," he said.

"You have a lot to see in life still," Samad responded.

"What about you?" Amir asked him.

"Amir, you don't know my story. I have suffered a lot. I have been charged with a felony and have been to prison too and once was creased by a bullet that could have been lethal. I committed mistakes and broke the law in my youth. You see, God may forgive you if you redeem yourself, but mendacity will come back to haunt you when you least expect it to. So, if you can be honest and truthful in this life, it is a big gift. A gift very few have. Now I want to settle down peacefully with my family. I want to build a tourist guest house. Maybe someday you will help me."

"Sure, I will," Amir said.

"When I finish studying, I will concentrate on business, and I will help you," Amir said. He genuinely meant it.

The next day was spent in forest bathing. Amir sat by the lake observing as a giant squirrel ran from one tree to another and the loping guard dogs barked and tried to chase and catch it.

The chirping of the foraging birds and the whirring insects moving about as well as the rich life in the lake and the sudden view of an eagle with a prey on its talon were all hypnotic. The soundtrack of wind in the willows played in his mind as he watched a bird preening its feathers. Amir incised the word 'Shen' on a grand old tree nearby.

They squatted in the jungle one more night lying supine and watching the stars and left for Kumily early next morning. Samad decided to take a longer and more difficult route for the wayfarers to cross the wayless jungle, this time. The verdant valleys and rivers and shallow lakes had to be traversed and Amir tripped a couple of times, once into a ford, making him partially wet. Khalid was more athletic and was almost at par with the waffle stomper shod Samad. Johnny gave Amir a stick and he used it as a staff. Half the way, they reached a small settlement and got a lift in a tractor, which after a turbulent ride, dropped them off at a farmland, and then they set out on foot again.

Eight hours later, a bull cart ride and a rickshaw trip got them to the village from where they took the bus. When They arrived in Kumily they all went to get sleep and the following morning Amir and Khalid left for Bangalore carrying with them cherished memories.

If there was disdain in my heart,

It has been washed away,

With blessings so astonishing,

The bonding of souls so alike,

Who knew each other,

Before Time and Forever.

A few months later Amir completed his final semester and returned to Maldives. He contemplated going to Kumily before leaving, however, the proposed business had still not worked out as the process was retarded because some members of Khalid's gangs were in trouble with the authorities. The plan was held in abeyance and Amir had to keep giving excuses whenever Samad called him. Samad always spoke about financial difficulties as his children were growing older and he had to think of their college and higher education. Johnny too called him occasionally, but he never spoke of any business. He would always tell Amir that they should meet again and recalled the fond memories of their visit to Bangalore. Amir though often wondered whether he knew exactly what happened during that trip.

However, Amir decided to visit Kumily once before finalizing the first drug deal. He was now exporting general merchandise regularly by air through Bangalore and bigger shipments by sea from Tuticorin port. Therefore, he understood all the procedures and methods of the ports and customs.

Back in Malé his mother gave him a lot of work in the company to keep him occupied. Amir suspected that she had learned about his partying ways as she had frankly told him that she did not approve of the crowd he was hanging out with after work.

Amir worked diligently in the office during the day. The company was doing well, and Amir and his family lived an upper-middle-class life. However, he did not manage to raise capital to start a new large-scale business. The Business from Bangalore earned him a few bucks to spend on his expenses which he now managed without asking money from his parents.

Amir had many business ideas but lacked the initial capital investment required to kick-start the projects. In addition, his parents were not interested in working on any new sectors but were concentrating on existing projects.

Amir met his friends for coffee in the evening and their meetings lasted till midnight. Most nights were spent high on joints and when he returned home, Amir emptied the refrigerator to fill his voracious appetite and fell asleep as soon as he hit the bed.

The urge to earn a fast buck and get into the highly profitable narcotics business was higher than ever. Just one shipment would give enough capital to kickstart a new project. Amir and his group had realized that they were on the radar of the drugs enforcement department of the police, and they had to be careful not to make any gaffes as they could be raided anytime. They had to be extremely careful. However, despite smoking in open places, none of the members of the core gang had yet been arrested.

Nonetheless, they knew and suspected that some spies had infiltrated the gangs and seemed like ordinary smokers but were giving tips to the police. Amir was warned by Shahid to not smoke so openly as he received a tip that Amir and the gang were being watched closely. Added to that, they felt their phones were tapped. However, they soon decided that they were just getting paranoid and to keep going the way they were until one of them got caught. Getting arrested for smoking Marijuana could get them out without much trouble, however, trafficking or doing business with drugs could end up in life imprisonment. The risk was very high but the profits to be raked in seemed too good to ignore. Besides, Samad was pressing him too much as he too wanted to earn some quick money.

It was Amir's father who changed his mind. One day after lunch he had a man-to-man talk.

"It's time you take over the family business," His father said.

"I am not ready yet,"

"Your business from India is going well, you can take over the other sectors too."

"The only thing is you are hanging out with the wrong crowd. You see, I have seen a lot in life. What you must understand is, never get into trouble with law enforcement. I mean, stay away from everything illegal. It's a trap. The police know everything, and they lead intelligent people like mice to a mouse trap. After that, you are under their control because they can convict you any time, so don't be an imbecile and tarnish your reputation." In other words, he was asking him to keep his nose clean.

Amir's father was not the type who would objurgate or deliver a sermon, rather he would talk sense into him.

Amir knew that his father had enormous experience in business and the organized systems of the world. This was an admonition.

"Your mother is getting old, do not do anything to disappoint her. You cannot abdicate your responsibility. She has sacrificed so much for the three of you. You must value it and give her a beautiful end to her life's story. That is why I think it's time for you to take over and be occupied doing the right things."

His father rarely gave him advice, although he always got the daily dose from his mother wherever he was. Amir knew that these words had to be treasured to lead a safe, successful life. There was no point in trying to exonerate himself.

He critically evaluated his father's advice and realized that for the good of himself and his friends, it was best to build his empire legally and professionally even if it took time. He was not so desperate that he had to look for illegal means. It was just peer pressure that was leading them in that direction, he apprehended.

He went for a coffee with Khalid and explained to him that he would take over the family business, which meant that he would have some control over the finances and so he could invest in different projects and build a legal setup in different parts of the world. Khalid also supported this idea and told Amir that once they became untouchable, they could carry out the underground deals easily. Despite trying to assist Amir with the drug deals, Khalid had never really tried to abet him to do the dangerous deals.

"The risk is too great now," Khalid agreed.

They both realized that they had to be fastidious.

"Yes, but we will keep connected with Samad and the gang. Maybe we can start the spice business we spoke about," Amir said. The areas around Kumily were known as cardamom hills and plantations of other varieties of good-quality spices were grown in the rich, fertile ecosystem.

The next day Amir told his father he was ready to follow his advice and manage all the business of the family. Amir was appointed as Managing Director. The first thing his father taught him was to handle the accounts. This was something his father had done by himself all through the years. Amir didn't like all the math but quickly got acquainted with debt and credit and liabilities and assets.

The more he got involved, the more interesting things started becoming, and by the time a few months passed by, he made good progress. This kept his family happy and that gave a sense of fulfillment to Amir. His only quibble was that he wasn't generating money fast enough to raise the huge amount of capital he needed.

Finally, after almost a year, Amir told his family that he needed a break. He decided to visit Bangalore where he could meet his business partners and then travel to Kumily to enjoy himself with Samad and the gang.

Amir took the flight from Malé to Bangalore. After having spent three days in Bangalore, he finished his work and took the flight to Madurai. From there he took a cab to Kumily.

On this trip, he would meet Aleesha.

Chapter 5

Aleesha was a Christian. Her father was an Orthodox Christian from Greece, and her mother was a Roman Catholic lady from Kerala.

She was introduced to Amir by Johnny. Johnny's mother and Aleesha's mother were sisters. Although she grew up with her father in Athens, she regularly visited her mother during the holidays.

Amir met Aleesha on this third visit to Kumily. Amir first thought that she was one of the many tourists who frequented Kumily, especially in the winter. She was accompanied by Johnny to Amir's room in the guest house where Amir was having a drink with Samad, Murugan, and friends. She was wearing a flippy green midi.

Amir welcomed them and when Johnny introduced Aleesha, he slightly shook hands keeping his gaze respectfully low as he always did with women. But, as time passed, he could not ignore the fact that Aleesha had been gazing straight at him since she came in. When he took a glance, he realized that she was a very beautiful woman. He tried to limn her beauty in his mind. When their eyes met, he gave a short smile and soon abased his head and looked away, most of the time at Samad, so that he could fake that his attention was not on her. She was maybe just an inch shorter than him, a brunette with a slender waist and an enviable figure. His whole body was urging him to be grandiloquent. Yet some force resisted him despite the blatant attraction.

The conversation going around in the room was about the next day's travel plans, Johnny had brought with him two other guides to join the party and Johnny was engaged in a jabbering in their native Malayalam language. Samad kept interrupting them and explaining the stuff they were talking about to Amir.

Finally, Amir decided to break the ice. He started forming a felicitous phrase in his mind and finally gave up and asked Aleesha, "How do you like it here?"

"Very much, it's my home!" she replied.

"I told you she is my sister," Johnny told Amir.

Amir was a bit surprised; he had thought that Johnny just used the term sister vaguely as brothers and sisters in humanity. He didn't realize they were biologically related.

"Mi casa es su casa." Johnny laughed at Amir.

"Johnny's Mother and Aleesha's mother are sisters," Samad explained.

"Her father is from Greece," Johnny told Amir. "They live there."

Amir nodded a bit, looked at Aleesha, and said, "Nice. Welcome to the party."

"Every night is party time when Amir is here," Samad said. It was evident that Aleesha and Samad had a good companionship, Amir could see it from their body language as soon as she came in.

He had an overwhelming desire to know more about her. Amir decided he would ask Samad more about her when they were alone.

The next day, Amir was woken up by a shrill jangle of the doorbell. He thought it was Samad and checked his watch. It was just eight o'clock. Amir thought of pulling the blanket over his head and trying to sleep a bit more but decided against it and pushed himself up as he didn't want to waste precious time on his holiday. When he opened the door, he was surprised to find Aleesha.

"Oh hi!' Amir said.

"Good morning." After a pause, she added, "I had to talk to you. Ever since I saw you, I could not stop thinking about you, When I shook your hand, I felt a sharp tingling sensation all over my body. My pulse has not been normal ever since. When it calmed down, I came to see you."

The sleepy Amir was amazed but then realized he had been dreaming about her at some point during last night, and he wasn't sure if he still was. Amir took a deep breath to test if he was awake, and he could only recall fragments of his dream. One thing he remembered was they were near a waterfall, kissing.

Amir realized that he had already been quite high when Aleesha and Johnny joined them the previous night and with all his plans on his head, he hadn't properly considered a relationship or friendship with the very attractive girl in the room. For all it took, she might already be someone else's. Now it seemed that something in him had subconsciously attached to her because the dreams of last night were rewinding in Amir's head.

As the rose in the garden

blooms into life,

it knows not

what tomorrow holds,

picked up for its prettiness,

or grow old gracefully and die,

either way

fulfills its purpose.

"Come in," he said. "Coffee?"

"Yes."

Amir made two glasses of black coffee and came to the room's balcony, the same place where they had gathered last night. Overlooking the balcony was the woods. It was possible to climb up the balcony wall and jump into the woods.

Aleesha took a big sip from her coffee and said, "Let's go into the woods."

Amir assessed the situation and decided to go with the flow. He climbed the wall and pulled his hand out to her. Together both of them jumped into the woods. This part of the woods was within the city leading up to the boundary between the town and the foreboding jungle.

They walked a few meters deeper, and Amir stopped beside a teak tree. He pulled out a cigarette and offered one to Aleesha. She accepted it but did not light it.

They had smoked a few joints the night before. Keralan marijuana and hash oil were becoming increasingly popular among Western tourists. Most of the travelers already knew the way to get some stuff as they had heard through fellow countrymen who visited the hill stations. Although by law the sale and use of marijuana was illegal and possession was a criminal offense, it was used habitually everywhere by the tourists. Most of them were backpackers traveling through various hot spots India had to offer for their type. It was indeed an incredible experience as Amir had found out. Most surprisingly, during his trips across India, he found the people he met were very intriguing and formed close bonds with people from various classes of society. Despite living in very different circumstances, they all had a common element, which was their approach to life. The hearts ruled them. Sometimes they were mischievous and greedy, but they always offered the best blessings.

Reflecting on these thoughts he suddenly realized that Aleesha too was from Kerala. Amir brushed away a serrate leaf sitting on Aleesha's shoulder and looking directly into her eyes asked, "So how are you feeling now?"

"Your eyes, they are powerful."

Amir was used to such flattery and wasn't going to let his mind illude him. "So are yours, they are beautiful." Amir knew it was an understatement. "They say the eyes are windows of the soul. My personal belief is that our soul is somewhere else. Trying to communicate with us from millions of light-years away. Like when we play a video game, we try to control the character, get it?"

She smiled, "Yes. But I think the soul is within us, but we can never be sure as long as we are here. My grandmother was a very spiritual lady. She was from Greece. Very knowledgeable in Astrology. I learned quite a lot from her. What's your opinion on that?" she asked.

"Astrology? I try not to give much importance to it. But I have been told it works whether you believe it or not," Amir joked.

"She told me that it was foreordained that I would meet someone very special, a soulmate when I was twenty-four years old. I am 23 now and will be 24 in two months."

"Oh, when is your birthday?" Amir asked.

"December 24th, I'm a Capricorn. Samad already told me that you know a lot about Astronomy, religion, and philosophy stuff."

"Oh, what else did he tell you? He also thinks very highly of me, although I don't think I have achieved anything great in life except having enjoyed it to the maximum with friends and lovers, many a moment, in place and time."

"So, isn't that what life is about?" She asked.

"Well, according to Samad, I will make a difference in the world. Maybe not that great, but something that will improve the human condition."

"That's not a mammoth task. You could be sitting here, under this tree, and conjure positive thoughts for the betterment of the world and you would be connected to the source of all life, if you avoid all unnecessary thought formations. That very moment, you change the world forever."

Amir realized that this was someone who thought like him. "Well, for me, meeting Samad was a life-changing experience," Amir said.

"I have known him since I was a kid. He is a type of shaman. Very intelligent. Also, working as a guide he has learned human personalities very well," Aleesha said.

Amir looked at her and wondered where this conversation was going. "You are very beautiful." interjected Amir.

"Physically?'

"Well, yes."

"Hmm."

"I expected you to be straightforward. I didn't want to waste time, that's why I came to meet you so early in the morning. Can I show you around the town?"

"Ma'am, this is my third time in Kumily, and I think I have been going around with the best guides."

"Guides, that's what they are. They will show you what interests you. I on the other hand will show you the things that interest me in my hometown and you can decide how good the experience was. All you must do is crease me up."

"Deal, I hope you can add some zing to the experience," Amir said.

She finally lit her cigarette. Amir sat down on the ground, and he realized his heart was beating a bit faster than normal.

"We'll escape Samad and gang. I have a Suzuki at home."

"Alright, but first let's have breakfast at the Hotel."

After breakfast, they started the detour.

Those twelve hours from eight in the morning to eight p.m. at night were a captivating experience for Amir. There was a beautiful, intelligent, and active woman who seemed to know exactly what he wanted to experience. Much of the talking was done by her and Amir kept observing as a birdwatcher would be engrossed when he saw a beautiful bird resting on the most unique of trees among a thousand similar ones.

He felt poetry slipping out of his mind.

Pierce my heart,

To produce the first,

With the thoughts of your mind,

Drink from the fountain,
A wine so rare,
For it is just you and me,
The server and the served.

She took him along a special path, rugged and muddy, to a beautiful spot near the Periyar lake. He watched as she playfully told him her experiences here as a child, played with the water, and excitedly waited for birds or animals to pop out so that she could show him.

She, like him, believed in moments. Moments that transcend time and space, because the soul will never forget them as long as it exists. She not only loved nature but became part of it, taking him to the waterfalls, elephant camps and hiking through the forest and leading him to specific spots, showing him different varieties of spice trees growing in the area and explaining the biology of other plants and herbs and their medicinal and other benefits.

Meanwhile, Amir kept asking her about her past and time in Athens.

She had completed her bachelor's in business administration from the University of Athens. According to her, her interests were in Arts and humanities though at one point she was interested in pursuing zoology. Her dream in life was to go and settle down in America. Therefore, she decided that it would be easier if she tried to get a Business Executive position in a U.S. organization. She was interested in completing her MBA before migrating to the USA. So, she was on vacation to spend time with her mother and friends.

Amir tried to ask her about her parents and family but decided that maybe it was best to keep it for some other time as he did not want to interrupt her cheerful mood with a serious topic as to why her parents were living apart. Also, she had not yet asked him to visit her mom and he didn't want to pry into her family affairs.

After lunch, they went hiking around through the forest for most of the afternoon. In the evening she took him to a café' on the outskirts of the city, designed within a garden of colorful trees and versicolored flowers. Aleesha particularly liked the yellowish ones and plucked one and said, "Xanthous. It means yellow."

They ordered two coffees.

"Samad told me you are single", "Tell me about your personal life."

"I am very ambitious, very possessive and I like everything to be in order and simple, don't like surprises, don't like confusion. And for these reasons, I have not been able to keep a relationship with a girl going for more than a couple of years," Amir told quickly, surprising even himself at the assessment he had made. "What about you?"

"I had my first relationship eight years ago; I was just sixteen. It didn't last a year. Since then, I have been with two other men, but for even shorter periods. I seek perfection, my dream is my life, if anyone is obstructing it, they have to move away". She continued.

"And what is your ambition? Your ultimate target in life?"

"To love a man so much so that I would sacrifice everything, all material pursuits."

"But isn't that contrasting? What if it is the one whom you love is the obstacle to your dreams?"

"I cannot seek perfection outside. If I do so I will lose control of my mind. Perfection for me is a personal thing. I can decide to love someone, and my every act will be based on this irrevocable decision. My soul will tell me when I find 'The one'. Whether he remains with me or cheats me is up to him. If so, I would leave him, for I don't want a noxious relationship, but I will love him even stronger from afar, to make sure he is mine in the next stage of life. In my belief, I have already loved this person in another realm, another time, and my time on earth this time is to connect with him again. It does not matter whether we find each other. It's just like the Adam and Eve story. When they were pushed out of heaven and onto Earth, they had to go for days frantically searching for each other."

"You are a Christian?" Amir asked.

"Yes, my childhood was a very Christian one. Both my parents are religious, following their versions of Christianity. I do believe in the hereafter, but I also don't believe that that again is the end. That will merely be another stage, another test. If we follow our heart and practice and preach pure love, we will just be doing fine. And what is your belief?". She asked.

"I am a Muslim and am happy to be one. Because it enjoins good and forbids evil. However, I have transgressed all limits. Even we believe that the Christ would come and save us. That day we will all be united despite all the unnecessary wars and politically motivated divisions and befuddling created by the power-hungry and rapacious individuals and groups who brainwash the masses into accepting their versions and ideologies. So, until Jesus returns, we can try and make this earth as livable a place as possible, for us and our children's children," Amir said.

"What are your career ambitions?" She asked.

"I want to build a business of my own. I want to be my boss. I don't want to work for anyone. I will be completely taking over from my dad soon. That's why I am here for a vacation to refresh my mind before I start work."

"Great" I am here for a break too before undertaking my MBA." She told him. "After that, I want to migrate to the U.S. and work for a big corporation. Retire by the time I am fifty-five and travel the world with a lover. You know I have this condition called xenophilia."

"That's a very practical dream," said Amir. His dreams weren't anything like hers. He wanted to be a modern-day conqueror. Be the number one in every domain he enters. Build his business empire and compete with the likes of Jeff Bezos, Jack Ma, and Elon Musk, the most successful entrepreneurial thinkers of the early twenty-first century. He knew that if he could sell his ideas to potential investors, he would not be far from achieving his dream as he believed his dreams were far more innovative than the current concepts of businesses the world revolved around.

His business acumen came from his father, who began his business in the nineteen eighties as an exporter of seafood from Maldives to Singapore. His partner, Mr. Mufeed, was a vivid personality and a visionary thinker who began the export of different species of sea cucumber to Chinese markets where it was a delicacy among elite diners. Mufeed spotted the administrative skills of Amir's father and made him his partner. His father soon became an expert in holothurians.

However, within a few years, they ran into trouble with local strongmen and unscrupulous politicians who wanted their cronies to control the seafood market which brought in valuable dollars.

This forced Amir's father and his partners to dissolve their company and relocate to other destinations and establish their businesses there so that they could keep supplying to their regular clientele in Southeast Asia without interrupting the supply. It was because of this need that they came to Bombay which served as a gateway for export from India to the rest of the world. During this time, Amir's father visited Pune, fell in love with the place, and brought his family to reside there. The city laid the foundation of what Amir would become in his life as he started crafting his dreams during his school days and while roaming the countryside and villages on the outskirts of the beautiful city.

Most significantly, Amir's father made friends with Mr. Isaac Rumin, A Jewish businessman who had settled down in Bombay. A Halutz in the early twentieth century, he was now a multimillionaire, and having learned about Amir's father Abdullah's business, courage, and ambition through mutual friends in Bombay, he had taken him into his fold and became a very good family friend.

Amir could remember many evenings when Isaac came over to their humble flat in Pune and had long conversations over tea with Amir's father and Mother. Amir's mother was a good hostess, and her pancakes were a favorite of Isaac's. He had developed a fondness for Abdullah's children Amir, his elder sister, and younger brother. Isaac was in his late sixties, and he used to recount his travels and adventures nostalgically to Amir's parents. Amir listened eagerly, especially to Isaac's philosophies of life. He was religious and sometimes he used to daven in their home.

Rumin told them of his many mistakes, and one of his quotes that Amir always remembered was, "If you never made a mess, you can't even prove that you ever lived."

Since then, Amir had taken Isaac Rumin as a mentor and started following in his footsteps to create his business empire and succeed, no matter what he may have to sacrifice.

My weapons are within me,

The iron armor is my heart,

My mind is the acuate sword.

Conqueror of fate, I am.

Now, looking at Aleesha, Amir became a little bit suspicious of himself achieving his dreams, as normal people thought very practical ones. On the other hand, no one tells others their wildest dreams, just the achievable and auditory ones. So maybe Aleesha was doing the same with him.

"You know, I have strange dreams, I dream of magical lands with out-of-this-world music playing in the backdrops, also they are very real as if it does exist somewhere and I feel I am there when my body sleeps at night, I want to transcend these dimensions, understand what life is about," Aleesha said. "But you need to earn your bread and butter first. Once I am free from worrying about all the worldly stuff I want to travel, meditate with a quiescent mind, and become an astrologer like my grandma. Which I hope will help me unlock some truths."

"I am not a seer, but I hope and believe, that the Great force is with you and hope you achieve your dreams" Amir added kindly.

"Thanks."

It was at that moment that their eyes met, Amir's attempt failed terribly as they both lost consciousness of the surroundings, engrossed in each other, reached out for a warm hug, and locked their lips with such a powerful energy bursting from their bodies and a fountain of bliss erupting from the brain. They remained like souls tearing into each other for what seemed like an eternity.

When finally, their lips parted, they realized the gravity of the situation. They had made a faux pass. They were sitting in the café', and two other tourists occupied a distant table, their waiter was at the counter going about with his usual activities.

"Aleesha," Amir said looking at her lovingly,

"Aleesha Bourantonis," she replied in her dulcet voice, smiling widely.

"Yes, Miss Bourantonis, I hereto pledge my unconditional friendship to you. Greece is such a fascinating country, the cradle of modern civilization and thought".

"Yes, but the Indians aren't far behind, Sanskrit is such a fascinating language, it could be argued to be the father of many developed languages."

"Hmm…you represent both. I on the other hand come from a very small but fiercely independent nation" Amir said.

"A nation of unmatched beauty, paradise," she said. "Enough complementing each other, now that we have gone so far why not talk about our dark sides." Her eyes narrowed and she chuckled lightly.

"No hurries, no worries," Amir added, replicating Johnny's normal advice to him. "I think we will make a great team together. So, let's leave as much as we can for greater moments, moments we can treasure forever and a day". When they reached Amir's hotel, it was already dark and Samad was waiting in the corridor.

"Why no calls today?" Amir asked him.

"Busy with some French tourists," Samad told him, but Amir knew that Samad was aware of Aleesha taking him on the excursion.

"Mr. Flint was asking about you."

"Oh, let's meet him tonight if he is free." Amir had not met Flint on this trip yet. It was one of the events he looked forward to eagerly on any trip to Kumily.

"Will you join us?" Amir asked Aleesha.

"Yes, but I need to freshen up, and I might need to help Maa with some chores. I will call you when I get free."

"Okay, thanks for the wonderful time today."

She smiled and left.

"Interesting, isn't she?" Samad asked.

"Yes."

"She is a good match for you. It is a good age for you to settle down."

Amir looked at Samad. In his fifties, Samad was a very conservative man. Although their philosophical views of life were similar, the young Amir was rebellious by nature and was not ready to tie himself up with responsibility yet. Like many a youth of his generation, he believed that he needed to be independent financially before tying the knot and having children.

"Maybe she just wants to be friends," Amir said, trying to downplay the scenario.

"Shall we have dinner?"

"Yes," said Samad, and they went to the nearby restaurant. Amir had lost count of the number of times he had food in this restaurant. It was the place where he had his first meal in Kumily on his first trip.

The restaurant was part of a three-star family hotel which was frequented mostly by local tourists coming from different parts of India. Kumily was the border of both Tamil Nadu and Kerala. Which made it an ideal location for many residing in developing cities in both states. However, most locals favored the neighboring hill station, Munnar.

At the restaurant, they called Johnny to join them and had a Kingfisher beer till he arrived. Which was about fifteen minutes later. Amir was grateful for these friends, as he navigated these risky territories without fear of chantage.

They ordered rice and curry with fried fish and after a hearty meal, they left and went to meet Mr. Flint. When they arrived, Flint was sitting in the garden of his cottage smoking a pipe. He had calipers on his hairy legs. "Hello, my boy!" Flint called when he recognized his face.

Amir hugged and shook hands, "So pleased to meet you again. How are you?"

"Oh, just trying not to be an old curmudgeon."

"Are they taking good care of you?" he asked pointing at Samad and Johnny.

"Yes, he is fine," Samad said.

"No need to worry, most qualified men up on these hills," Flint added, laughing. He then asked his servants to light a bonfire for them.

"Amir has been hanging around with Aleesha," Johnny told the old man.

"How is she?" Amir asked Flint.

"Now my boy, she is a rose. Look from a distance, it gives such a beautiful feeling, but if you try to pluck it by the stem the thorns may injure you. The petals, the stem, and the thorns are all part of the flower. I beseech you to accept that."

"She is very much loved by all the friends you meet here because she is one of theirs. Her mother like Johnny's is from the indigenous tribe of this region."

"They are like queens. Even the tribal people have kings and queens," Samad added.

Samad had told him that these royals lived many kilometers yonder in the deep jungle, difficult for the normal person to penetrate.

Amir reminisced about the time he spent deep in the jungle along with Samad, Johnny, and Khalid. The tribals and their ritual dance around the fire and the food served to them. It was one of the most fascinating events of Amir's life. Amir wondered why the tribals still lived deep in the jungle. The only contacts they had were the guides and the guests they brought. For some reason, they had treated Amir like a king.

After that, the conversation was mostly about events happening around town, Johnny's single status and unemployment, and to Amir's interest, some philosophical views of life.

"The also-rans, it is them we have to concentrate on if we want to develop an enlightened society," Mr. Flint told him.

"Because they put in the effort and touched many a life while they were at it."

"Society only honors the victorious but sometimes the victory is just by a sheer stroke of luck and not individual brilliance."

"The average student may be average because he puts more effort into making sense of things which maybe were not taught in his school syllabus but what his curiosity about the world he lived in made him interested in."

All the while the main thought going on in Amir's mind was about Aleesha. She had not called, and it was almost time to end the party.

When they left Mr. Flint's house it was almost eleven at night. Samad and Johnny dropped Amir at the hotel, said their goodbyes, and left him, telling him that they would come to pick him up after breakfast for a jeep ride across the tea plantations in Murugan's Jeep.

Amir went to his room and got ready for bed. His phone notified him of an incoming message. Amir looked at it eagerly expecting a message from Aleesha.

It was a message from his mother. She was worried because he had not called home for the past two days. Amir called her right away and after a normal conversation of everyday talk, she told him that she had a dream about him last night.

"Oh! A good one or a bad one?" Amir asked.

"You were in a small boat, paddling through a big river, surrounded by forests and wetlands. There was a girl with you. Your father and I were on the other side, you were sailing away from us."

"How did the girl look? Anyone you know?"

"No, she was beautiful, but you weren't very good at sailing, and we were a bit scared. It looked as if it might capsize…"

"Maybe you are too worried because I am traveling through the hills," Amir said. After that, Amir spoke to his dad for a while, discussed business matters, and kept the phone. Reflecting on what his mother had said, Amir wondered whether it was a sign. Maybe Aleesha was the girl.

He took his phone and typed in her number and then decided against it. He went through this process twice more and finally rang her. She answered almost immediately.

"Hi, sorry I could not make it! I had a long conversation with Maa tonight and had to neaten my room."

"It's ok, should catch up tomorrow.'

"Yes. You must be tired, take rest."

"Ok," Amir exchanged goodbyes and hung up the phone. He fell asleep almost immediately. He woke up at dawn the next morning, prepared a joint and a coffee, and went to the balcony to have it.

Sitting in a corner, looking into the mystical woods in his THC-induced lethargy, he realized that this trip was again going to be an enchanting one just like every trip he made here. He felt the connection between him and Thekkady forest was timeless. He had experienced such strong emotions, feelings that brought tears to his eyes, marveling at nature's beauty. The forest always rewarded him, and it was not just good oxygen and fresh air or good physical exercise hiking through mountain ranges. This time it looked as if it was going to be more special. He was building up a good chemistry with one of its own. A daughter of the jungle…

Amir reflected on the wonderful times he had spent relaxing on the pristine beaches of the islands in Maldives. Enjoying the never-ending blue seas reaching up to the horizon and beyond.

He remembered what Samad usually told him when they looked at the mountain ranges from one hill. They could grasp the landscape with groups and groups of mountains in the backdrop forming a boundary.

"Megamalaya" Samad called it.

However, across the region and nearer to towns, the hilltops seemed to be losing their natural wilderness and becoming huge tea plantations without ends in sight.

Amir's thoughts drifted to the development the world was experiencing and the creation of giant corporations which in his opinion were trying to control the masses. The Orwellian concept described in the book '1984' and the dystopian world forecasted by him were prevalent in all societies, although the shirt was tailored to fit different sizes according to country and region.

The world was becoming obsessed with Western ideas such as its fashion and culture. Amir reflected on the great nation, China's influence. Well into the second decade of the twenty-first century, China was running past the U.S. as the most industrialized nation. Despite its strict adherence to Maoist principles and communist policies, it could not find a cover from the winds of the westerlies. The way of life of the Chinese, including the way they dress up had all become surprisingly Western. The espousal of Western beliefs was not just in China, but the whole of Southeast Asia had fallen into this rabbit hole of foreignism.

It may have been the films and Televisions along with the West's advancements in technology, that had made the Chinese race idolize Western concepts and individuals, promoted by the entertainment industry and media.

Added to all that, the West was seeking a new World order which faced strong opposition from the more conservative nations, religions, and those fighting White privilege or White supremacy. Not surprisingly, Islam was one of the enemies of this new concept of governance. The highly liberal principles of human rights and scientific developments conceived by men and sabotaged by a group of elites whose only primary interest may be to retain their nefarious hold on power had become the fate of the Earth. Islam had their undisputed holy book as a constitution which according to the followers, would remain valid and effective till the Apocalypse. This was also the ultimatum in the other major religions of the world. Even the Hindus believed that the world was in the Kali-yuga, after which the present world would be destroyed and a new one recreated. However, some Islamic scholars laid out Jihad as the one-way ticket to paradise. Which appealed very much to factions of the youth of almost every Muslim community that promoted Islamofascism. They had nurtured negative views of the world. These weltering thoughts were bred into their young minds by extremists who in most cases had vested interests and inveighed strongly against the West. However, with billions in their fold, a collective Muslim population would be a formidable force, and the powers that be did not take too long to realize this. Although in the aftermath of 2001, there was a strong campaign against extremist Islamic ideologies by George W. Bush, the U.S. administrations that followed decided to take a different approach to coexistence by advocating peace. The Obama administration carried out campaigns targeted at Muslim youths in deprived parts of the world. Tried to teach them the values of the U.S., and their culture, and that they were not enemies but friends. The Access program funded by the State Department was one such program that Amir knew of as it was carried out in his hometown of Addu City, in the Maldives. There was still a ray of hope. A common ground. Human civilization should not fall into labefaction.

Now into the second decade of the twenty-first century, the world was becoming highly liberal. The LGBTQ+ community was becoming a strong force everywhere, even in many cultures where it would have been blasphemy to even mention it, even as recently as the end of the twentieth century. The new man had to be uber-sexual. Women's rights were gaining momentum and feminism was the next "in" thing. A sharp contrast from a century earlier when women had to fight for woman suffrage.

Technology was the newfound religion. Everything was being virtualized. Everyone from babies to adults to grandparents was hooked to their smartphones. One thing Amir frequently thought was that the ruling class could have all the information about any specific individual they chose because their entire search and surfing history was available to the intelligence agencies. We were all covered through IPs, processors, and e-chips, and now with the advent of technologies such as 5G, even the mind may be monitored. Amir shuddered at the thought. Before, at least Facebook had to ask you 'what's on your mind'. Now, they would probably know it before the thought was constructed. The way things had progressed in the past decade it was very certain that the future belonged to Artificial Intelligence. A world where humans and technology will have to learn to live together or perish. Giving rise to a race of cyborgs. Amir thought of the effects chemicals called party drugs, were having on the youth. According to him, it was a social experiment. At least his generation where more inclined towards natural stuff like marijuana and shrooms. These were topics he and his close friends discussed for hours without an end to calm their restive minds.

One such friend was Anand. He was an eccentric fellow. Another of his housemates during his college days in Bangalore, Anand was one of the few close friends Amir valued, who were much younger than him. His best friends, Aman, Khalid, and Johnny were all almost a decade older than him.

According to Amir, Anand could be a savant if he got the chance to pursue his passion.

It was the creation topic that they used to expatiate frequently and ideate on. He remembered many a night they spent long hours on the balcony discussing the various possibilities of creation and engaged in contentious debate. Everything from the Old Testament and the Bhagavad Gita to Darwinism and the Quran, to Tao to Nirvana and fortuitism was scrutinized and explored to the very limit possible.

One such evening, the topic was about whether we maybe were just another race controlled by higher beings from another planet, where we derived our powers from them.

Amir's answer to that was the very simple theory that even if that was so, there would be some source from which these beings got their power. So, it would be a never-ending examination, even if anyone could ever go beyond their level of imagination and realm. It was just as the universe was. It had no boundary and without a boundary how was it even possible that anything could come into it? This was why Amir believed in God.

"Then I think there is a God particle, which is the source of everything and whose existence all the imaginations depend on and become an infinite reality," Anand responded.

As Amir finished his coffee, he reached out to his phone and called Aleesha.

"Hello," she replied sleepily.

"Good morning. I was wondering if you would be up for a morning walk through the woods."

"Sure, give me 15 minutes."

Amir prepared a joint while waiting for her. He didn't want the friendship that was blooming to falter. She came within thirty minutes and shared the joint until they felt the kef. They went out in the direction of the forest.

"I am thirsty," she said, "shall we have tea at the stall?"

"Of course."

They reached the roadside tea stall selling milk tea, otherwise known as chai, and milk coffee in old but dainty cups. It also had different varieties of cigarettes, snacks, and some biscuits on sale.

They asked for two chai's and nibbled on some biscuits. After tea, they proceeded towards the forest again. On the way, Amir showed her the first guest house he had stayed in the town. "That was before meeting Samad. After that, it has all been his arrangements. I think I can agree with his choices, except for the squalid toilets" said Amir laughing.

Samad was adamant that he stayed in guest houses run by the locals rather than going for the bigger hotels run by corporate businesses from outside the city. He was quite good at identifying people's choices, which may be the result of years of experience in guiding travelers from around the world.

Amir on the other hand had experienced all classes of hotels. With his parents he would normally stay at five-star accommodations, while traveling with his friends, they normally went to middle-class hotels, where the group could crash after long nights of clubbing.

In the last few years of his studying days in Bangalore, he had started finding solace in traveling alone and cheaply. Saving the money for greater experiences that almost always popped up on the way.

"What's your program for the day?" she asked,

"Going for a jeep ride, and maybe join Mr. Flint in the evening, That's all." Amir was eager to ask her to join him at night, but he didn't want to hasten things up.

"You should visit my home and talk to Mom," she said. "You have become a very close friend already. But you must be sober enough when you meet her."

"Oh, I'll try," Amir laughed. "Make it in the morning, maybe tomorrow".

"I was wondering what she will think of you," she said slowly.

"What's her story?" Amir finally asked.

"It is an interesting one. She is fifty-two now. She met my father during the eighties. He wasn't a hippie but toured India with a young group who were experimenting with all types of herbs. It was the winter of 1982."

He met the young Samad who became their guide. Samad took a peculiar interest in my dad. My dad also trusted him very much, straight from their initial meeting. It was my dad who helped Samad to acquire the land at the entrance to the Jungle. Samad's dream is to build a guest house there.

Amir knew that already. He had even asked Amir for help. Amir thought that once he built his business and saved a comfortable sum, he would donate some to Samad and his family.

"Samad told me you resemble my father in his young days," Aleesha said. "Samad took my dad to visit Johnny's parents. Johnny was just a toddler then. It was just a few years since the family settled in Kumily town. Johnny's mother and her sister belong to the native tribe. It was Johnny's grandfather who welcomed the first outsiders to the town. Since then, the town has been developing very fast, it was a hill station during the British time, and now it is a town, as you can see. If the long road to reach the top of these hills were easier, this town would already be a city. What is sad is that the real locals or the tribals have lost their stronghold of the town and surroundings. People from different parts of India had come and started businesses. Large corporations have bought vast areas of land for farming and tea plantations for a trifling sum. Even the country's mafia had taken control of how things operate. Of course, it is in partnership with the local governments and venal police forces. Tons of marijuana, hash, and heroin are produced and transported out of these hills."

"Anyways, during the visit to Johnny's house, my father developed a strong bond with the family. The family were Roman Catholics and spoke English as they read the Bible regularly at home and in the mass. Johnny's father was a convert, one of the first from his family, whose ancestors from his mother's side were originally from the city of Ernakulum".

Amir had visited the city now known as Kochin. A thriving city situated on the east coast of Kerala facing the Arabian Sea, overlooking the Indian Ocean. It was also a major port and Amir knew a thing or two about the smuggling business of the famous Kerala Ganja.

"So, my father regularly visited the house, many times for breakfast. It was my mother, who served him, and they developed a close friendship. By the time my father completed the two weeks his group was to spend in Thekaddy, their friendship blossomed into love. My mother tells me that when he left, she cried for two whole weeks, I am not sure whether they had any physical relationship during this period, but according to my mother she felt that he had taken her heart away. He had promised her he would be back. Those days there were no telephones or internet as we have now. The only way to communicate was by letter. He had given her his address. In the first few months, she posted letters to him but when she got no reply she stopped writing. The cithara he had given her as a present became her most loved possession, which she guarded fiercely.

"It took three years for him to return. My mother was married by then. She married a local constable in the police force. She told me it was just because of family pressure that she got married. She could not love anyone but the Young Greek man who had stolen her heart. When my father returned to Kumily, Samad explained the situation to him.

My father confessed his love for her and told Samad that the only reason he took so long was because of the financial troubles his family was in when he had returned to Greece, due to which they had to change their address. The exigency of the family made him take over responsibilities. It took him two years to get their business back and rolling and when he was financially stable and could afford a family of his own, he told his parents about having fallen in love with this beautiful lady from Kerela. His family didn't protest but asked him to be careful.

"So, you see, this was a perplexing situation. A married Indian woman marries for life. It's like a nailed and sealed coffin. There was no way out. Within a few days, the truth was out and there were whispers across the town among relatives and friends of my family. Johnny's family and my mother's family lived side by side. My father was regularly visiting Johnny's home and thus was able to talk and meet with my mother. A few of the locals spotted them alone together on a few occasions.

"Then one day her husband confronted her and asked her to decide. Her husband loved her dearly. Despite not getting the same feelings back from her, he had worked very hard to give her all the comforts of life. He believed that someday she would value his efforts and love him back. Despite loving my father a lot, she could not garner the courage to let go of her husband. Maybe what society would say also frightened her.

"Anyways, my father left for Greece, heartbroken. But my mother's trouble just began. Within a few days, she realized she was pregnant. Despite being with her husband for two years they had no children. So, my mother knew the child was my father's. She had a decision to make as she would have to face calumny. Then she realized that this child was a blessing from God. A living sign of her love and passion and if she was able to give her a good life it would be a symbol of her love which will go on for generations. So, she told her husband the truth and said that she would bring up the child irrespective of what anyone said or what the society thinks."

"Impressive," Amir added.

"Yes, a true feminist. So, she brought me up and I was her life. Astonishingly, she got a lot of love from her relatives and the locals. Her husband too was one of the best stepfathers anyone could have. His kindness and understanding made my mother indebted to him for life. However sadly, he didn't last long and died when I was just six years old. I was seven years old when my mother finally mailed a letter to my father, revealing the truth.

"He told me he was not only overcome with emotion but also enraged that she did not let him know earlier. When finally, he could think sense, he was immensely proud of my mother for her courage and the true love she had for him in her heart. Tragically, my father was married by then to my stepmom. They were in the third year of marriage. They traveled from Greece to Kerala within a month of having received my mother's letter. He tried his best to take me with him to Greece. My mother cried uncontrollably and told my father that I was all she had in life and that she could not live without me near her. All my father's efforts to convince her went in vain. It was Johnny's mother who stepped in to make a truce. She told my mom that I would not be able to get the best education if I stayed in Kumily and asked her not to thwart the opportunity. My mother agreed to send me to Greece by the time I was ten on the condition that I would visit her every year during the holidays."

The strength of true love,

A desperate desire,

Destroyed in each other

To rise again

From the flame of eternal love.

"It was in 1996 that I left for Greece. A whole new world lay waiting for me, but my roots are here. Johnny, Samad, and the others accepted me and loved me as one of their own ever since I was born. What I learned in the early years in Kumily laid down my foundation despite going to Europe and living with the cream of society and graduating from the best schools. But the wisdom of the people who lived in these forests and their connection to nature and compliance with its ways was always spellbinding. Especially Samad. He seems to have a cure for every disease ready in some herb or some aseptic in complex mixtures."

"I heard so, Samad, the medicine man," Amir said.

"I am indebted to him too, I used to have very bad Asthma since I was a kid, and my parents took me to the best specialists in different parts of the world, without any good results. I developed nosophobia. I used to feel suffocated after walking for just a few minutes," Aleesha said. "Samad prepared an antidote, now I am fine, can hike for hours without any trouble, a true shaman he is."

"Their kind wouldn't last though. It's the age of the big pharma." Amir said. "Anyway, your parent's love story is engrossing."

"Yes, I love them both very much. They are both perfect in their ways and have taught me so much about life. Both from their personal experience and through their ideologies.

I guess we truly love only once in this life," Aleesha said quietly.

"Have you?" Amir asked her.

"No!" She answered without any hesitation. "What about you"?

Amir had to reflect. But he knew that he did not miss anyone from his past relationships in that way. "I don't think so, but I have no regrets."

"But you affect me," Aleesha said.

"Eyes can deceive," Amir added with a laugh. He could not help but wonder why she looked so carefully into his eyes. When he looked into hers, she always shuddered and looked away.

Samad and Johnny had told him that he had powerful eyes but Amir wondered if that was of any use as he still hadn't mastered the art of controlling himself in difficult situations.

"No, eyes do not lie, it reveals what's in your heart," she said.

"Hmmm. I think Samad would be at the hotel now, for the ride in Murugan's Jeep," Amir said. Amir felt satisfied because Aleesha had shared such a sensitive and personal story of her life with him.

"I'll join you when you guys come back," Aleesha said.

When Amir reached his hotel, the receptionist told him that Samad had not come yet. It was almost ten o'clock in the morning. Amir waited outside the hotel for a while. It was almost eleven o'clock when Samad and Johnny came. It was an aberration for Samad to be late.

"Sorry, got a little busy."

Johnny piped up, "Some Austrian tourists, sightseeing around the cardamom hills."

"No problem, I was with Aleesha."

"How is it going with her?" Johnny asked.

"Fast," Amir divulged.

"She told me her parents' story."

"Oh, then you are a lucky fellow, she is very reclusive. Never discusses personal things, except maybe with Samad."

"You too," Amir said.

"I am her brother, she respects me," Johnny said.

"Amir, don't mess around with her unless you are serious," Johnny said, placing his hands on Amir's shoulder. "I trust you, Amir."

"Well, it's all up to her, whether she wants to be serious or wants to have fun. I won't force anything."

"No Amir, she does not want fun only. I see her eyes when she is with you," Samad said. Samad was wise and his knowledge surprised Amir who, himself being an avid reader and thinker of almost every aspect of human existence, was among the most intelligent in any group where he had found himself in since his childhood. Samad, however, was practically from the jungle. Therefore, advancements in technology and its ramifications were convoluted for his naturalistic mind. Other than that, his knowledge of religion, society, and the human character to love, was second to none Amir had ever known. Thinking of love, Samad's love story, which he proudly recounted on many occasions was worth a song in itself. He had spun a yarn about how he saw his future wife for the first time, how he wooed her, and how difficult it was to get her parents to accept his offer of marriage.

However, this obsession with the eyes was sometimes annoying. He had reflected on it many times and realized that maybe they noticed something he didn't or saw things he couldn't. Besides, these were strange people with an intense connection to nature. The mystic hills and the forests were part of their being. The ombrogenous plants and silver oak and rubber trees were their friends. It was so perplexing how they made their way through the forests, they knew every bend and corner and straight path to their destinations, the same way people in the city rode their motorbikes or cars in their hometowns and cities. However, here there were no boards or landmarks but millions of similar-looking trees, rocks, and innumerable collections of water streams.

Just like in the Maldives, during the days of his grandparents, the men went fishing early morning and returned in the afternoon with the God-given catch of the day. When they set out, they had no guarantee of the bounty they would be blessed with. So, there were rituals conducted before the boat sailed the sea. Every island had at least one healer or a Magus who would recite incantations.

The people of these mountains were similar too. Samad told him stories of his younger days when he would be sitting outside his hut, when suddenly a hen would run into his veranda, and how he would swiftly grab it by the tail. That was lunch for the day.

Thinking of all these thoughts, Amir decided he should ask about the lives of the Greeks from Aleesha.

Murugan arrived in the Jeep that was to take them around the Annamalai hills. Jeep rides around the hills were one of the favorite recreations of the tourists. Several jeep drivers were trying to lure the tourists for a ride. Murugan was one of the best drivers among them. Amir remembered his first jeep trip with Murugan where he courageously drove through dangerous paths within the forests and took rarely used tracks which provided the path to unimaginably beautiful views and landscapes. Surrounded by the misty hills and fluffy clouds hovering above the head, they had gone running from the top of one hill to another where cows and goats grazed the soothing green grass patches that covered the hills for miles and miles.

At the end of the trip, Samad had asked Amir to pay Murugan four thousand rupees, which at that time was close to eighty dollars and although he was a student traveling just on his pocket money, the amount was quite big for him, in reality for the experience he had, it was worth every penny.

As Samad treated Amir more like a friend rather than a tourist, his group also treated Amir as one. So, they never asked him for money but would eagerly wait to be invited to one of his parties. It was always Samad who decided what was to be paid and whom to be paid and when.

Amir liked this arrangement. With Samad by his side, he knew he would not have to deal with flannel mouths and knew when to sever ties with and move on.

Murugan greeted him with a hug. He didn't know much English and said some stuff in Tamil to which Amir smiled and nodded an acknowledgment figuring out that it was some sort of greeting.

Despite having many close friends among the south Indian states of Karnataka, Kerala, and Tamil Nadu he hardly knew the meaning of a handful of phrases. He always communicated with them in either English or Hindi and let his felicity and lady luck do the talking.

All along the jeep ride, the only thing running on Amir's mind was Aleesha. He was dreaming while still awake. Fabulous ideas of what he will make of life with her by his side. He had found 'the one'. The Shen of his childhood dreams. The Shen was his assuage whenever things went wrong. His soul mate will dwarf all his other relationships. The Nightingale call heeded. He felt galvanized.

A feeling of bliss,

An unearthly emotion,

An ardor so dear,

A heart illuminated,

My soul is free,

Singing and flying

Amongst the fae,

Having found

That this body was sent to search for.

By the end of the trip, Amir and Aleesha had become extremely attached and inseparable. She took him to meet her mother. Amir noticed a Greek flokati rug on the living room floor and several plaques on the wall. Her mother made tea for them.

"She says you are special, I hope you get married'."

Amir looked at Aleesha, who was sitting with crossed legs on the floor, and chuckled. "It's up to her," he said.

"She is getting old now. Have to settle down. Better."

Aleesha's mother was still very beautiful, and Amir recognized that their faces were pretty similar, despite the Caucasian features she inherited from her father.

When it was time for Amir to head back to the Maldives, they had formed a bond so strong that every cell of their existence demanded them to be coalesced. She decided to come to Maldives with Amir. Amir arranged for an employment visa through a job in his company.

Aleesha was going to be busy doing her online masters. Amir offered her a salary, but she said her father would pay for her stay and expenses until she finished her degree.

Chapter 6

It was the summer of 2012; Amir had finally managed to set up his global business venture and got it systemized. Aleesha was matriculated to an online MBA from the University of Liverpool and after her final exam, she wanted to take a long holiday to revitalize her mind and body. Amir decided to make this a memorable experience as he realized that they were both going to be busy with work in the coming years. He reflected on his ideal vacation spots and countries with cultures and natural beauty that interested him. He had traveled extensively in India, Southeast Asia and Eastern Europe. However, the West always fascinated him, and his dream and ideal vacation was traveling in the heart of Europe with the love of his life. So, on this particular trip, he decided to choose Switzerland. He also considered a tour of Europe but decided against it and purchased two tickets to Zurich via Dubai from Maldives. Amir had been searching for images of Switzerland on the internet and locating and identifying the most beautiful landscapes and he felt an instant longing. It was like a calling he had to respond to. He had seen similar sceneries and views in parts of India where he had spent many days thinking about his life and existence. Having come from an island nation with islands just a few meters above sea level and mesmerizing views and bewitching beaches, Amir's fascination for the mountain tops was like an urge to reach for something great, something which resides very high, above the skies and stars and the weirdest boundaries human logic can ever imagine. This interest, developed as a child while studying in school, had become a hobby that made him take a detour from the normal routine wherever his business or studies had taken him over the past several years. More recently he had also developed a great interest in understanding and comparing different cultures, although in his assessment humans were more alike than different whatever the geographical location or circumstances. One thing he had unearthed was that in some parts of the world, the people were very adamant about speaking the local language. Amir preferred not to learn even the most basic phrases and tried to communicate mostly through expression, an art he had mastered and successfully carried out in almost every circumstance in cities, towns, villages, and even the jungles.

There was a language without words, he recognized. Humanity was handicapped by ineptitude to understand this language.

Amir purchased the tickets for the 15th of July, which would be summertime in Switzerland, and he was searching for a hotel room in Zurich when Aleesha entered.

"I have taken the tickets," Amir said with a wide smile on his face.

"Where to?" Aleesha asked looking at Amir with the glint in her eyes shining brightly.

"Switzerland. All across the country, Zurich, Bern, and Geneva."

"Yahoo!!! I will help with the itinerary," she said eagerly.

She kissed him on the cheeks.

Beatifying her always gave Amir a special feeling. A feeling he knew he did not experience with another being. He had known love from his parents and was lucky to have three or five people whom he could call true friends. He also believed that he loved his ex-girlfriends when he was in a relationship with them. However, this was special. She was the yardstick of his peace. His heart told him so because it behaved differently and reacted uniquely to her gestures and show of affection.

It was during this trip to Maldives that they understood the psychology of each other's character. Up until then they had grown very close as friends and looked to each other for sexual and mental comfort. However, they were both ambitious and the main concentration was on their professional life. They understood that they loved each other and would one day start a life together.

The majority of their time spent in Kumily was with their mutual friends and once Aleesha accompanied Amir to the Maldives, she stayed in a separate apartment a few meters away from Amir's home. There she spent most of her time studying and Amir was working hectically on his business ventures. He would explain to her during their late-night yanks that he worked hard so that they could move out of the country and settle down in a major city like Dubai or Singapore, which suited their lifestyle. It would also be a place where he had his business interests as when his setup was complete, his friends, who were also his business partners, would handle the Maldivian side. This was acceptable for Aleesha as she could get a chance to work as a business executive in one of the corporations in these big cities. They would share the accommodation and be partners. However, up until then, there was no talk of commitments. There was a deep respect for each other. Maybe because they did not want to lose something this special. Both of them had a lot hidden inside them and their sentimental selves found comfort that was surreal through each other. Which was dangerous. For it was something that could surely never be replicated. They had spent hours talking to each other about their dreams. Amir had decided that he would do all he could to help her. He had fallen in love with her in Kumily itself, but he knew he had to handle it with sedulous care. Aleesha was a very sensitive girl and Samad had advised him not to go too hard on her. As usual, he valued Samad's advice. After more than a year of the relationship, Amir was convinced that it was imperative to tell Aleesha the true depth of his love for her and his desire to marry her, have children with her, and grow old with her. Which was something they never talked about. Amir sometimes wondered why, because he thought this was something every young girl had on their mind. He was her best friend and why she avoided such talks didn't make sense to him. However, he had restrained from asking her and was careful not to importune. Instead, he doubled his work on his business front and started making plans to settle down in one commercial hub by leaving his businesses in the Maldives to his friend Hamdh. This required him to raise a considerable amount of capital which he would have within a few weeks. So, before he shifted his residence, he needed a holiday. He chose his dream destination, which was Switzerland. There he would completely spill his heart out to Aleesha and explain to her his situation and dreams for their life together.

Aleesha immediately started her searches on the internet for the most visited spots in Switzerland. Just like Amir, she loved beautiful natural scenery. They also loved visiting Malls and chic coffee shops across cities and towns, and this was all on offer in Switzerland.

"The big cities are Zürich, Geneva, Bern, Basel, and Lausanne," she said

"Haven't heard of Lausanne. What's it famous for?"

"Don't worry about it. You will learn when we are there, let it be an adventure to remember," she said.

"Alright, madame," said Amir.

A week later they took the flight from Maldives to Zurich via Dubai. They exited the plane holding hands, "Welcome to Helvetia, my love," Amir said.

She held his left hand harder and Amir felt his adrenaline rising inside his bloodstream, anticipating the adventure that awaited them.

He had first learned about Europe and its geography and history in his grade school in Pune, but it was through Asterix comics that he felt intrigued about the continent. There was a very small library that had almost all the comics of the series. He and his sister were able to go there once a week and took two books at a time. Amir always chose one Asterix comic and his sister took a Nancy Drew or a novel. Enjoying the comic was the highlight of his week. Ever since, he always wished to tour Europe and this time he knew that while in Switzerland he would be revisiting his childhood and memories of his time in Pune. How life had changed how he thought it would be and how it was, was so different. If everything he had planned worked, he would be married now to his first girlfriend, be a business magnate, and be an influential figure in the politics of his country.

The reality was that he had had multiple girlfriends with no relationship lasting more than a few years, just a medium-sized business and a handful of friends working as political activists. The past decade had led him down a path never dreamt of. In trying to find the purpose of life and existence, he found likeness in strange minds, who had drifted from the path of the masses as they could not find meaning in the standardized lives people were leading. These groups had led him at first, away from his principles, then from his religion, and then into the rabbit hole of no return with drugs and substance abuse and their baneful effects.

However, Amir was clever enough to steer clear of addiction. He managed to stick to his whiskey and cigarettes and marijuana joints unless there was some big occasion planned with his trusted best friends, especially by his side. During such times he had tried LSD, magic mushrooms, and other psychedelic herbs which took his mind on trips that traveled deep into history and the future trying to discover answers to the biggest mysteries mankind could fathom and at times just laughing away the times with dear friends to the littlest of jokes or utterances that popped out of nothing.

Now he had Aleesha, a stronger intoxicant, an enchantress. Ever since they met, she had ruled his very existence. His priorities changed, his character changed, his friend circle changed, and his relationship with his family changed. Amir knew her influence on his life was increasing day by day. He had the inveterate tendency to be possessive. Being intelligent and a logical mind, he knew that the physical relationship alone was so addictive that giving it up would require a long road to recovery. However, the problem was that he was getting too emotionally attached. More than he had ever been to anyone else. Including his best friends, whom he could trust with almost anything. The good thing was that it gave him the motivation to work harder and stay away from hard drugs. The businesses were almost set, he now had to settle his personal life. His belief in the fantasy of his 'Shen' was renascent. He was well into his late twenties and maybe it was the right time for him to marry or settle down permanently with a life partner. Aleesha was extremely intelligent, beautiful, and caring. There was no point being irresolute.

Despite being together for more than a year, they didn't exactly know each other's past too well. The sex was good, and the adventures together were even better. It was as if they could read each other's mind when it came to making plans for the day and spontaneously jumped to conclusions like running away into the wilderness, stopping their bike halfway through a deserted highway and making love there and once when by the beach at midnight, they threw off all clothes and made love again and again in the lagoon on a dark moonless night and later sat at the beach hugging each other and letting the waves hit them one by one and consuming the darkness of the night as the stars above watched them. Every day, they did something that made it memorable, something different was their motto.

If I could get a chance,

To be with you,

Just for a moment,

My soul will suffer,

A million years,

Just for a moment,

To be with you.

This life,

My epistle to thee

When they did talk, they talked about the world. This was because that's how their friendship began. They could answer each other's questions about the world. Amir realized that just as he sidestepped questions about her personal life, she did the same by not trying to delve into his past.

This holiday was planned to take care of these thoughts that were negging his mind. Amir was a very practical person. He could not let a worrying thought reside in his head as it normally took away his peace of mind and blurred his thinking. He was going to speak his heart out to her and make her tell him all about her and her past. However, he didn't want to be persistent.

They arrived at the hotel in Zurich. It was a medium-sized hotel with facilities just below the 5-star standard. It had delicately designed spacious rooms with all the required amenities and a small balcony showing a view of the modern side of the city with a distant view of the brown tile-roofed homes.

It was almost first dark by the time they freshened up. The journey of more than sixteen hours, which included a stop in Dubai, was a bit mentally stressful and to feel the comfort of the hotel room with its palatial furnishing, was a welcome breather for them both as Amir thought he felt a bit jet-lagged. Especially the cleanliness and ambiance of the country were something they would soon start taking for granted but at present welcomed wholeheartedly as they realized that this destination was a great choice for this important trip of their life. Until then they had spent time together only in India, and Maldives and made two very short trips to Sri Lanka and Singapore.

Amir was the first to get ready and was waiting to drink a cup of coffee when Aleesha came out of the washroom. She was in her undergarments and her body was vibrant with sexual fervency.

Knowing that she was looking at him invitingly, he asked "Aren't you even tried".

"Hoi! The first time in Switzerland. Can't wait."

Soon, they were kissing each other all over and the bed was a total mess when they were done. They lay on the bed quietly for a while until Aleesha yelled "God, I am hungry!"

Amir gathered enough energy to get up and gulped his coffee. Aleesha sat up on the bed, put on her thong, and sang 'How Do I Live' in a cantabile tune. Coming up with sweet melodious songs occasionally was a quirk of hers that Amir enjoyed.

By the time they were down at the hotel's restaurant, it was dusk, and the night was entering to cover up the city.

"Let's finish dinner and go for a stroll for a few hours, then we can come back and have supper."

"Here again?"

"Depends on how things go. If there are good restaurants close by, we could try one of those also," she said.

"I think nearby there are all the hotels," Amir said.

The waiter came and Amir ordered a Polenta and braised beef and Alisha asked for veal and mushroom.

"Is this place much like Greece?'

"Sort of. It is Europe, after all."

They finished the dinner hurriedly and went to perambulate the town. Near the hotel, there were modern buildings and branded cloth stores.

They walked through the roads and lanes interestingly absorbing the scenery and taking photos with their phone's cameras.

After almost one and a half hours they decided to head back to the hotel.

"Would you be able to find the way back," Aleesha asked teasingly.

"Nope, but I have the Hotel card with me," replied Amir cheekily.

He believed that he knew how to get back as he had paid attention when they were strolling aimlessly. When he used to travel alone or with his male friends, he would not have bothered as he would normally be intrigued when he visited new cities or towns. Here, with Aleesha depending on him, he could not afford to be so negligent.

"I think we will have something light and go back to the hotel."

"We need to get a good sleep, tired, after the long journey," she said.

"Yeah, yeah, I know, what with the exercises at the hotel and these long walks, we certainly do need good sleep."

"I am not hungry though."

"I saw a small haute restaurant not far from the hotel. The second left we took, just the street across the hotel's entrance."

"Yeah, I think I saw it too," Amir said. "A small, homely café" They found the restaurant without much difficulty.

A young waitress welcomed them. Amir was awed by the surprising care for detail in every bit of design. Spotlessly clean with a wonderful chandelier in the dimly lit dining area. There were two tables outside.

Aleesha decided to settle for a comfortable table inside, which was in one corner of the room. "I love this place," she said.

"It's great," Amir added. He thought about the city and its economy. He recollected what Mr. Rumin had told about what he called the gnomes of Zurich.

They gave the order and Aleesha pushed her chair closer to him and hugged him lightly. "I am loving this holiday already," she said.

"Well, we have a lot of work once this holiday is done. So, I guess we need rest the most."

They both laughed together. From their time together, they knew that rest was the last thing on their list.

Amir waved his hand lightly at the waitress who was serving them and when she came, he asked her how far the Lake Zurich was.

"Oh, just walking distance, around fifteen minutes."

"Can we go now or what's the best time to visit it?"

"I suggest the day, you can have enough activities for the whole day. It's quite vibrant this time of the year," she said.

"Thanks," Amir and Aleesha said, almost together, and smiled.

"I read that we could ride bikes around the lake," she said.

The next morning Amir woke up at fifteen minutes past nine. Aleesha was up and having her morning coffee. She was superimposing various photos of the trip on her Instagram.

"When did you wake up?"

"Just twenty minutes back, let's go for breakfast before they close the buffet".

"You should have woken me up," Amir said.

"You were sleeping like a baby; I didn't want to disturb you. Anyway, we have thirty minutes to get ready."

They went to the hotel restaurant and realized that they could see the lake of Zurich from one end of the restaurant. They had not noticed it when they were there the previous night.

They had a good breakfast of buns, croissants, eggs, sausages, and varieties of cheese with orange juice and coffee."

"Okay, so what we do is take a walk up to the lake and do our excursions around it until evening. It seems there are bistros, bars, and restaurants by the lakeside. We can grab lunch there and sit by the lakeside."

"Alright."

On the way to the lake, Aleesha bought a basket from a small store and filled it with some snacks and juice packets. Amir calculated the parity of the currency and realized it was more expensive than even Maldives.

When they reached the bank of the river, the view was mesmerizing. It gave a good idea of the topography of central Europe.

"Wonderful, isn't it?" Aleesha said, after like ten minutes of silence.

Amir nodded in agreement.

"All this lovely nature surrounding us sometimes makes me feel I have ecoanxiety," she said.

Amir laughed and said, "Just relax, don't be so serious about everything."

"From Lucerne to Bern and Geneva, we will be traveling through the Alps," she said.

"Yeah, I checked it out too, your itinerary is fantastic."

They picked up bikes and followed the bike routes and peddled till they found a nice spot overlooking the lake and a panoramic view of the old city and mountains in the distance.

Aleesha pulled out a rubber sheet from her basket and laid it on the floor. The greenery of the grass, the colorful fragrant flowers nearby, and the majestic mountains in the distance were a treat to the eye and heart and Amir knew these were moments he should savor. The "feel' he took in now will remain with him in his old age if he is lucky enough to live a long life. Taking the "feel" was a term his gang used mostly when doing a cocktail of drugs, drinks, a wonderful scenery, music, and the sense of freedom. Sadly, drugs had already killed some of them and others were not mentally fully stable. One thing Amir was sure of was that just as he remembered those moments, his friends would also do so, wherever they were and whatever situation they were in.

With this thought in mind, he looked at Aleesha and realized how important it was to have a stable life. A wife and kids and a home. This would give him a sense of responsibility so that he would not dare to tread the dangerous roads he did in his youth. Besides, the feeling he had for her was truly magical and he could live the rest of his life away from any substance or thing that could put her and their life in danger. He realized that the past year he had toiled so hard to set up the business primarily because he wanted to settle down with her.

They were both smoking a camel cigarette.

"I love you," he said, stroking her long brunette hair.

"I love you too."

"Really, how much?"

She turned to him. "Do you doubt it? If you do, you are crazy," she said. This time she was a bit more serious.

"What is love according to you?" Amir asked innocuously. He immediately knew that Aleesha realized where this was going to go. Although he dodged philosophical questions when he was alone with her, she would have noticed that he selected people as friends only if they could satisfy his thirst for knowledge and the obsessive interest of the unknown. Those who shared strange ideas and outlooks of life. Also, he highly valued his friendship with Samad. Almost as if he was a blood relative.

The other character of course was Khalid. Despite his down-to-earth attitude and no-worries nature, he was damn pragmatic, yet a unique character.

"It just means that you care for someone almost as much or more than you care about yourself," she said.

"Is that possible? If I don't love myself, how can I love you?"

"It's perfectly possible. I can hate my existence but live it because I love you and want to see you happy. Like maybe a mother may love her children and live her life just for their sake," she said.

"Yeah, I see. But that's a very different kind of love. That's where you have a responsibility."

"That's a male chauvinistic view. Even fathers have a responsibility," she said. "What's good for the goose is good for the gander.

"I am not denying that," Amir said, "but motherly love is special. Maybe because women can love and sacrifice, more than men do." He looked at her straight in the face and their eyes met each other's.

As always, Aleesha shyly looked away. "Why you're looking like that?" Aleesha imitated INNA's song.

"See, my life has been one roller coaster ride so far, with its highs and lows, but I want you to be with me at the highest point and in the scariest ride."

"I will be there for you always. But I think we need to know each other a bit more," Amir blurted out directly.

"What does that mean? We have been the best of friends for months," She frowned at him.

Amir realized he needed to hit the nail on the head. "I want to know everything about you, your past, and your dreams, especially your past."

"I told you my family history."

"Yes, that was interesting, so I guess yours would be something like that too," he chuckled.

"Hmm, you never told me about your past either. You just say you had several girlfriends. What about the special ones? I mean, there would have been many like me." She was playing his game against him.

He smiled. "No, there was no one who came even close to you."

"Well, let's start with you".

"But why now? we are having the holiday of our life. Let's take things slowly, we have got a lifetime ahead of us," she said.

"Who knows? Maybe there might be no tomorrow."

"Stop being melodramatic."

Amir laughed. "That's the thing. The intensity with which we feel the earth, and the sky, and bond with the person near us. Take all this as a gift God has given, divine mercy, who knows what tomorrow will bring? Maybe the variance in intensity will burn you or destroy a relationship but the beautiful truth is that this moment will last forever. When the heart is pure. Maybe we may have to go separate ways, maybe life will show us different roads, but we will cherish this moment for we love every bit of it. The lake, you, the mountains, the songs of the birds, this ant trying to conquer my shoe, and every movement of every being we witnessed, this has all been written. If we did feel this beauty, the feeling of being alive, what is there to lose?"

"You would know, in the remote villages in Kerala and Tamil Nadu where we traveled, there used to be a tree where especially the old aged would sit under. For them that was the place of serenity. Generations of people would have sat there, taking a break from the stress of life, feeling one with the beautiful nature around them, knowing that whether they remained or not, the sun would rise tomorrow and if they were lucky enough to see it or feel it, the day will give them their due."

"Yes. Faith will lead us to the truth. I believe," she said.

"So, the point is, let's take our relationship one step further."

"Yes, maybe let's have a drink first," She chuckled.

'Yes, there is a whole country to see, no point in staying in one point for too long."

They rode the bike for a while until they found a bar by the lakeside.

It was a perfect spot for refreshment. They had a quick bite and a few drinks.

Once they had unwound and lit cigarettes Aleesha said, "I had a few relationships until I realized I enjoy my own company more than having just anyone by my side. It was then that I met you."

"I would like to know about the ones before you realized you are your favorite companion," said Amir smiling.

"Yes, I know you well enough to know what you are getting at. I knew this day would come sooner or later."

"Good."

"I was sixteen years old when I had my first relationship."

"I was seventeen," Amir said.

"Wait, this is my story, I want to hear yours completely later. I was in high school in Greece. Andrew worked as an assistant manager in a nearby supermarket where I and my father used to shop. I always liked mature men more than the young boys in my school. I liked the way he looked at me, we used to visit there at least twice or thrice a week. After around six months or so he finally gathered the courage to speak to me. He asked me for my number. I had just got a mobile phone of my own and he was the first guy I gave my number to. Since then we started dating. I thought I was in love."

Amir could feel the jealousy rising in him and the energy surrounding him warned him to relax and fight the bad vibes and quash the thoughts.

Aleesha didn't seem to notice the change as she seemed engrossed in her story. She told him about how she used to lie to her dad that she was going out with her best friends for studies and used to roam around with Andrew.

"And then it happened. It was in his garage where I had my first sexual experience. We made love there; it didn't last too long and the stuff on the ground hurt my back when he forcefully thrust himself inside me, pushed my body hard as he was not able to control himself, and then he ejaculated all over my tummy. We lay there for a long time. I was home two hours later than I should have shown up and Dad was extremely stressed and worried."

Amir knew that someone as beautiful as Aleesha would have had many experiences of physical pleasures, but he was right on target as he knew the strength of a girl's first love. Humans grow up as ingenuous beings until they realize the things adults tend to hide. For instance, it starts with covering the private parts. Then the differentiation of sexes and the curiosity it gave rise to. Then you realize that's how families are formed, and you picture yourself as a mother or a father and having children of your own. This gave rise to the idea of your prince charming or princess. Most people depend on ineluctable fate and luck to give them their life partner. These people accept what comes their way either through marriage arranged by parents or family or someone special they meet through friends or by chance at their place of work or through professional commitments. Then there are the others. These people have a clear idea of exactly whom they want to be their life partner. Until they do find that someone, they may get into relationships but never wholeheartedly accept them as their life partner. Most of the time it is for temporary benefits if ever they do get into relationships with people who are not exactly the person they have imagined in their mind. A compromise. These people do not mind having to lead life solo even right up to old age. This second type was a rare species before the twentieth century, however of late, these independent individuals were increasing in number as people preferred to end toxic relationships rather than blaming fate and carrying on with what was not working. Amir knew he belonged to this second category. He had started dreaming of his life partner very early. Although he now no longer remembered how he was able to do so, he knew that every night he fell asleep dreaming of his wife and how he would live his life with her. This carried on until his late teens. It was only then that he started realizing that his dreams were the product of the fairytales of his childhood. But Amir was a stubborn individual. He was determined to find a girl who was exactly the Shen of his dreams. He wasn't going to get spliced just for the hack of it. Shen was the name he had given to the love of his life. Aleesha was not only the closest he had ever met in resembling his Shen or soulmate physically, but she matched him intellectually as well. She was tremendously fascinating and the energy they shared was out of this world. It was so powerful that Amir wondered whether they had met before in another world and loved each other because he felt that their souls seemed to know each other. He avows to love her forever.

living this life,

For your sake,

That is easy,

For I breathe,

just for your love.

My life,

Just a paean for thee.

A simple hug from her was like switching into another realm, where nothing existed except them and bliss. Amir was afraid. He was intelligent enough by now to realize that all good things had a big price tag or were surrounded by the likes of fire or danger. It was for this reason he didn't ask her about her past before.

Now when she was telling him of her past, he studied her closely. He wanted to feel her emotions. It was one thing for him to believe she was his Shen. If she did not have a mutual feeling, it simply was not going to work and he would lose his soul mate, at least for this lifetime. Whatever the outcome, he would be thankful. Thankful that he had met her. At least for a second.

Amir realized that he should take things slowly. As the vacation lay ahead and there were going to be a lot of opportunities to understand each other completely. Amir was strangely satisfied because she was being very frank with him and telling him things she had not even mentioned in all the past months they had been together.

"He was six years older than me," She continued.

"Six months into the relationship, things started to change, I am not sure why, but I think he had an inferiority complex, I was from an affluent background, and he was from the lower middle class. Also, my father didn't like him much."

"He started drinking insanely, and we started getting into arguments. As you know I am very ambitious. I was focused on finishing my studies and leading an independent professional life and later becoming an entrepreneur. My life was pretty much set up in my mind. Andrew just came along the way, and I accepted it. Loved him. Did all I could to satisfy him. Somehow, he didn't understand it or didn't believe it. He started jeering me, but it was when he started hurting me physically that I realized that it was going to end. I warned him many times, but he would repeat it and he would apologize profusely, and I would accept it and exonerate him."

"He would normally blame the beer after he was sober and I would accept it, cause people don't behave rationally when drunk. Slowly the respect was lost, and I realized that there was nothing left to fight for as he had a yellow streak in him. He was insecure. Despite that, I stayed with him for three more months to give him a chance."

"Until a frightful day. He was not drunk, and we had a long argument. He was big and strong. He took me by the hand and threw me at the wall, I almost hit the nearby window and could have fallen off and died. I quailed at his heartlessness. I was in terrible pain and cried uncontrollably for around fifteen minutes. Andrew realized the gravity of his actions and apologized."

When I had cried enough, I got up and took my jacket, looked at him and said, "Fuck you.".

That's the end of the story. He tried to reach me through all possible ways, but I was no longer interested."

"But since then, I have been extremely careful before letting any man influence me emotionally. I realized that I liked to be around men and loved them as friends, but opening the door to my heart has been a no-no"

"Until I met you," She said, finally looking into his eye for the first time since she started talking about Andrew."

"Love you," was all Amir could utter at that point, and smiled. He realized it would not be easy for her to go back to a past she had buried under the soil.

"Your turn."

"What's the hurry? We still have a country to explore, give me a hug."

She came to his arms and they lay cuddled up on the chair Amir was sitting in for a while, looking into the beautiful surroundings, but their minds completely calculating the words that were just spoken.

Amir observed her as she lay in his arms. This was the woman he was going to grow old with. He said a silent prayer to God to give her a long life. Thanatophobia was Something he had gotten accustomed to since childhood. Whenever he remembered death, he would pray to God to give his parents and loved ones a long life. He knew she was special, but she was also like most of the girlfriends he had had and now that she was telling him of her past, he understood that behind the smile and beautiful face lay a hurt and bruised heart that was putting on a brave front.

Amir had decided long ago that he would fight for her. Unless there was a betrayal, or she was unfaithful there was no way he was going to leave her. Even if that happened, he didn't know whether he could let go of someone whom he knew was his soulmate.

He knew that she was ambitious and had a stubborn mind. She wanted things her way almost always. The fact that their relationship had no strings attached until then made things easy for both of them. Amir was an easygoing person. He could put up with almost anything. A trait he had gotten used to when he used to lead the boys and girls studying with him in Bangalore. The challenging times managing people with such weird characters when he was just a teen made him very understanding, which he realized was not a character he was born with. He was a restless person and although he did put up with people's stuff, there was a limit he would let people play the game for. Once he had decided he was right and ready to fight for it, he would be ready to face the world for what he believed in. Now he was ready to believe in this relationship with Aleesha. He realized that learning about her past may change his perspective a bit. The only time when he felt jealous was when it concerned the one whom he thought was his girl.

A bittersweet melody,

Sung by sirens,

Burns a desire within me,

Ensanguined with the blood of love,

mine alone,

And for me,

You manifest on earth.

Aleesha yawned and Amir decided that they needed to change the topic. "Let's walk back to the hotel," he said.

She agreed and after a little help from the locals, they were able to find the route and were back in the hotel in less than half an hour. "Let's spend some time in the hotel," Aleesha said when they were in the room.

They were going to check out the following midday and were scheduled to travel to Lucerne, which was about an hour's ride. Aleesha had booked a boutique hotel there. Amir decided he would read a bit about the cities they were to be traveling to in the next few days. According to Aleesha, she had made a round trip from Zurich to Geneva and back to Zurich with several stops on the way, which covered most of the major cities and the areas of notable natural beauty and Swiss culture.

They both freshened up, switched on the television and lay on the bed. Aleesha put her head on his chest and asked, "So, what do you think?"

"About what?"

"About what I told you, my past."

"Am happy you told the truth; I want to know everything about you. Just as I want to know every inch of your body, every tiny bit of emotion of your heart, and every thought of your mind."

"Well, there's a lot to share then."

"Don't worry, we have time," he said and kissed her hard. After a strong and passionate kiss, they looked into each other's eyes and Amir kissed her lovingly on the forehead for a few seconds and let go.

"Let's enjoy Zurich at night. Maybe there is a disco somewhere nearby.

"After dinner," she said.

"We can ask at the reception."

"Just google it," she said.

He did. "There's one quite close by called Jade with rave reviews."

She popped up behind his shoulder, checked it out, and gave a thumbs-up. "What about dinner?"

"We'll have it early, after about an hour." When they left for dinner, it was about seven p.m.

Aleesha wanted to do a bit of shopping before leaving for Lucerne, so they had a quick dinner and went shopping in a supermarket and returned to the hotel to get ready to go to the club.

Amir was ready in half an hour, but Alisha took almost an hour in the washroom. When she came out, she looked ravishing, in a dark green floral top and a blue and black mini skirt, with her beautiful hair styled into shaggy layers, which had a careless and sexy look.

"Wow, you look stunning," he said.

"It's all for you," she said.

The club was posh with white fabric upholstery with a carefully designed bar with pleasant white aesthetics.

There was a DJ playing techno music and the dance floor was occupied by a youthful energetic crowd grooving in electronic style. Amir felt comfortable instantly and to go with the vibe, chose a few shots of Tequila rather than his favored whiskey. Aleesha too had a few shots of vodka, took his hand and dragged him to the floor. Amir was impressed with the chromatics in the club.

As they danced, the floor was getting packed and the club bustling with more young men and women by the hour. The crowd was friendly and decent despite the intoxicating environment and Amir was happy with their choice of club. He could dance away the night freely without having to worry about guarding Aleesha, which was not the case when he used to party with her in many Clubs in the sub-continent. Besides, techno was his favorite music to dance to as it required less effort. He could just keep beating a leg to the rhythm of his heart and let his mind loose.

After about forty minutes on the floor, Aleesha told him that she needed a rest. They found a table in one corner and Aleesha went to the restroom.

Amir lit a cigarette and ordered a Whiskey for himself and a Martini for Aleesha.

Aleesha returned and threw herself down next to him on the sofa. They kissed each other, first in slight labial movements and then a total French kiss froze the time until Amir pulled back after more than a minute.

"From the beginning, time with you has been such a dream. I sometimes have to pinch myself to confirm that all this is real," Aleesha said, laughing and giggling in shrill gaiety. She had had her shots too quickly, was a bit high and was in a jocular mood.

"Yes, it is all real. Very real." he said and pinched her.

"Let's order something to eat."

He didn't want her to get drunk too soon as the night was still young, and he was just beginning to enjoy the disco. Besides, according to Aleesha, the next few days would be spent enjoying the natural beauty of the Swiss countryside and away from modern urban life. Amir had since his late teens needed to party with friends in clubs to rejuvenate himself when he felt drowned by the stresses of life. This Zurich club was comforting, however with every sip of whiskey he was recollecting what Aleesha had told him about Andrew. He wished he had met her when she was younger and innocent and pure. He soon realized these sudden thoughts that billowed in his mind were a result of jealousy and tried to get them out of his head. But he realized that she had told him there was a lot more about her past she had to tell. He comforted himself by thinking that there could not be any worse and anyway, she was his now. She belonged to him, and he would fight the world for her. He looked at her and was amazed by how beautiful she was. He felt grateful that he had her as a partner. It was then that it dawned on him that he should propose to her. Ever since meeting her, Amir had decided to take things slowly.

Now it was over a year and even this trip was aimed at getting to know her more. However, looking at her now, he had the urgent desire to make this beautiful, intelligent woman his partner for life. Amir raised his eyebrows, took a deep breath, and decided maybe it was the drinks and the environment affecting him. He had forgotten that he had ordered some food until the waiter came and laid down the dishes.

"We will eat and dance again," Aleesha said.

"Yes. We will dance the night away. This is becoming a great holiday."

"It's just been two days," she said.

"Yeah, but I already feel at home."

"Maybe we could shift here, I could get a job."

"If I could discover a good business opportunity and set it up here from the capital I have, then it won't be a bad idea."

"We could live a quiet, happy, and quality life here," he said.

"Maybe, but some beautiful things are better to look at from far. If you hold them too hard, they will be destroyed because they are delicate. Maybe we could use this as a getaway for holidays when we feel down and enervated due to workload."

Amir pondered over her reasoning.

It didn't seem so delicate to him. Here, he could lay a good foundation for a life with a wife and family. Amir was open to all possibilities. He was certain that he would not live in Maldives once his groundwork was done there and the business set up. He had his family and enough reliable people who would look after the operations there. What was most important, he realized, was who was going to be his wife. That would be a big factor in deciding where he would settle down.

He recollected his time with his mom and dad in Pune. It was his dad's choice and Amir spent some of the most beautiful days of his life there. This evoked delightful memories of time with family and friends. Going to nearby hill stations and to the grand city that was Bombay with its numerous towers, condominiums, temples, mosques, Parsee towers of silence or dharmas and parks, were highlights of his childhood and he believed that his children needed to have a similar experience to make them dream big. In his childhood, there was no internet or mobile phones. Now the times were different and even Malé was undergoing gentrification and was on the verge of becoming a booming metropolis within the coming decade. So, he needed to give his children something different than what was on offer for one and all. For all these reasons he still had not decided on the future. Sitting in the club, he realized that he needed to discuss all this with someone and that someone was Aleesha, who was now not only his girlfriend but also his best friend. He reflected on the past year and realized that she occupied more than half of the time he gave everyone else collectively. Except Khalid, whom Amir made sure he met at least every other day.

Suddenly he realized the power she was having over him. All his emotions after hearing about her past had seemed a bit strange. Yet he was getting more and more attached to her. What if she betrayed him in the end? Amir involuntarily shook his head along with a flexion of the limbs, a sudden reaction to the negative thought.

"What happened?" Aleesha asked surprised.

"Maybe the whiskey," Amir said and laughed. He promised himself not to let negative thoughts overtake him that night. He stood up and held his hand to Aleesha who took it, and he led her again to the dance floor. He was a bit dazed and just stood in a spot making gesticulating motions.

They danced till midnight, had a couple more shots, and took a taxi back to the hotel with their hair and clothes disheveled.

Aleesha crashed into the bed after just removing her shoes and jabbered a bit before she fell into a deep sleep. Amir though was not feeling sleepy yet. He sat in the armchair and smoked a few cigarettes along with some leftover whiskey from the minibar. He let his intoxicated mind wander. Here, he was with a woman he loved. One with whom he had a special telepathic connection. With her he was undisguised. Letting her know his desires without shame or discomfort. He had practically set up a successful business. The money was coming, and he could settle down and lead a comfortable upper-middle-class life. But that was not his target. He wanted to get the feel of the power held by the world's elite. This was not going to be easy. He had to be a cutthroat businessman like Isaac Rumin and build a conglomerate resembling and based on the mafia system and principles. However, here he was getting attached to a woman. A force that could stand in the way of his ambitions. He had witnessed such a scenario in his childhood, where his over-ambitious father and his very practical mother had several disagreements and arguments which he used to hear secretly. His nature was such that he was always curious about the lives of the adults. He would sit with his toys and act as if he was immersed in them when guests visited his house, and he would carefully eavesdrop on the conversation between them and his parents. This was where he learned about the practical and realistic nature of life. While these thoughts were running in his mind, he suddenly remembered that they had to travel the next afternoon.

He quickly changed, used the washroom and lay beside the sleeping Aleesha slowly so as to not disturb her. She sleepily opened one eye and put her right arm on his shoulder.

The next morning, Aleesha was having her coffee when Amir woke up. It was almost ten. "We missed breakfast," she said, noticing that he had opened his eyes.

"Aagh, you should have called," he said wiping his eyes.

"No, we need the rest, I think today we will have many activities."

They checked out of the hotel and left for Lucerne after lunch in the hotel pavilion. The route was filled with panoramic views of mountains, lakes, and small villages. They reached the city within an hour. The Lucerne city situated by Lake Lucerne had its old city characterized by medieval architecture. Aleesha had planned just one night in Lucerne and had a trip to a Ski resort in Zermatt planned for the next two days. However, Lucerne was offering a tasty mix of activities, like exploring the town, boat rides in the lake and hikes, and many scenic spots to stop by, according to their taxi driver who took them to their hotel. The hotel was neat, and the ambiance complemented the beauty of its surroundings. The view from the room which was delicately designed and furnished in eau de nil with flooring made of flitch veneer, was spellbinding.

They settled down in the room and discussed the plan for the day. They decided to take a cruise by the lake in the evening, explore the town, and visit the museums.

The lake cruise was a memorable one. They had a satisfying meal aboard one of the steamers which served tasty European cuisine. After that, with the help of a guide, they toured a couple of museums.

While observing the art on display Aleesha told Amir that this was going to be her hobby once she retired. Aleesha was a creative artist. Her drawings, stippling art, photography, paintings, and craft never failed to impress Amir. Although he never gave much thought to it before, while observing the finesse of the drawings in the museum he realized that she could do well in creating inspiring art that could sell for high prices.

"Yes, with your flair for art, you could strike it rich maybe."

"'Maybe'? That's such a strong word," she said.

"It is the 'Maybe' that holds all of us back. In life, there are no guarantees. When we are about to take a drastic step that might change our lives, the "Maybe' factor suddenly stops us. It is because of this that most people choose the tried and tested methods like getting a degree and working in a stable nine-to-five job." Amir reflected on what she said. He wouldn't let the 'maybes' of life get in his way. He thought.

"People like me," she said, as if reading his mind. "I know that if I followed my passions and worked on them alone, I could create something as good as the work of the grandmasters, but that would require complete dedication and tireless effort and discipline every day. So, I will now work on my Masters, get a job, and earn enough money to retire early. I also want to be a part of a classical ballet dance performance. After that, if life gives me enough time, I will spend my old age creating beautiful drawings inspired by memories made like the memories we are making in these wonderful landscapes with the love of my life. These memories will be cherished, and I want to make them immortal through my art." She thought for a while and added, laughing, "And then maybe climb Mt. Kilimanjaro."

"I hope you realize your dreams and I will help you fulfill them," Amir promised in a more serious tone. He recognized the fact that their dreams had to be closely knit together.

Her explanation made sense. She was going to work hard now and follow her passion later. The problem with Amir was he was trying to do all this together. He couldn't depend on tomorrow. For tomorrow may never come. Even if he had to sacrifice his dreams, he would follow his heart today. He knew this could be his hamartia.

He also felt that it was the reason he had little regrets in life. He gave his maximum to please those around him and to satisfy his own heart's cravings. He did believe that life was beautiful. Especially now, because life had given him such a beautiful and amazing companion. Aleesha was all that and more. Amir justified his wandering thoughts, because at the back of his head, there was the story she told him about Andrew. He suddenly even felt that she had changed a bit after telling him about her past. She was trying to please him but was not her usual chattery self, giving the weirdest of reasons for every little thing happening and the circumstances they were in. Maybe these were just figments of his imagination and labile emotions, Amir thought. She could just be feeling the weight of all that traveling and the difficulty adjusting to new environments.

They returned to their hotel by dusk and sat on the balcony sipping coffee along with a fondue. As they sat there Aleesha observed the sky and pointed at Venus and said "The Hesperus'.

"Beautiful and peerless, just like you," Amir responded.

The view was beautiful, and the comfortable room made them decide to spend the night near the hotel and come back early after dinner. The town was saturated with fascinating charm. Aleesha even suggested room service, however, Amir reasoned that they would be there only for one night so it would be best to explore as much as possible. Besides, Aleesha also didn't want the room untidy and messed up before they got intimate. Which was obviously what was on the back of their minds.

Amir tried to limn his desire with words in his mind.

This hunger,

Insatiable and voracious,

Devoid of reason,

A peculiar sensation,

Sawdust in the wind,

A magic spell,

For, control not,

I have of my feelings.

But wonder I do,

Is it the same for you?

They finished their coffee and freshened up and Amir took a card from the reception, and they went for an aimless stroll around the town. What they witnessed was a medieval city sitting within fragments of urban development. Aleesha was more familiar with such architecture, and she compared it to the buildings in her hometown near Rhodes in Greece. Amir on the other hand compared it to cities he visited in Asia. It made him a bit nostalgic remembering the tourist towns he had visited like Pondicherry in India, the nice little French town on the eastern coast of India, facing the Bay of Bengal and also the beautiful town of Bogor in Indonesia where he had traveled with his father and his business partners, a town full of reminiscences of Dutch colonial era.

As a student of history, he had often wondered about the evolution of man and how different kingdoms rose and fell. Looking into the recent factums from the past or the last millennium, it certainly was evident that it was the civilizations or states with the most advanced and lethal weaponry that ruled other weaker ones. Which was different from the years before Christ, where the organization and the general's art of war were the principal factors in defeating enemy armies. The Roman Empire was built by the disciplined soldier's organizational structure and the visionary tactics of the commanders. However, in the East, the culture and traditions made the foundations of magnificent kingdoms which coupled with great centers of learning withstood foreign attempts at control bravely. The invention of gunpowder brought a quantum leap and changed the whole concept and methods in which wars were fought. The old practices of turning the soldier like the samurai into a master of sword and martial arts and mental supremacy over opponents could no longer withstand the development of machines that could be used for mass killing and destruction of fortresses and nuclear hecatombs. Amir contemplated that the European colonization of the world may have only failed because they couldn't match the numbers of the Indian and Chinese races as they had to employ local soldiers and give them the weapons that had to be used against rebellion by their kind. The implacable Mongol conquests and the Leadership of Genghis Khan always fascinated Amir. Despite his deep research into the history of the time of the Great Khan and the culture as well as civilizations that existed at the time, including the powerful Arab and European states, he had no answer to the successful onslaught led by the Mongol ruler despite the castigations. This made Amir realize a long time ago that it was not only weapons and tactics or gunboat diplomacy but the birth of great leaders that made civilizations flourish and vanquished others. It could be written in the stars. Amir looked up at the stars as these thoughts crossed his mind. Immediately he observed the Orion, the most familiar constellation to him since childhood. He had read a lot about the constellation and the role it played in ancient religions and cultures. He felt nostalgic remembering the times he and his friends looked at the Nebula through the telescope from the coffeeshop in Malé, heavily smoked up.

Now looking at it from a continent far far away from his homeland and as an adult, he felt grateful for the life he had lived, although things had not gone exactly the way he planned. Most gratitude was not for the material success he had along the way but for the beautiful people he had in his life. His mother and father, brother and sister, his wonderful friends, and right now, this amazing person that Aleesha was. She was leading him into fantasies, holding his hand firmly. Making him believe that the greatness and love he desired could be achieved. Holding her hand firmly he realized he was lost in thoughts and could not properly recollect the way back to the hotel as they kept taking turns left and right aimlessly. Surprisingly less was said. It was as if they were both lost in their thoughts. Maybe it was the Swiss effect and the tiredness.

"You know the way back?" Amir asked Aleesha with a big smile.

"I think so", I noticed a small art gallery not too far away. If we could get there, I can find the hotel easily."

"I wanted to have a peek there, but you seemed lost in thoughts!" she teased.

"Well, I am not the only one. You aren't your talkative self either."

She had to agree, because he was normally the listener, and she could go on talking about things she liked endlessly, and Amir would never stop her. He loved the glint in her eyes and her feminine ways of expressing herself. What a work of art the human female was! He always saw his Eve in her and imagined himself as her Adam.

"Well, am just happy. Traveling my home continent along with you after being yours for such a long time."

"Not much different right? Only much cleaner." The landscapes they traveled together in the hilltops of Kerala and valleys of India had similar scenic views.

"Well, yes we are actually in an immaculate country even by European standards," she said.

"I like the way how everything is arranged and landscaped."

"Yes, it is, but sometimes letting nature be wild and carefree brings with it its own Magic. That's what I experienced in Kumily when we walked into the Thekkady forest. Maybe being a daughter of a woman of the valley makes me so attached to the woods. But I always feel a welcoming hand leading me deeper and deeper and the benign climate and the halcyon weather are perfect for every molecule in my physical body. I cannot express it but the times I was with you alone in various spots of the jungle were unimaginably perfect. I didn't think we could ever experience such a wonderful feeling, such captivating moments except maybe in heaven."

"It's God's own country. I too feel the same whenever I visit the valley and hills. Coupled with such wonderful friends and company, those are the highlights of my life."

"But to me, this journey with you in this beautiful country will always remain the epitome of my trip of existence. I don't think anything can dislodge this experience" Amir said.

"We still have around a week."

"That's including the journey back home," Amir pointed out.

They had booked ten nights in different cities in Switzerland. Aleesha had planned the itinerary and chosen various types of hotels based on the city they would be visiting. Their next stop Zermatt was a ski resort, which would be the closest they would get to the Swiss Alps on this trip. As per her plan, they would take a taxi to Zermatt the next afternoon.

They found the hotel sooner than they had anticipated and realized that they had not had dinner yet. There were a few dining spots nearby, but they had not decided on one yet. So, Amir told Aleesha that they would try the one nearest to the hotel and get back soon.

"I haven't arranged the taxi yet. Maybe we should speak to the receptionist, so we will be set for tomorrow."

At the reception they learned that a private taxi would go up to the town of Tasch, from thereon they would have to travel by train to Zermatt, near the Matterhorn mountain, which he described as the jewel mountain. It was a journey he recommended highly, and Amir asked Aleesha why they would be spending only two nights there. She looked at him amazed and said that they still had to explore Bern, Lausanne, and Geneva before flying to Basel and then going to Zurich to take a flight back home.

"I see, looks like the days are too less, we require months to explore this stunning country in depth."

"And to think that you were considering a European tour in ten days," she teased.

"Well, that's about taking just a slight feel of the air of every city and keep moving on. I have traveled that way many times. Especially when I was a student who broke the rules and went on adventurous trips, mostly on a low budget. But I did realize one thing though. You do not need to go so much in-depth in every place. There is always the familiar similarity to one or other places that you have been to that you could link it to along with familiar habits."

"But I have already fallen in love with this country. And when you love something, it gives you the license to break all rules for a divine dance that will linger timelessly in the story of the world."

"You just have to know how to follow your heart. It speaks the language of your soul. The soul I believe is somewhere out there up above. Not some spirit in our bodies," Amir said.

"About time, I have missed your philosophical stories. They always inspire me." Aleesha said.

"I know, that's why an introvert like me blabbers so much when am alone with you."

They found a cozy Swiss eatery with pleasant views and had a light dinner and a few glasses of wine. Aleesha found a guitar that was placed on the wall and got permission from the Manager of the restaurant. She slowly played the guitar to an allegretto tempo as Amir set there enjoying the moment.

The next day they started the trip to Zermatt after breakfast. The friendly hospitable staff at the hotel arranged the taxi and made their departure as swift and comfortable as possible. The drive was filled with fantastic views and was quite a memorable trip. The driver was friendly and spoke good English. They spoke about Swiss culture and lifestyle, and he gave them some tips and advice about what to do in and around Zermatt. They reached the town of Tasch, after a little more than four hours. Aleesha had stopped in between to take photos at regular intervals. They then took the shuttle to Zermatt.

Their hotel styled as a chalet was in Zermatt city center. When they had settled down with their cups of coffee in the room, Aleesha told Amir that there were fabulous resorts in the mountains, but she had decided against it because she wanted to explore the town and its people and go for excursions and escape to the mountains with a guide. From both of their experiences of traveling, they had been lucky in finding helpful and kind guides and they decided to gamble on it during this trip too. It added to the experience because once the guides started liking them, they gave them in-depth details of the culture and tradition which cannot be found or read anywhere.

They sat there looking at the Alps and the slopes.

"I think this is a wonderful place for you to tell me the stories of your love life so far," Aleesha said.

"Here?" asked Amir, surprised. "I thought this was a town for adventure. Exploring the Alps, I mean."

"Well, yes. We could mix it all together little by little, we'll get there."

He reflected, trying to decide where to begin. He was twenty-eight now and by now had around three serious relationships and a few affairs and one-night stands of which he had lost count.

He quickly told Aleesha about Seema and then about the affairs in Bangalore. When he had finished telling his narrative, he realized that he had told it to Aleesha almost without any emotion. As if it was someone else's story he was reciting to her.

"So how special was Seema to you?" Aleesha asked, observing him intently.

"Not as special as you. I didn't even try to appease her," Amir added almost instantly.

"Maybe, but that was your first emotional experience of the feminine kind."

"I had a mother and sister who loved me deeply. From their story and life, I learned the psychology of the feminine mind."

"They must be strong characters," she said.

"Why do you say so?"

"Because sometimes you seem heartless." She said laughing and punching him slightly on his shoulder. Especially in your business deals. You are a ruthless leader."

"Maybe it is all the weed that I smoked. Heart is petrous," Amir joked.

"Wish we could have a joint up here on the mountains," she said.

"So much for your break," Amir teased.

On Aleesha's insistence, they had stopped smoking marijuana and hash oil since their last trip to Kumily.

"Anyway, Better stay on the safe side while traveling," Amir said.

"I want to create lasting memories of this trip. It would help if we were both sober the majority of the time," she said.

"Agreed!"

"These mountains are meant for meditation, yoga, and a somatic experience. Quiet contemplation and sacred bonding. Something we need badly in our lives, because when we get back, we will both be engrossed in work, work, and work."

"Yes. We can have a small excursion and find some good spots where we can camp and meditate. Of course, we don't have to stick to the codes. We can try some germane tricks.

They asked the hotel for a guide and a robust young Swiss man of about twenty-three greeted them with a wide smile. He led them from their hotel to the village areas recalling stories of the past and the legends of the Matterhorn. He told them some stories about some huge giants or knave demons and their feuds, which Amir found a bit difficult to grasp but kept nodding as if following the conversation eagerly. They stopped at regular intervals of the hike to absorb the natural beauty. This quiet contemplation made Amir think. He was entering the fourth decade of his life, and he was in Switzerland. Was this all written somewhere up there? Are we all just following a script that was written by a greater force and even if so, do we have free will?' These thoughts made him remember the past days and nights he spent with likeminded friends like Anand discussing their existence, trying to find the meaning of life, disregarding all theories and explanations given by scientists, philosophers, and preachers of great eloquence and examining every facet of the conundrums and arguments.

He was reminded of a Sanskrit mantra used commonly by the Hindus in India. "Satyam Sivam Sundaram." which translates as 'Truth is eternal and beautiful'. The truth will last. It was always going to be there. So, all he had to do was look around and wipe off the dust covering the light. The underlying truth cannot be destroyed, for it created everything and came out of nothing. The rest are mere assumptions of weaker minds. Even the great prophets had to wait for divine revelation in most cases through an intermediary and even Moses when he needed to speak to God for a second time had to go and meditate for forty days and forty nights before he had the opportunity.

This God is close to his creation. Amir remembered the verse from the Quran where God says he is closer to man than his jugular vein. If he could fathom this language of God, he would have the answers to all his questions. Year by year he was dwelling further into this concept called 'language without words.' If man understood this, he could talk to animals and all living beings and fulfill his purpose of life by being the most intellectually advanced living organism. This made him think. The trees he was passing by may also be very wise if they understood their creator. Time, space, and abilities may have limited their activity on Earth and their vagility, but not necessarily their wisdom. What it may have witnessed staying in this one spot for years may have been more spectacular than the adventurous life led by many a brave man. In any case, when man wanted to understand nature they went into the woods or a cave or mountain and sat in one spot contemplating before they achieved enlightenment. That is the story of humanity.

"I wish we could stay here longer," Aleesha said, adjusting her muffler.

"In Zermatt?" Amir asked.

"Yes, I think I vibe well with these mountains and the cold."

"Imagine, coming here in Winter!" Amir said.

"We should try it, someday," Aleesha said.

"Well, we still have another day here."

"We need to take good photos with the Matterhorn backdrop".

"Maybe some more interesting events will come up along the way," Amir added.

Amir started talking to the guide. His name was Eric. He had a florid face and he spoke fluent English. He was telling Amir about the Foehn winds in the Alps. Sitting beside him while Aleesha lay on the mat engrossed and fixated on capturing the scenic beauty, Amir was reminded of Johnny. Johnny had opened to him the treasures of the Thekkady forest and had turned from his guide to one of his most trusted friends. Amir had traveled alone frequently and made strong bonds with the locals he met on the way, but he kept the impromptu meetings short and kept moving from one town to another unless he came to a place that was rather special or met a person who his instinct told him could open a whole new interesting chapter for him to explore. He had almost always been right. It may be because of his travels within India during his childhood. Those long journeys taught him when to be on his guard and he learned the kind of people to trust and whom not to, although in those times the troubles were handled by his parents and uncles, he always had a sense of responsibility for protecting his mom and family, as the oldest male child.

Eric asked them about lunch. After discussing with Aleesha, Amir told him that they would explore the villages and mountain ranges a bit more and have a late lunch before going back to the hotel. They trod the valleys on foot for a couple more hours before heading back to Zermatt center and having lunch at a small café'.

After lunch, they bade farewell to Eric who promised to be back the next day for another excursion to a different area of the valley.

Amir and Aleesha had decided to spend the night in the hotel. When they got back both were tired and sloshed into the bed side by side.

"Was an interesting day," Aleesha said. "Loved the countryside especially".

"Yeah, the villages were straight out of movie sets. Eric is a nice chap. Maybe should have a drink or two with him tomorrow."

"You do that," Aleesha said.

She knew that Amir was reminiscing about his drinking binges with his male friends. At such times she had to be on alert because he never seemed to have enough.

"Maybe", Amir smiled.

"Quisaz, quisaz , quisaz" Aleesha sang in Spanish. Her pellucid singing was always mellifluous to Amir's ears.

They lay in bed until it was past six in the evening. After that, they refreshed and got ready to go out. Amir went down before Aleesha and struck up a conversation with the receptionist. He asked her about the surroundings and interesting places.

When Aleesha came down, Amir asked her whether she was hungry. His stomach was borborygmus. She said she would like to have a stroll and have dinner after dusk. They walked a bit and found a bar where Amir had a whiskey and they sat and smoked while observing the surrounding activities.

"From your experience, how do you think of me as a girlfriend?".

"You want me to be frank?" Amir asked.

She nodded.

"I am very careful with you because I valued this relationship a lot, initially I didn't want anything to happen that would ruin the friendship. I fretted about not being about to please you enough. Later on, I fell in love with you deeply, for I saw my soulmate in you. I am a very possessive person. I needed to tell you that. Maybe this is the right occasion." He continued, "I could get jealous of the smallest of things. Even when you spoke of your past, I started regretting the fact that I didn't meet you before you met Andrew."

"Does that change the way you see me?" Aleesha interjected.

Amir paused a second before replying equivocally, "Not really," with a smile that Aleesha understood well.

"I see. I wouldn't want to say anything that might make our relationship weak," she said.

"Even I have a past," Amir said. "That shouldn't change anything. What would matter is that we maintain the respect we have for each other."

They were both very frank, and Amir realized that he should go slow on the whiskey. Aleesha was just having Aqua. Amir suddenly thought that she was being more serious than usual, but then decided it was the tiring tour in the afternoon and the stunning environment having its effect.

Their eyes met and for a moment, they looked at each other with an unexplainable emotion as if two energies were entwined in a cosmic entanglement void of all reasons and beginnings and endings. It was then that they understood that their lives were much more than the physical presence on this earth. They were two souls sure to meet and love at every new birth or after death and rebirth. At that very moment, in the distance, a bright star fell slowly, plummeting down into the horizon. Amir almost showed the magnificent event to Aleesha, but he was stopped by a secret he knew. A secret he dared not think about, let alone share with anyone. Not even his Shen. But he knew that he had disinterred a mystery of the universe. This was his apotheosis. Sitting with his soulmate and witnessing a sign from the universe.

He understood the power of their union and there was no need for more explanations and looking back into the past. The need for details had just disappeared into the astounding Mountains of the Alps with the emanation of love from their hearts. A sanctified love. The magical land had given their life new meaning.

Just now a lamp was lit,

I fear not the darkness,

For you have created,
Within me a joy,
With no bounds,
I ask you for your sorrows,
My love will be your syrup,
Courage will be with you,
For my spirit is your guardian.

Amir felt an ease, a peace of mind. He realized the trip was worth it. They didn't say much for the evening had dinner and returned to the hotel. The next day they traveled from Zermatt to Geneva via Lausanne. After spending one night there They took the flight from Geneva to Bern. They spent a day touring the famous landmarks in the capital and traveled to Zurich to take the flight back to Maldives.

Back in Maldives, they were both engrossed in work.

Two months later, Aleesha told Amir that she wanted to visit her dad in Greece, saying she'd be back in a few months. She said that she needed some time alone to plan her future. Amir agreed. They had been together since they met in Kumily and didn't go a single day without meeting each other. Amir thought that this would be a good break for him too. Maybe he could plan on settling down for good. He needed to decide where and whether to get married. It all depended on what Aleesha wanted to do next.

A week after she left, Amir received a message from Aleesha saying that she had decided to follow a spiritual path and had found a Guru who would help her in the endeavor. She said that marriage and the pleasures of this world had no meaning for her anymore. She also said that she wished him all the joys of life and wished that he would soon find a life partner. She ended the text by saying that they will meet for sure in the next life and will be with each other forever.

The initial shock made him petrified. Amir was anguished and his mind began to festinate. He was hurt but not rancorous.

Black,

Not blank,

Questions,

Without answers,

Finally lost grip,

Of dear life,

The determination destroyed,

Fetters in my legs,

A fall so severe,

Even the tooth,

couldn't withstand.

A facula lit,

On My mind.,

As I observed,

The funeral pyre.

Aleesha's text was so full of paradoxes, as was the situation. They were madly in love and were going to settle down in life. But now the debacle left him jilted. Amir tried hundreds of times to reach her, but she did not reply, and she deleted all her social media accounts. Amir thought of calling her mom through Johnny but then after days of debating it in his mind gave up the idea. Finally, he had to digest the fact that he had lost his true love. There were no arguments, no litany of complaints. His heart was heavy, and he could not help but think of the moments they spent together. Did it not mean anything to her? He was sad. If it was spirituality that she wanted, they could have tried it together. He knew that she was far from being a cloistress. Finally, he thought that it may have been his religion. Amir was a Muslim, and he was intransigent about it because he firmly believed in its tenets. Aleesha on the other hand was gnostic. Although she was born to Christians, she had always spoken about the power of the soul and that this body was just a temporary one that would return to earth and the soul would be liberated at death. She believed that the soul was part of the divine and was eternal. They had had such discussions, but Amir's logic was always based on what he had learned from Islam. Aleesha had respected that, but Amir always knew she didn't agree with him, although their beliefs weren't antithetical, they were disparate. Despite experiencing drugs and other forms of mental pleasures, Amir believed he was a Muslim, and his mind was pretty much ossified in this regard. Now he had had the kiss of death. No Nepenthe could give him peace. She was his peace.

Despite all this, Amir thought that Aleesha left him in a search. Maybe he could not lead her to her peace. At least not in this world. Amir wondered whether they would ever meet again and what the circumstances would be. Maybe he was Bluebeard, and she was his Fatima.

He had to regress and reflect.

Only the survivor realizes the deep lesson behind constantly losing the plot. For he learns the divine decree and its magical ways. Only if he continues to strive.

He kept worrying and pined for the lost love for days without any work or enjoyment. Maybe whatever he had with Aleesha was too good to last forever on this earth. You cannot create heaven on earth.

He knew he would not be able to Love anyone the way he loved her. So, he decided to give all his attention to his work and dream of establishing his business empire. Wealth and power will compensate for the lost love, he thought. It would almost be impossible for him to give his heart to a woman now. It was no longer ignescent.

The tale of sorrows,

Written in blood,

wounds all around,

The wise heart stoned,

Through the pain,

Legends arise.

Chapter 7

2013

The plane landed at Jakarta airport at dusk. Amir wound the knob of his watch to set the time. When Amir and Khalid reached outside, Mr. Suharto was waiting for them. Suharto was an elderly, short, thin man who would be accompanying and guiding them throughout their stay in Indonesia. Amir guessed that he must be in his early fifties. He had met him briefly during his previous short visit. He was sent to pick them up by Amir's father's business partner in Indonesia, Mr. Tusiman.

Mr. Suharto apologized that Mr. Tusiman couldn't make it to the airport as he was busy handling an urgent shipment to be sent to Japan. He said that he would meet them in the night in their hotel.

After a short trip, they arrived at the Batavia Hotel. The hotel design was highly influenced by the Dutch Colonial period architecture. The friendly staff and auxiliary helpers immediately started attending to their needs and after the formalities, they escorted them to their room. The room was convenient with two beds and all the required facilities.

As they were settling down Suharto handed over to them a call from Mr. Tusiman. He told Amir that he would be at the hotel in another half an hour and invited them for dinner.

After the call, Suharto left them, saying he would wait in the hotel lobby, and asked them to freshen up and get ready for dinner. They thanked him and let him go.

Amir looked at Khalid and told him, "Two weeks, might as well make good use of the time and start operations tomorrow itself".

"Let's see how this Tusiman guy can help us. Tonight, we can find that out."

Amir nodded in agreement. "Dad says he is a canny negotiator."

Khalid was very different from him in some respects despite their close friendship. Khalid found it hard to trust people until he had checked them out properly. Usually, during meetings, it would be Amir doing the talking and him observing and giving the verdict later when they were alone. In Amir's case, he trusted people but if he ever got finagled, that was it. He didn't believe in giving second chances. Amir looked at Khalid. He was grateful that he had such a cool friend who understood him.

Growing old together,

The adventures,

The dangers,

Learning from each other,

Soldiers of light,

Brothers in arms,

With you by my side,

Even the devil is afraid.

Their task at hand was to create a shipping channel between Indonesia and the Maldives. This was Amir's dream project, as from his previous visit to Indonesia and through his dad's business contacts it was very evident to him that Indonesian goods could be exported to Maldives instead of catchpenny Chinese products and earn good profits. However, the problem he faced then was the absence of direct shipping from Indonesia to Maldives. Container loads had to be shipped from Indonesia to Malaysia or Singapore and then to Colombo and then from there to Malé. Thus, making the shipping rates too high to be feasible and the time for the goods to reach Malé was too long.

Amir was able to convince his father and the Board of Directors of the company to invest in the project. Accordingly, a subsidiary company for import and export would be set up in Indonesia. They would purchase a vessel with a capacity of a minimum 500 metric ton load. The ship will sail directly from Jakarta to Malé and to Addu city, the southernmost Atoll of the Maldives, which was the second most developed city in the country.

Their first mission of the trip would be to inspect a few ships that were for sale and about which they had communicated with the owners through e-mail. Secondly, they would negotiate with Mr. Tusiman about setting up the foreign investment company. As a longtime friend of Amir's father, Tusiman had been chosen to be their local representative. In addition, he had his shares in a Tuna processing Factory which was at present exporting fish to Japan. Mr. Tusiman had many a time used Amir's father's assistance in selling his goods by using his father's contacts in various parts of the world. Especially in the yellowfin tuna trade. Therefore, it was presumed that he would assist them to the best of his ability in this project. Amir decided to agree with his dad's idea despite having been warned many times by business associates in Singapore and Malaysia to be careful in dealing with stingy and rapacious Indonesian businessmen.

After having freshened up, they went down to the Lobby. Alongside Suharto, Mr. Tusiman was waiting for them. He greeted them and again apologized for not being able to go to the airport to pick them up. He told them that the shipment was being palletized. Amir told him that it was fine and told him that he hoped his shipment went well. Amir introduced Khalid to him and as they were about to sit down, Tusiman told them that he would be taking them to a restaurant a little bit far from the hotel so they should leave as soon as possible. He went out to get his car and returned driving an SUV.

They reached the restaurant in little less than half an hour. After they ordered the food, Tusiman initiated the business talk and Amir gave him a rough idea of the project he had in mind.

"It will take about a month to get done with the formalities," Tusiman said.

"I will arrange for a meeting with a lawyer who will explain all legal matters."

"But all we have is two weeks," said Amir.

"And I think inspecting the vessels and their fitments at different ports is going to take up much of our time."

Tusiman gave a thoughtful look and replied, "Let's see how much gets done, once we speak with the lawyer, he will do most of the government work, meanwhile we can travel to see the vessels."

"Good," Amir said.

The restaurant was a high-end restaurant with female Indonesian waiters mincing about. A beautiful young waitress came over to greet them and served the plates.

Khalid gave a satisfied smile, and Tusiman winked and as she left, he asked "Good? Is it?"

Khalid responded with a short laugh and a thumbs up.

Suharto said, "Plenty plenty, you no worry!"

"Indonesian women are beautiful," Amir said, reminiscing his previous experience.

For most of the rest of the evening, they discussed tourism and Indonesian cuisine, with Mr. Suharto serving them different varieties of seafood dishes, from catfish to cuttlefish, reef fish, and some strange-looking species and sundry assortments which Amir didn't know but gulped down quickly, to be polite.

After the meal, they were dropped off at the hotel and Tusiman told them that he would be at the hotel by ten in the morning. They went to their room and Amir asked Khalid "What do you think?"

"Mr. Suharto is a jolly old man" was his reply.

'How many cities do we have to travel to to inspect the boats?"

"At least three," Amir replied.

"I will have to call the vessel owners in the morning and then we can plan the itinerary".

Little did Amir know that the next day was going to be a day that would change his life forever.

The next morning, they were hardly ready when the phone rang from the reception telling them that Mr. Tusiman was waiting in the lobby.

When they reached down Suharto greeted them at the elevator and took them to meet Tusiman who was with the lawyer. After greeting them Amir told them that he and

Khalid had not had their breakfast and invited them to join them. They politely declined and said they would have coffee. They went to the hotel's main restaurant and ordered a la carte.

Amir always enjoyed meeting with lawyers, as the law was one of his favorite subjects despite having once dropped off halfway through an LLB program due to his avid business activities. Also learning about the commercial law structure of different countries gave a good insight into the economic mindset of the populace.

The lawyer introduced himself as Mr. Danny. He explained the procedure for foreign investment, the deposits and opening of bank accounts, and the registration of the company. He told them that normally it would take five weeks to complete the documentation and procedure but through his channels, he could have it done within two weeks. Which of course happened with an increased price.

They agreed on the fee and Amir told him that they would be there for only two weeks and that he should complete the process through Mr. Tusiman and that whatever letters and signatures required should be taken within the week as they would have to travel out of Java the next week.

Amir had done his research over the internet and despite being a very flexible traveler he knew that traveling the length and breadth of the country to at least three destinations within less than two weeks would be a challenge. As a last option, he had prepared in his mind to increase the duration of the trip to another two weeks as they had travel visas for a month. If they stayed longer than that they would have the additional burden of going through various procedures to get the business visa and extend the stay.

With all the negotiations done over breakfast, Danny told them that he would meet them again the next day with the necessary documents to be filled in and signed and left. Amir asked Khalid to wait downstairs and he went up to the room and used his laptop to update his dad about the meeting, the procedures, and the minimum capital so that he could get the final confirmation before giving the advance money to the lawyer.

With that done, he returned to the lobby.

"How long is the flight to Cirebon?' Amir asked.

"Around an hour," said Tusiman.

"You want to go today?"

"No, I think we will start the travels after doing the documentation with the lawyer tomorrow. I will make the appointments through mail today and then we can plan the trips. For the rest of the day, I think we will go sightseeing in Jakarta, what do you say, Khalid?"

"Will be good," he replied.

"If Tusiman is busy Suharto can accompany us," Amir said.

"I am free today, what would you like to see and do?"

"Your choice," added Amir and everyone laughed realizing that they were in for some leisure time.

"Let's go to the Mall of Indonesia. They have a kermis there today," Tusiman told Suharto.

As they were going to be business partners in quite a big project, Amir wanted to study Mr. Tusiman's personality, which was the reason he decided to spend time off work and was glad he agreed to accompany them.

Tusiman took them to a few malls, they purchased their mobile sim cards and after lunch, they spent time sightseeing in his car watching the mélange of architectural flairs. Like most capital cities, Jakarta was vibrant and welcoming with ultra-high buildings, shops, and multi-cuisine restaurants. They went around and reached back to the hotel at around quarter past five in the evening. During this leisure time, they didn't discuss much business, so when Tusiman asked about the plan for the next day, Amir suggested they sit down in the restaurant and have coffee.

"Should I take tickets to Cirebon for tomorrow evening?" Tusiman asked.

"Yes, once we finish the meeting with the lawyer we can leave, and if there is a return flight, we can come back at night."

"I will have to check that out," said Tusiman and he called his secretary to check out the flight availability.

Meanwhile, Amir called the vessel owner in Cirebon and asked him whether he would be available and whether they could inspect the vessel the next day. He replied in the affirmative and said that he would wait for them and asked them to send the flight details so that he could pick them up.

After that, they discussed the business prospects of import and export between Maldives and Indonesia, and Khalid inquired about the sources of products so that they would be able to get the best possible prices.

After finishing his coffee and before taking his leave Tusiman looked at Amir and told him, "Mr. Amir, this is a very big project, and you are bringing a big investment into the country. It's not as easy as it looks on paper. We will meet many challenges and it is going to require great courage if we want to pull this through successfully. Again, it all depends on you."

Amir bowed down a bit and acknowledged the advice.

"let's try our best, I think we can beat the competition and if we get the best prices, we can succeed in the market, it depends a lot on you as the local party in sourcing the goods as cheaply as possible.'

"Call Mr. Suharto if you need anything or want to go out anywhere tonight," Tusiman said and after handshakes, they both left.

They returned to the room and relaxed for some time smoking a few kreteks they bought at a local store and discussing the events of the day and Indonesian culture, which was quite similar to their own Maldivian culture as both were Islamic nations and people observed similar preferences in food, dressing, and outlook.

They decided that they would look up a restaurant nearby on the internet and take a taxi for dinner rather than call Mr. Suharto.

Around eight-thirty, they took a taxi to a restaurant near the hotel, with good reviews on the internet. The restaurant served Indonesian and Thai cuisine.

As they were entering, a tall, thin man wearing a designer suit and glasses walked up to them, pulled out his hand, and greeted them "Mr. Amir?". Shocked and taken aback Amir asked him as politely as he could "Who?"

I am a friend of Mr. Kuan, whose boat you are going to buy.

"But how did you know we were coming here?" Amir said realizing that he could be trying to dupe them.

"Let me take you to a good place for dinner and we can discuss business," he said.

Not knowing exactly what they were into, Amir looked at Khalid. The smooth operator he was, he did not show any emotions, but from years of camaraderie, Amir knew he was ready for whatever was to be faced.

So, Amir said, "Okay", but Tusiman's warning rang in his head.

The stranger led them to a black Mercedes Benz and asked them to get in. He took the front seat next to the driver and instructed the driver in the Indonesian language Bahasa, where they were to go.

He pulled out a card from his wallet and turned and gave it to Amir. His name was Firaz Ahmet, and he was the chairman of a resort supply chain called Quantum Supplies. Amir tried to connect the relationship between his company and his business to identify where his interests lay.

After about fifteen minutes they reached their location. It was an open-air restaurant that had a barbeque, a buffet and a band playing slow music. A waiter approached them and guided them to a table for three. It was obvious that he knew their new friend.

As they settled down, Amir pulled out his wallet, took his card and handed it to Firaz. He smiled as he took it and told Amir, "I already know everything about you and this, your right-hand man."

"Your family, your education, and all your adventures and business activities. Your love life, your family, everything is recorded in our files. Your intelligence is conspicuous."

"You have lost me," Amir said surprised.

"Your friend here is seven years older than you. You met each other many years before in Bangalore where you were a student, and since then you have been involved in various types of business and activities, some I rather not mention here."

By now Amir knew he had to be very cautious. If he knew this much, then he was telling the truth about knowing more.

Khalid also looked bothered.

So, Amir asked him, "Why this interest in us"?

"You," he said.

"We were in on your case since you were a student in Pune, India. We have closely observed all your businesses and the deep travels and inquiries you made in various cities of India and Sri Lanka, especially the port cities, planning your business empire, taking over from your father. We know how you have planned it all, my dear, but let me tell you 'Everything is planned, and everything is controlled' by a system and there is a commission running it. It would be an injustice to your intelligence to think that you didn't already suspect it despite our very careful and foolproof procedures to remain hidden. However, this is your foretaste of the actual realm of things."

"Thanks for the encomium, but Let's talk business".

"You are here to buy a boat, so might as well do that."

"Is anything going to stop me?"

"No, in fact, you will get the boat for free, however, you would need to get the amount into the country to clear tax purposes, but the amount will be sent to an account you will open in a bank in Singapore. You will meet Mr. Lim in Singapore who will arrange it all for you."

"500 tons capacity, good condition, made in 1976. It will have a Maldivian ensign."

He had already decided on Amir's boat!

"Why this generosity? What is our task?"

"All you need to know is, you need to pick up our cargo and make sure it reaches the waters of Indonesia and back on every trip."

Amir was getting the idea; this was the smuggling he was suggesting.

"It's not like I will be on the ship."

"Each and every member of the crew will be chosen by Mr. Tusiman."

This was another surprise. There was no point trying to whitewash anything.

Giving a knowing smile, he said to Amir, "Call of us the Delta force, we are present in every country, anyone of substance must be signed up for us. We are soldiers doing the work for a system that controls everything, we are just below the top brass, more than that, even we have no clue. We just follow instructions."

If you want an example, take Microsoft, they were asked to develop software that would reach into every house, every room. Facebook asks you "what's on your mind" and your smartphones know you better than yourselves. Through these and more, every person is covered and caught in a grid, and all these are the brainchild of the commission that controls the system. Of course, you are paid well when you do a good job, and you have insurance and security, and your families are protected."

"You may think this is outrageous, but if humans were not monitored and there was no control whatsoever, how do you think seven billion humans would live together peacefully and in harmony? Impossible. However, humans need to develop, and every kind of thought needs to progress till we uncover the true secrets of the universe, for despite the years of research and works by great scholars, we know so little about over existence and the universe. So, this is a search for the truth. To get there, every form of human instinct needs to be fed. Every war that has been fought in recent times has been directed and produced by the system. Terrorism and the mafia are tools of the system. Although most of the terrorists and mafioso would have no idea they are doing the bidding of some other people who have no interest in their ideologies. It is only the top tiers of the pyramid that know of the system. That's my purpose here today, to welcome you both into it."

He looked at Amir and again gave the same smile that Amir was growing accustomed to. Confusion was fogging Amir's brain with questions and memories. One thing was for sure, once he got into it there was not going to be any way out. This was like being incarcerated. "What if I refuse?"

"You would never be able to achieve your dreams. At the most, you would get a 9-5 job in a good company doing prosaic duties and then retire someday. Which I think is not your idea of living."

Amir had to agree with him on this point. If he didn't agree, years of hard work would be undermined. Defiance would be a dead end.

He always knew that things everywhere were controlled by some forces but to this extent that you are just a puppet dancing to the tunes of your masters is not what he expected, for he wanted to be the puppet master and not the puppet they tantalized, which he guessed Firaz and people already knew and Amir couldn't help but feel helpless because he knew that all these years of research and finally reaching here was not a coincidence, but he had been lead all along.

"Where do we need to pick up the cargo? and what is the nature of the goods?"

"Sri Lanka, a place you know very well. Trincomalee port, our agents will be there."

"Sometimes gold biscuits, arms, sometimes drugs"

"Don't worry, everything will be meticulously planned by our people in Maldives, Sri Lanka, and Indonesia, your job is to just sail the boats between the two countries at least once a month, That's our command." You will receive half a million dollars for every trip, which will be transferred to your account in Singapore. Before you go to Maldives, you need to go to Singapore and make business arrangements there too, you will be guided throughout by our people although they won't mention anything about it. So, this is your dream setup. You don't have to deviate from your original plan. You can keep doing your trade and you are getting the license for it. You can make it big, and no one will suspect you as you have the necessary legal set up everywhere."

"What if we ever get caught?"

"Smuggling I mean! Serious offense"

Firaz laughed and looked at both of them. "Luck is very important in life and lady luck is with you now. You will never have to face a trial regarding this business. If you do get caught for any breach, which is a very unlikely event, we will make you disappear from the system. You need to be careful with people, as although everything will be planned by our personnel, each doing just their task in interim arrangements, the "Normals" as we call those outside the force, are the majority and if they ever get suspicious you will have the intelligence systems after you. Need to learn to be discreet and live a low-key life despite the wealth you will accumulate. I don't think it's necessary to warn you both about that as the films you see and books you read must have taught you all mafia rules and policies. We have our own Magna Carta."

"Mario Puzo," Amir smiled for the first time since meeting him.

"Omerta," he said, and looking at the food that arrived a few minutes back, he said, "shall we?"

They ate in silence, and Amir suddenly realized the driver was at the entrance, arms folded and staring steadily at them.

With the band playing a slow rhythmic Indonesian song in the background, Amir tried to relax a bit, however, the man in front of him would not let him do so. His concentration now was only on the food. He looked nothing more than a professional miserly business executive of Chinese origin but had a no-nonsense attitude and a flair for style. Amir wondered whether they would meet again. Also, he wasn't exactly asking Amir to agree to his deal, to him it was almost a complete and done project. What worried Amir was that he had no idea to whom he was promising fealty.

"You both should find good wives and get married". He says after a long pause." It helps you climb up the ladder. I know you are ambitious, but the system requires people who are settled and serious about life, not youngsters venturing into trial and error, perhaps, and perhaps it took so long for us to reach you is because you had not started a responsible life. We do know about your hippie days too."

Amir started getting anxious and rewinded to his past life and the affairs that he thought were his matters that others had no idea about, but here was a man talking as if he had read Amir's autobiography!

After dinner and smoking another cigarette, Firaz says, "So it's all done, maybe we may not meet again, however, you must leave within two weeks, you will go to Singapore and meet Mr. Lim, who happens to be your father's friend before you go back to Maldives. He will mail you within this week."

Khalid gave Amir a sudden glance and smiled.

"It avoids suspicion when you go through channels you have already known in the past." Mr. Firaz said, reading their mind. Amir tried to ask about his father and then decided against it. One thing was for sure. If Amir was going into this, he would have to take total control of all businesses and keep all family members out of this project so that no one else gets into trouble if ever things went wrong.

Firaz paid the bill, and they left the restaurant. He dropped them at the hotel and after giving them both a quick hug he told Amir, "You have no idea, it was a great pleasure meeting you, I wish you all the best!"

Amir could feel that it was a genuine remark.

After he left, Amir walked out to the road instead of going into the hotel. He lit a cigarette. Khalid too did the same and followed him. When they glanced at each other, they burst out into laughter as they always did in such situations. Together they had faced a lot, and even in dire circumstances kept their cool. For the ambitious Amir, it was such a great blessing to have a friend to whom he didn't need to explain using too many words. They understood and read each other well and most of the time just used signs to express their thoughts or next action.

However, this time they needed to talk and talk seriously.

"So, what do you think?" Amir asked.

He shrugged and asked, "What do we do?"

"Once we get in, there is not going to be any way to wriggle out."

"I think we are already in it, there is no escape. If we want to go for the bigger things there is no other route and they have pulled us in, it's not an offer, I think it's an order," Khalid said.

"Well, then tonight is the last night of our previous life".

"That calls for celebration," said Khalid, spelling out the mutual thought.

"Floreat Nusantara," Amir said to acknowledge his agreement.

They quickly checked out the nearby nightclubs and nightlife in the city and settled for a discotheque fifteen minutes away from the hotel. In the club, they were greeted by tall slender beautiful Indonesian ladies who accompanied them throughout, and they danced the night away.

When they reached the hotel, it was past one thirty in the morning.

They said good night to each other and lay down to sleep. However, sleep eluded Amir. His past life was withering away and events of it were recurring in his mind. His mind was trying to make sense of all the things that happened to him and the reasons for it all. It was also irritating to know the project at hand was not only legally but also morally wrong.

O dear life,

When I was at the door,

Knocking on freedom,

You lead me to a cave,

Of riches endless,

But a traveler I am,

What shall I do here,

I cannot take the gold,

Where my soul resides.

He looked back at his life and realized the offer at hand went against all his principles in life and the things he had always stood for. Deep inside, he believed that he was a good samaritan, although his actions didn't align with his religious beliefs, he always hoped that one day he would start dedicating his life to serving mankind to wash away his sins and mistakes committed in this provisional existence and prepare for the next life. However, there were things he wanted to achieve before that and now in his early thirties he was far away from achieving his dreams Tonight, over dinner he had realized why, and had been forced into an arrangement made not by him but by some other forces, for the first time in his life and he was facing a test of his probity. His infrangible confidence had taken a blow. In his vacillation, he finally drifted to sleep.

Chapter 8

It had been two years since the meeting with Firaz in Jakarta. Amir was a successful businessman running a trading conglomerate with subsidiaries in various countries on four continents. As per the deal that Firaz laid out, his only job was to keep the trade between Maldives and Indonesia going, which meant he had to make the boat sail with goods from Indonesia to Malé and back, at least once a month. The rest was taken care of in smooth operations and despite the initial worries it had become a norm hardly given consideration and inadvertent. However, the money kept coming and he could invest in several projects in Central Asia, Africa, Europe, and North America. All well-set-up legal subsidiaries with head offices in India and the Maldives. It was grand larceny. It wasn't exactly duress as per legal terminology, but his hands were tied.

Khalid had started a family and settled down in Sri Lanka and handled the company offices there and in Singapore. He too had given up drugs and marijuana use because of which he had to take Zoloft to calm his anxiety. Apart from the job he oversaw for the company, he was also launching his operations and opening a chain of retail stores for garments and arts. Art was his hobby and when he suggested the idea, Amir promised him his full support. However, they hardly got to meet each other ever since. Amir missed having a close friend nearby to release the stress of work. He often remembered the times when they used to talk so freely about everything from politics to astronomy to quantum physics and philosophy.

Amir arrived in Mumbai for a series of business meetings after having spent some time in Mauritius. A major segment of the business was concentrated in exports from India, for this reason, Mumbai had become the capital for his business activities. As the plane landed, Amir looked at the magnanimous city from the sky. The resilient Bombay, as it was previously known was the city of dreams for Indians, and it was not just merely a title, it truly defined the city. If you were tough and believed in your dreams and worked hard, the city did reward you. But it did test and tire out even the best of the best, Amir reflected.

Amir was picked up at the airport by his assistant and they drove straight to the office where Amir signed some documents and held a staff meeting. The company had underbid a potential mega project and there was a final opportunity to present a fresh one. After completing the meeting, he checked into his hotel and went to his room. Out of the twentieth floor of the tower, he looked out at the great city. Here you can find every flavor of human existence. The richest with the world at their feet, the poorest surviving years of penury, people of every race and color mingling, every form of luxury to the poorest slums. Every kind of art, every cuisine, to the most varied assortments of palatable street food. All this, he had experienced as a child when he visited the city with his dad when he was just eight years old. He had sat at the Gateway of India and experienced the same feeling as he did now, as he stared at the city. Only the child had grown into a man.

Almost thirty years later, Amir had earned wealth and achieved material success. His undisguised zeal to be a business magnate was achieved. He was turning into an expert analyst, calculating yield to maturity precisely, and was judicious in his investments. He avoided ostentation although he was not very frugal. However, he felt that he had lost his freedom. He had lost his innocence. There was no other level to climb. His life was sabotaged by a system. He even suspected that he was becoming effete. Everywhere he looked, he saw people caught in a trap and enslaved in something they had no idea of. People struggling to make ends meet, people who believe they will get lucky someday and will be able to lead the life of luxury they want to provide for their family. He felt the urge to hug such people and tell them to be satisfied with a simple life for if they tried to break into the higher life of extravagance, they would have to sell their morality, and freedom and above all forfeit their faith.

He returned and lay down on the bed staring at the ceiling.

Spiritually and mentally, Amir was a total mess. He just carried on with quotidian tasks and there was no spice or adventure anymore. Although the wealth managed to hide the worries from showing externally through makeup and being well-groomed, it was when he was alone in the bathroom, when he looked at the mirror that he realized that he had created a huge void in his life and unless something filled that void, it would not be long before he lost it all and collapsed for good. The stress was inextricable. It didn't help that he had let Khalid and the few other friends he could trust go to different countries to look after the different branches. He had his vested interests; he didn't want them working together in one place, so that they could not nurture any common thoughts against him and his hegemony. Amir highly valued the people he could trust and didn't want them to change. Therefore, he made them feel important and gave them the best possible positions and perquisites from the company. However, experience had taught him that it takes a second for a human being's thought to change, a friend can become a foe anytime. Therefore, he needed to be extra careful as the leader of the pack, as if one of them turns bad, its effect could be felt throughout the organization like an earthquake where it's tremors are felt far and wide. Therefore, he periodically recasts the important characters in his life.

Amir went through the itinerary for the week that he would be in Mumbai. His mind was always occupied with adjusting assets and liabilities. He hoped he could get some time off for a short leisure trip so that he could reflect and overcome his weariness and make some good plans for the future.

It had been almost four years since he had a girlfriend. The failed relationship with Aleesha had chastened him. Since the day in Jakarta, when his life changed forever, he had directed all his concentration to work. The first year was full of apprehension and worries, the second on expanding the business further and further. He had been so busy that his sex life had become dormant. He had no time to even check out the escorts or prostitutes in the various cities, unlike his younger days with friends when they never left a town without checking out its women. Not necessarily for sex but to hang around with and go clubbing and only if they did find some who were extremely good enough did, they take them to their hotels. Which was a rare occurrence and one high on the pocket.

Amir decided to give it a thought during this trip but immediately decided to get it out of his head. He was approaching middle age, and this was the time for him to find a suitable woman who would be his life partner and settle down.

His mom was very much on this case, telling him that she and his father were growing old and that it was time for them to play with their grandchildren. His sister was married and had a daughter and a son, and his younger brother was about to marry within a few months. Amir always told his mom that he was married to work for now. Truth was, he could not settle down with just anybody.

He needed to love a woman for him to get married to her or to spend his lifetime with her. He had a robust idea of an ideal wife. Growing up made him understand that such people exist only in fairy tales. Thinking rationally, he thought that was how grown-ups should behave. Today he realized that people do not want to grow up. There is an inner child within everyone who follows the cravings of the mind without caring how many rules they break or how many hearts they destroy or how difficult the road ahead would be if they do certain acts without much care or worry.

He also learned that people do not change, although their behavior does evolve based on circumstances and experience. However, the inner self remains the same and you can be certain when all the masks are removed and every bit of hatred and remorse taken away, there remains the same person we were as children, with the same innocent dreams and hopes. Therefore, Amir normally could judge people based on the first meeting, when they are not ready and do not know what to expect from him. Especially with women, there was a strong mental and physical connection he had experienced occasionally, telling him that this was something he should carry forward as far as possible.

This instinct had never been wrong as he was able to discover wonderful women who told him their unfulfilled desires, dreams, and their dark secrets. This discovery of the nature and physics of the human female may still be the most intriguing and enticing knowledge he had ever come across. There was a species because of whom there have been wars and murders, for whom palaces have been built, and for whose love, songs, and turgid poems have been written and the bravest hearts crushed. Most importantly, each relationship that ended did leave him heartbroken despite him refusing to acknowledge it externally. Every time a relationship broke the "no strings attached" barrier and developed into something special, there was a promise to give all they had to make it everlasting. In the initial relationships, it was downright honest. However afterwards the promise was made with fingers crossed.

Until he met Aleesha six years back. The romance lasted less than two years. Since then, he has kept himself away from any commitments and has spent his energy on building his business empire. 'Laborare est orare' was his solace. He didn't think he could fall in love with anyone as much as he had loved Aleesha. She had taught him many things. Pride, not hubris, was an essential touchstone of a faithful woman. Every time he ever thought about a new woman, it was Aleesha he would see in her smile, the way she spoke, the way she dressed.

Work was the refuge he had from the ghost of this past. Which was one of the main reasons he didn't give a second thought in Jakarta after meeting Firaz. For he believed he had lost so much, there was nothing left to lose. He would not say he had lost his heart, but it was turning into stone, and he was becoming increasingly world-weary. He had to find a remedy before all hell broke loose or he lost his mind.

In his last meeting with Khalid, he realized Amir's condition and urged him to start a new relationship and end the sabbatical. He believed that the ghost of Aleesha would leave him as soon as he found care and got love from another woman who could take her place. Amir knew

Khalid was being optimistic. The quagmire of emotional distress she had caused had destroyed his peace and harrowed him with misery.

Amir's thoughts are disturbed by the ringing phone. It was a Facebook messenger call from Aman.

"Where are you?" he asked.

"In Mumbai."

"I need to talk to you soon, when is the earliest we can meet up?"

"I think by the end of this month, have got some necessary work to be done here. What's up?"

"Nothing serious, the government is getting weaker, which means my job is in jeopardy, so just want to discuss things. Also, the court has placed a lien against my resort."

"Ok, will call you as soon as I get back to Male."

"All right, take care."

"Take care."

Aman was into politics and was a prominent member of the leading Political party which was ruling for the past ten years. He had a good job as a state minister of the president's office. However, in recent times, the opposition parties joined together to form a strong alliance which was proving to be a tough challenge to the ruling party which was facing a slate of critics and analysts. The opposition leaders were trying to incite riots.

Aman and Amir shared a friendship of two decades. It was during his pre-university college days in Bangalore that he met Aman. He was ten years older than Amir. Amir was just seventeen at that time, however a budding friendship developed immediately. In the boarding house, they had initially shared a room. It was during these days that they had long discussions, marked with an asterisk in Amir's life diary, which eventually would shape their futures. When Amir met Aman, he was innocent and immature but being an ardent reader with a keen interest in politics and current affairs since he was a kid, Amir and Aman made great company. Where Amir had theoretical expertise, Aman had practical experience of life's journey. He had divorced his wife and decided to go for higher education primarily because his ex-wife had taunted him for his lack of education as she had a doctorate. Having joined the Maldivian armed forces straight after school, he was a trained military personnel before dropping out and joining his brother's business. During those days he met Mauna and fell in love with her. After a few months of dating, they decided to get married. It was only a while into the marriage that Aman learned about his wife's first lover and her feelings for him. Being madly in love with her as she was his first serious girlfriend and with whom he had his first sexual experience, he hung on to her despite the marriage going through rocky stages. One of the main factors at hand was money and Aman believed that if he could give the lifestyle that his wife demanded, she would remain with him faithfully. Therefore, he worked harder and tried to expand his business further by going into bigger projects. However, risk-taking proved to be a big blunder for him and the business started spiraling downward forcing his brother to take responsibilities away from him.

At the same time, his wife had started seeing her first lover and friends started informing Aman about these meetings. It was only when he caught them red-handed, did he finally divorce her. She left without any remorse and Aman was left heartbroken and engulfed in sorrow. It was these circumstances that made him decide to leave the country for some time and therefore higher education seemed the best option as he would have something to occupy his thoughts and would be a time well spent and an investment for the future.

"Don't you let a woman destroy you. Always remember they have many options…you are just one of them." Aman told Amir.

Aman chose to study Business administration. After days and nights of conversations over coffee Amir and Aman realized that to make a mark on society it was essential that they have a strong link within the political spectrum. Amir was always interested in Arts and humanities therefore he was doing his PU course in Arts. The curriculum included topics in Political science, Sociology, Psychology, History, and Economics.

It was during one of their everyday discussions that Amir decided that he would go forward as a businessman like his father and Aman decided that business was not for him, and he wanted to make it big in politics. Somehow, they knew that they would in the future complement each other through their chosen field of work. They had big dreams and during their group discussions in Bangalore, they laid the foundations of their very own 'la cosa nostra'. They promised themselves not to be assailed by doubts and regrets until they found the efficacy. Since then, Amir has been on the lookout for 'qualified' men or women who would complete the team. It had been many years since he developed a flair for spotting this type of character. He learned soon that what he was looking for was a rare species. Therefore, he valued these 'loving friends' just like family and they never disappointed him. At least not until then.

Meanwhile, Aman became more and more punctilious and ready for the political warzone.

Amir made a mental note to meet Aman as soon as he reached Maldives and concentrated on the work at hand.

He needed to go to Colaba with his assistant, Raju, who would be there to pick him up in an hour. He had a meeting with an exporter of seafood over dinner.

He was ready and waiting in the lobby as Raju arrived thirty minutes later than he was supposed to. Amir was accustomed to his ways as he was his usual company during his visits to Mumbai. Despite many flaws, he was a very useful guy who was always ready to help with anything Amir required during his stay. Raju told him that the restaurant was pretty far away, so Amir winded down and relaxed. Raju played a slow Hindi song. Amir was more fluent in Hindi now as he was interacting with many Indians to source goods for his exports.

Suddenly, Amir realized Aman had spoken of the political situation back home, so he searched on his smartphone and read the news from back home. There were continuous protests against the incumbent government and according to many reporters it may not last the term. The critics lambasted the rising corruption within the government despite having pledged zero tolerance to exploitation. The citizens had learned the political chicanery and made tall demands from the candidates. A no-confidence motion had reached cloture, and a vote was on the agenda for the next month as populist nostrums gained momentum. The disagreements had reached fulmination. This was a bit of worry for Amir as he was working closely with the government on many projects and most of his friends had influential positions in the government. A change in government would mean an abrogation of many signed MOUs. Also, Aman was an influential figure among the party cadre, and it was a dream of theirs that one day he would run for the President with Amir's financial backup. However, that was not on the cards as of yet and they needed to make sure the party stayed strong. The country, despite its transition in 2008 was still an inchoate democracy. Amir had met the current president occasionally before he was elected and once during the past three years of his tenure as president. Although the president was a man of principles, the liberal policies of his party were attacked strongly by the conservatives and the joining of forces by all the opposition had given momentum to the protests. Little was being done to quell the hostility and attempts to discredit the president, who planned to run for a second term.

The Maldives was a predominantly Islamic country, hundred percent as stipulated in the constitution, a person had to be a Muslim to be a citizen and had strong laws against apostasy. It had been so for almost a millennium since the country converted from Buddhism to Islam upon the order of the king of the time. Since then, the culture was taken over by Islamic rituals and traditions and peripatetic Sufis who rested on the Maldivian shores brought their insights into the local way of life. Thus, it was a rather peaceful and moderate version of Islam that was practiced in the country for centuries. However, of late, Saudi Wahhabism or extreme Sunni philosophies were becoming predominant in the country just as the wave was spreading throughout the Islamic world as the only true form of Islam. Although the majority of the Maldivian populace didn't agree with the extremist version, the past decades had seen the citizens as individuals and groups becoming very religious in their outlook and behavior. Contrary to the late eighties and early two thousand, the number of women wearing hijab, burqas, and yashmaks increased rapidly. Preachers also took advantage of the disastrous Tsunami of 2004, which plunged the populace into turmoil and revealed how delicate its existence was.

However, there was a section of society that was battling this conservative system. Highly educated and intelligent individuals were questioning every pillar of the system and setup. Questions were being raised to which scholars and followers had no answers. The internet and satellite television had a strong impact on the youth who went looking for answers about their very existence and developed profane ideas. A strong liberal brigade had risen and was mostly using social media to promote their views and impugn the fundamentals. However, despite their discretion, a few of them fell into the hands of extremist nationalists and were murdered for expressing their 'un-Islamic' views. There were allegations that extremist forces were acting within the military and security forces of the country. Many youths who found westernization and materialism as a form of some pernicious evil force, were giving up worldly matters and going to fight supposed 'Islamic' wars in the war-torn areas in the Middle East and other pariah states, looking for jihad and redemption from a world that was making it impossible for them to stay steadfast on their religious beliefs. One of his closest friends, Shahid, had fallen into this trap. Frustrated with life, he and some other members of his gang went to Syria to join the Jabhat al Nusra organization as belligerents. Others who were absconding due to several crimes also took this route and joined them. He lived in a war-torn city for a few years and got trained in the use of guns and rockets. A few years back he was killed in an exchange between the Al Nusra front and the ISIS fighters.

Several individuals took advantage of the confusion to create schism and upheaval in the society. Others used it as an opportunity to earn a few bucks by supplying the terrorists with personnel and taking money from the youths going there as recruits as well.

Amir sighed and shook his head lamenting the situation the world was in. As it was night, the Mumbai traffic was dying out and they were having a smooth ride and reached the restaurant sooner than expected.

At the restaurant, Amir met Mr. Shenoy, a middle-aged potbellied man. He was dressed casually in a satin shirt and jeans. The restaurant was a cozy one with a good atmosphere for intense conversations, with Hindi music playing lightly in the background. As the waiter led them to their table, they noticed that the place was almost full, with people busy in animated talks.

Raju, Mr. Shenoy, and Amir sat down at a table in a corner. As soon as they settled down, they spoke about the current market situation and the possibility of exporting seafood from Mumbai by air to Amir's buying offices in the West. Mr. Shenoy assured him of the best price quality and regular supply. Amir asked him to e-mail him the details including the price. After a good exchange of details, they ordered food and relaxed.

Shenoy asked Amir when he was leaving and whether he needed any help in Mumbai before he left. Amir told him that his company had taken care of everything. However, Shenoy insisted that as the next day was the weekend, he was free, and he wanted Amir to travel with him to his farmhouse near Uruli Kanchan in Pune. Amir reminisced about the vibrant city close to Mumbai with good weather and scenic beauty. Shenoy was originally from Pune and began explaining to Amir that it was a hill station in his childhood and how it had developed into one of the most modern metropolitan cities, much thanks to its proximity to Mumbai and the highly educated middle class and an influx of people from different parts of the world for education and tourism, making it a very livable cosmopolitan city. Shenoy insists that Amir visit the city with him and take a break from work in his farmhouse. Amir reluctantly agreed and Shenoy said that he would be at the hotel by six-thirty in the morning in his car. The journey would take around three hours and he insisted that they take the road so that they could enjoy the natural scenic beauty on route.

They finished their dinner and said their goodbyes for the night and as Raju drove Amir to the hotel Amir asked him to accompany him on the trip to Pune, to which he pleasantly agreed. When they reached the hotel, it was past eleven p.m. and Amir quickly undressed and got ready for sleep with the journey on his mind. Despite his reluctance, a break had come his way and now he was quite pleased that he agreed. He fell asleep easily as his thoughts versified into poems.

A drifter,

Flowing in this direction,

The wind takes him,

The rebel in him,

Dead and extinguished,

 Fading away with his youth,

What he had dreamt,

And what he became, Alas

The alarm woke him up at five-thirty. Amir got up, had a bath and prayed his morning ritual prayer. Over the past year, he had started to pray as frequently as he could. However, he still was far from being regular at the Islamic obligatory five prayers a day. The ibadah gave him some peace and escape from work and other worries of life. Sometimes he felt that if he invested his time in spiritual growth as he did in his work, he may be happier. He was not the person who would take the path of a monk or priest, but he was a curious learner of the spiritual paths and had read about almost all the great spiritual leaders who have changed the world, mostly for good. It is due to these towering figures that cultures had their morality and humanity intact, Amir guessed. However, he still needed answers. Therefore, he decided to be temperate. Despite never being able to follow the Islamic teachings, it was always at the back of his mind. However, the teachings and the writs were almost thousand five hundred years old and although still practical, it was facing challenges from the much-developed liberal philosophies and scientific developments which were advocating freedom, not only of thought but action too and requiring exigent answers to all religious dogma which had put not only Islam but all other religions under threat. It was as if there was an agenda in the past few decades to make religions as elusive as possible. However, it could be said that it was backfiring as there was a strong growth in interest in spirituality despite the dislike for organized religion. Especially among the youth indulging in drugs like hash, marijuana, LSD, heroin, and other mind-altering chemicals and experimenting with their existence. The power of the untrammeled mind, dimensions of time and the existence of spiritual beings were becoming fashionable talk among youths. A trend that became the rage in the sixties and seventies during the growth of the hippie culture was now decades later returning in a more modern form, developing into a modern club and rave party culture. Amir too had been caught in this web but was about to get out safely at the right time, much thanks to close friends and family. Aleesha played a pivotal role in getting him back on track and back to work properly on his business. However, dear friends were still victims of drug addiction. In addition, they were struggling with anxiety and schizophrenia.

After getting ready, Amir made a cup of coffee and waited for Raju and Shenoy to arrive. Fifteen minutes later he got a call from the reception informing him that Raju had arrived. Just as he got to the lobby, Mr. Shenoy arrived and told them that the driver was waiting in the car just outside the hotel. It was a spacious BMWX X5 and they settled down inside quickly. Mr. Shenoy introduced the driver, whose name was Babu. Amir enjoyed long rides across scenic routes. It stimulated his mind's vivid imagination and filled him with ideas. Many a great project he had completed were ideas that spurn out through such enjoyable rides. He preferred bus rides alongside bloke-ish commuters, from one city to another rather than taking the short plane journey as the time he got travelling by road through various geographic plains and viewing natural beauty across highways always refreshed his mind like nothing else does. This journey was such a blissful journey across what Mr. Shenoy explained as the Sahyadri or 'benevolent Mountain' ranges. There were two famous Hill stations, Lonavala and Khandala on the route. Amir, as usual, was mesmerized by the beautiful views seen through his window. Raju told Amir that they would reach Pune within two hours. Amir kept looking out and let his mind venture freely into various fields of thought.

He decided to think about the current business ventures, trying to get more ideas that would be accretive to the earnings of the company and make it a well-known global business empire. He knew that things were smoother for him than they would be for most people as he was working within the 'system', and it certainly was helping him in the expansion. He wondered what the price of further development would be and knew that he had to be ready anytime for a meeting like the one with Mr. Firaz in Jakarta. So far, he had not received any further instructions, so he believed that he was doing fine. The business was expanding with major exports to Europe and North America and through investments in Africa. In a short period, the company had grown manifold internationally and if he continued at this rate, within the next few years, he would have a strong international business empire under his name. However, he knew that this would come at a cost and also, he was not so naïve as to believe that everything was going so smoothly just by coincidence. His sixth sense had warned him even before he met Firaz and discovered the 'delta force' that there was a sinister order controlling everything that was happening on Earth. The meeting only confirmed his suspicions. He reflected that even this day, the meetings, and the person with him may all just be doing their 'task'. In the beginning, he would try to test everyone out by bringing his detective skills to use. However, gradually he realized it was better to act as if everything was normal and we were all humans battling against life's adversities and trying to keep our homes running safe and in harmony. Since then, he had respected everyone for who they were and tried to empathize with people who were financially weaker than him and also with people who lived lives of luxury but were still not content, for their circles were filled with people like them who competed against each other for the finer things of life and power. Power –the word struck him as it came to his mind. Those with luxury battle with each other for power or rather for more power. Power is as primitive as existence. It was the power that decides the order of things, the weaker becomes subjects of the stronger, and wars and battles have killed innumerable people just on orders of power-hungry individuals during different ages and civilizations of human existence. In later centuries, power was accompanied by money and wealth. Those with wealth buy the allegiance of the weak and force them to obey the rules and act as per their command. Also, the mandate from the heavens or religious authority was the quintessential remedy for individuals and groups in power who control the masses and amass wealth through their allegiance to the rules set out by these people. The Roman Catholic church decretals and its power-hungry Pope of the Renaissance period and those ultra-rich royals controlling the Kaaba of Mecca, the class controlling the temples of Hinduism in India, and the Jews indebted to Zionists controlling the city of Jerusalem to the various Buddhist orders and East Asian religions have such powerful authority that the business of Faith has been, is and will be the most profitable business and source of power as long as humans exist and spirituality is felt and experienced. This will certainly happen forever as, despite the developments in science, humans of every age and culture have experienced Magic which exasperates all forms of knowledge known to man and Miracles as the touch of the divine keeps people of intelligence attached to their religious sacraments, practices, philosophies, and thoughts. However, religions and cultures from west to east, north to south, were so diverse and different that it was going to be almost impossible for humans to find a common ground and follow one system of thought or religion, and create a Utopian civilization based on peace and love. John Lennon's "Imagine" came to his mind and he hummed a few lines. Even if the truth was crystal clear it was going to be impossible for the people of power in their respective right to give up their belief, so the saying that there is no one more hated than the one who speaks the truth was a fact. Great philosophers, prophets, and saints had come with the truth only to be manipulated by the power-wielding rulers and priests of their generations and the generations that came after them. These conspirators lead the masses forward from the true teachings and embellished history. The religions that they brought have been modified and made tools to carry out the agenda of a group of prevaricated individuals hungry for power to control the devotees and create a system of wealth collection that was to keep them and their families wealthy and powerful for generations to come.

The beautiful truth,

So divine and pure,

Those who discover it,

Fall into the trap,

To make it their own,

Like treasuring a diamond,

But is that the purpose of the truth?

Wake up O human,

From the illusion.

His thoughts are interrupted by Shenoy who says that they will stop for a chai from a small stall on the roadside. They got out and had a strong tea and relaxed looking out at the majestic mountains lying before them. Coming from the Maldives, which was all about beautiful beaches and lagoons and the compelling sea, Amir again felt a certain connection with the universe when he looked at the endless spaces of ranges of mountains and the distant skyline. These jungles, full of life and ageless mountains provide home to thousands of trees that have weathered all storms and witnessed many a wonder of life, contributing their bit to the ecosystems of the world by providing the oxygen necessary for life, making our planet the unique one, in the endless universe having millions of planets like our home.

"You must visit Raigad Fort sometime. It was the castle of our Maharaj Chatrapati Shivaji," Mr. Shenoy said. He then narrated the fulsome saga of the heroics of the king against the Mughal ruler of the time.

"The old highway took almost twice as much time to reach Pune, but the view used to be very beautiful. Marvelous ride," said Mr. Shenoy, and Amir and Raju nodded in agreement."

"How much longer?" Amir inquired.

"Very close to Pune now, will take another thirty minutes to reach the farmhouse though," said the driver. It was the first time he spoke to them.

Babu was a man in his early late forties. In striped shirt and brown trousers with the typical look of a local Maharashtrian, a people Amir had grown accustomed to during his various trips to Mumbai. They had a yeasayer attitude which Amir found amusing. Babu spoke to Amir in English, and he wondered whether he was just Mr. Shenoy's driver or a more senior employee.

"Babu is from Pune; he located the farmhouse and got me a good deal. I bought it last year."

"We have constructed a sort of hacienda with five bedrooms there, amid sprawling acres of plantations of various types of fruits and vegetables. We get very big guavas also there. You like Guava?" asked Shenoy.

Amir nodded in agreement. It was one of his favorite fruits.

After the tea they left and finally reached the farmhouse sooner than expected. Mr. Shenoy's staff were there to welcome them. A young man of around thirty and an elderly couple. Mr. Shenoy told Amir that they did the cooking and cleaning and would look after everything during the stay. They guided them to their rooms. Shenoy showed Amir the available rooms and asked him to choose one. Amir took the one in a corner with the balcony with the best view. Raju was given the room next to his. Mr. Shenoy asked them to freshen up and come to the dining room for breakfast. Amir realized that he wasn't too tired. He used the toilet, washed his face and went and sat down on the balcony for a while. The place was filled with wonders of nature's design and Amir observed some evergreen fagaceous trees and shrubs. The different varieties of green trees and orchards covered sprawling acres of land. Being amongst the verdure gave him a lot of peace of mind and meditating within such environments could lead to a transcendental state. He recalled his younger days when he had jumped at every opportunity to travel to a hill station, beach, or village on the outskirts of cities. Since he started earning, he made it certain that he traveled to a new destination at least once every year. That was until he took control of his father's business. Since then, the only travel had been for business purposes on important ventures. Earlier, he used to manage some time off on business trips and visit holiday spots in the destination. However, of late it had only been calculations on his mind and time itself had become money. Traveling and taking time out had become a luxury he could not afford, as he was always needed in different branches of the company. Amir wondered how Managing Directors or CEOs of the past managed their jobs before the advent of the internet and smartphones.

Amir's thoughts again slid back to business and the various projects at hand and the shipments that had to be carried out within the week. He opened his laptop which had become slow due to overuse, and he had to find a kludge. He then went through the bordereau. He always tried to keep his work prepared one week ahead of the actual execution so that when the tasks came by, he was already ready with a foolproof plan. Amir had an increased workload because he tried to avoid cumbersome hierarchical structures. He had found a gem of a secretary in Jane, who knew exactly how he wanted things planned and done. She was officious in a pleasant way and would organize all his work so smoothly that he just had to follow the given order. She wasn't a mere toady like many of his academically qualified employees. She was a stickler for perfection. She was stationed in the main branch in Malé. Jane was from England, a graduate of Liverpool University who responded to Amir's company's advertisement for Director of Operations in its London branch. Amir was so impressed with her during the interview and later with the work she did for a year in London that he asked her to shift to Malé and work as the director of operations of the whole company. That being her job title, she was Amir's assistant. With a grand salary and good package, she accepted the offer but told him that she would be stationed in Malé for a maximum of five years. Amir said that that was enough and that they would decide on the future later. Two years had already passed, and Amir already feared not being able to replace Jane. She was the powerful stick he danced around during tough meetings. She was his floodgate of information who collected all the details of the organization and presented it to Amir in condensed form. She would reply to all the laudatory mail he received from customers and staff. She would have every minute detail taken care of and every point that they would take as advantage would have been tackled by her before the meetings, so that whenever he found it abstruse, she would put in her inputs, and he could take off again from there. She had impressed him often and whenever he asked her how she did that, she humbly replied "I learned from you".

She was a good-looking woman in her mid-thirties. She had a boyfriend who was an investment banker back in Liverpool. A relationship, which was once a movie-style romance, gradually turned into one of horror as her boyfriend repeatedly cheated on her and lied and blackmailed her. The strong woman that Jane was, she could not take it for too long and that was when she decided to shift to London and applied for the job that was on offer from Amir's company. Jane and Amir had a very professional relationship, although he wouldn't call her a close friend, they did have quite a few close conversations about their lives and life itself, especially over drinks when they traveled together. Amir was careful about the relationship he had with her, as losing the fiery assistant who by now was an important asset for the company would be too big a loss to overcome. Jane understood his position and she marveled at the freedom he gave her and she once told him that she never felt so liberated, handling so many issues and people and that she loved the life she was leading. Living in the Maldives, she took regular intervals from work to holiday in many luxury resorts in the beautiful paradise which always left her rejuvenated and ready for the battles of executive life. Lately, she has developed a deep interest in Jainism and its concept of Lesya. It gave Amir much joy that one of his best employees was satisfied with her job. He made a mental note to buy a kincob for her as a present.

His thoughts are interrupted by the knock on the door. The servant was there to tell him that breakfast was ready. When he went down, Shenoy and Raju were waiting for him at the dining table with brass plates in front of them. It was a good breakfast with Indian as well as continental varieties available. He was pretty hungry, so he started eating quickly and gobbled up a Dosa, and few slices of bread, an omelet, and ended it with yogurt, and then started sipping his coffee. He guessed that everyone else was also as hungry as him as they all ate quickly in silence. Once they were done, Shenoy told them to take their coffees and come to the garden in the backyard. It was a beautiful garden with various kinds of floriferous plants including floribunda roses and some strawberry bushes.

Mr. Shenoy asked Amir about the tourism sector in the Maldives. Amir gave him a thorough briefing, starting from the beginning of tourism in the 1970s when the first tourist resorts were opened to the establishment of a luxury resort and high-end tourism in the subsequent decades that followed to the current establishment of guest houses in inhabited islands catering to backpack, middle income, and budget travelers.

"I would like to plan a trip with my family. Which resorts do you recommend and what will be the budget."

"A good five-star resort would cost at an average, USD 1000 B&B, exclusive of taxes," Amir said. Mr. Shenoy was in Indian terms a 'crorepati' or a millionaire, so Amir knew that he could afford the luxury despite the exorbitant prices. However, Amir put in "I could get you some discounts through my contacts if you want."

"My friend, Mr. Shivraj from Delhi, is in the hospitality industry. An adroit investor. He operates several 3–4-star hotels in all major cities in India under the brand Blue Mango Hotels. He is a very rich man and not stingy like most of the businessmen in the country. Therefore, I spoke to him about you, and he insisted that I ask you about the tourism sector in Maldives and whether the returns of investing in the Maldives would be good. He is looking to invest his money outside the country for reasons best known to him."

"The returns are good and even in the worst cases, a resort would make a profit of at least a few million dollars annually. Some good ones make several million. It's a good industry. One of the best in the world. The service is impeccable."

"How do we enter the industry? Do we have to develop our property, or do we outright buy an existing resort?"

Amir realizes that he is serious about the venture.

"I would recommend developing a property. It won't be too difficult to get an island through my contacts, but the location plays a significant role in the volume of customers. Resorts with propinquity to Malé will get more tourists as they are close to the airport."

"I will set up a meeting between you and Shivraj. You can discuss a possible collaboration. We have to be careful of bogus claims and offers, that's why I need a trusted person like you to help him."

Amir nodded in acceptance. Amir's business had developed from import-export to retail, wholesale, construction, and various other fields. However, he was yet to get into the lucrative travel and tourism industry of the

Maldives. So, if the offer was good, he was determined to make a deal or else he would just introduce Shenoy's friend to his friends already in the tourism business back in Maldives. A new venture would certainly need a lot of concentration and commitment on his part, and he already had so much to look after. 'When you have the money, the world is full of opportunities and however much you earn it never seems to be enough,' thought Amir. He was going to be forty soon and he again recollected his recurring thoughts of the past few months of retiring. But retirement could only happen once he had earned enough to last not only his lifetime but also at least two other generations. Despite the great success of the past few years, he had not yet reached there. He was technically a millionaire, but he needed to step up and invest in different fields, which also meant he had to take huge risks if he wanted to retire at least by the time he was fifty. By that time, he wanted to get married and have children, so that when he was in his old age, the children would be grown up and he could spend his time traveling the world and in contemplation and worship. The growing irritation was that he may not be able to reach this target despite working so hard. He needed a project that would earn him easy profits and beat the competition. The business world was getting more and more competitive day by day and the businesses out of touch with technology were going bankrupt. Most startups do not last long and even to start a small business, huge investments are required as customer confidence is achieved through investing heavily in outlook. More importantly, large corporations were taking over most of the businesses previously controlled by small and medium enterprises, like retail, and he had a presage that some of his investments might go in vain if he didn't diversify. Giving thought to all these, Amir judged that maybe it was the right time to enter the tourism sector in the Maldives.

"Maybe we can arrange for a dinner, on Monday night," Amir said.

"Yes, will be good, I will talk to Mr. Shivraj."

After the coffee, they went for a stroll on the farm. The farm was filled with fruit and vegetable trees and plantations, and all the lush greenery was soothing to the eye and brought calmness to the mind. Amir felt he could spend hours just sitting there and admiring nature.

After the stroll, Amir went to his room and decided to take a rest for a while and lay down for a short nap. He almost immediately fell asleep. In his sleep, he dreamt of Aleesha. He was with her on a beach on an island. It was an afternoon, and the sun was scorching hot. She had her hands around him and was lying on his chest. They were in a candid conversation about shifting to Mumbai where she was eager to pursue her career in the fashion industry. Amir tells her that she is so beautiful that she could be a top model as she dresses with such elegance. She asked him whether he would let her. Amir without replying got lost in thoughts. If he let her pursue her dreams, she was capable of making it big. Having an eye for talent he knew that investing in her would lead to success. However, it would also mean she would have an independent life of her own and would be very busy with her work and the popularity would certainly transform her into a different character. In addition to it all, there would be a lot of men interested in her and Amir thought of the jealousy factor too. With all this going in his mind he tells her "I'll make your dreams come true". She pecks him on the cheek, and he kisses her slightly on her lips.

The next moment, he sees them in the house, where they had spent most of their time together. They were arguing about something. She lashed out at him, blaming him for not trusting her. Amir hated her scurvy behavior and was retaliating saying that it was all her fault that she was never satisfied despite all he did for her and that he was possessive because he didn't want to lose her. The argument got very heated, and Amir was feeling very frustrated and decided to leave her and get out of the house and have a smoke. Then he realized that he had still not stopped smoking. It was then that he realized it was a dream and he opened his eyes. He checked his watch. It was one o'clock in the afternoon.

He freshened up and went down to the living room. The others were still in the room. Amir went out into the yard and met the servants who were outside a crib with goats and cows grazing. Some hens were looking molted, running around. The servants offered him a chai which he politely refused and chatted with them. They were speaking Marathi, but they could understand his responses in Hindi. He observed a nearby derris tree. "Karanjvel," one of the servants told him.

Amir saw Mr. Shenoy coming bustling hurriedly. He greeted Amir and said "I have good news. Shivraj was on his farm in Khandala, he will be with us in the evening."

"Oh, that's wonderful."

"He is a jolly good man. We can arrange a good dinner and drinks for the night."

Amir had quit drinking habitually for two years. However, there had been a few occasions when he let go and had a drink. It was a far cry from the younger days when he could not close his eyes without finishing all the liquor in the room. It was a tough habit to obviate.

Amir thought of the old days. How he and his friends enjoyed and danced away the hours. Those wonderful untamed memories. Now he had responsibility. He looked after the family business and his actions would affect hundreds of employees on his payroll. In addition, he needed to pray to keep his focus. But the environment was too inviting, and he didn't want to be a killjoy. The thought of whiskey in his brain once again leading to a fountain of trenchant thoughts and numbing of the stress was too appealing. He remembered what Samad had told him when he asked why he always had rum."

"It is the first drink that remains the best drink."

In Amir's case, it was whiskey. He had seen a bottle of Jack Daniel's in the bar in the living room of Shenoy's house. However, he decided against it as it would be extremely difficult to realign once he started. He decided that he would just have a good dinner and sleep early. So, he decided to carry on with his adipsia for spirits.

Mr. Shivraj arrived at the farmhouse in the evening. A tall potbellied man wearing white pants and a filoselle silk shirt strut up to them and greeted them. He came with two servants and a ponderous German shepherd. He called it Jai.

The servants brought a flagon of tea immediately and Amir, Shenoy, and Shivraj sat around a white steel table and accompanying chairs.

Shenoy introduced them.

"What a beautiful country Maldives is," Shivraj said.

"You have been there?"

"Just once, Rihiveli resort," he said. "I wish to go again, but time hasn't allowed me."

"Maybe if you could help him set up business, he will visit more often." Mr. Shenoy said laughing.

"Yes, that's a good idea. I hear a lot of Europeans invest in the resorts. I also want to check the possibility."

"The returns are good," Amir said. "And the value of the property will keep rising for the years to come. You can sell it any time."

What about the legalities?

"Foreign Investments are very welcomed by all authorities. You wouldn't have to worry too much about that but the Maldivian party you share the company with must be trustworthy."

"That's why we need you, isn't it Shenoy?" said Mr. Shivraj.

"Yes, but I am not exactly from that field. But I can point you in the right direction."

"I want to build a resort targeting high-class elite Indians. I have got good contacts in Mumbai and Delhi. We can do good business by promotions and tie up with the travel agencies. I have experience in this industry, so I know what Indian customers will want."

"Yes, many of them are vegetarians and conservative," added Shenoy.

"Yes, you can build an island based on your concept and provide the required service," Amir said.

"The country must be developing fast now," Shivraj said.

"Yes, things are pretty much developing. Democracy has brought modernization to the islands. Fifty years back the islands were like small villages and the natives had a tribal lifestyle. Things have changed. People are educated and there are graduates in every household. Even in the islands."

"Good, but with that you will be losing the beautiful culture and tradition also. I heard people in Malé are very westernized."

"It was, back in the nineties and early years of the twenty-first century. Now there is an equally strong religious wave. So, it's kind of balanced." Amir said. "What I fear is it might become a kleptocracy."

"Yes, we in India are also losing our culture. Kids nowadays follow everything Western, even food." They all laughed.

"The main thing is technology. I think the world is becoming very small. You have so many options available, and you can readily choose whatever you want," Shenoy said.

"Yes, very true," Amir put in.

"If I may elaborate, I think before long, globalization will take over and the so-called new world order and one world government may be a reality and supersede the current multi-nations system. Although it is in a premature stage, those who don't comply will have to face sanctions."

"Well, we like our culture and unless we get a significant say or share, our kindred will resist any such thing as we resisted the Britishers," said Shivraj.

"Mr. Shivraj is a nationalist. He has good political clout, especially in Maharashtra. He has a brazen disregard for foreignism.'

"Yes, my father was a freedom fighter who boldly upbraided the British."

This interested Amir, as many of his businesses were now headquartered in Mumbai and his Indian partners were originally from Karnataka. He was looking at investing more money in projects in Maharashtra. Therefore, he had thought of diversifying and establishing companies with strong local parties in the state. If he could help Mr. Shivaraj with his plans to open a resort in the Maldives, he could set up a business with him in Mumbai. He trusted Mr. Shenoy through experience and knew that he had suggested Mr. Shivaraj to him as he was capable and experienced.

That night the servants prepared a fabulous feast made from all natural organic products made on the farm. Even the roasted chicken and mutton were from animals raised on the farm. It was one of the best meals Amir had had in a long time. He had grown tired of eating at various restaurants as he traveled the world for work.

Amir was fast asleep when he received a call from Khalid. He took it instantly.

"I have sad news," Khalid said.

"Tell me."

"Ihusaan has died of an overdose. Heroine. He was in Sri Lanka."

Amir was stunned.

It had been a long time since he had met with him. Amir had tried to pull him into his fold and even tried investing in some projects for him. But Ihusaan's mind was always wandering, and he was feckless. He could not find the discipline as he lacked any motivation. Life was just a bad dream for him of late and he was back into hard drugs. He even talked about Euthanasia. His only entertainment of late was droll self-mockery.

"Have they buried him?" Amir asked.

"Yes, I attended the funeral."

They were both at a loss for words. He was a special friend, one who left an indelible mark and made a strong impact on their lives. Amir felt penitent for not having done more to help him. They had to digest the fact that he was gone. There would be no more 'programs' as Ihusaan used to call their endeavors.

Chapter 9

Amir was waiting in his hotel room in Munich when Shivraj rang him up on WhatsApp. He told Amir that Mr. Ramanov would be at the Hotel Bavaria, and that he was to meet him in the evening at 4. Amir had become an increasingly itinerant trader over the past few months.

It was almost lunch time in Munich, and he headed for lunch in the hotel restaurant. He was dressed in a suit with a cravat and decided to take his diary to make some notes. In this particular trip to Germany, he met some investment bankers of the Deutsche Bank regarding amortization. He had visited and met some of the richest men in various parts of the world and the reciprocity he had with them entitled him to many privileges. However, he was eager to meet Ramanov, about whom he had read a lot about. Amir didn't completely understand the theories he spoke about, but he knew that his ideas were helping take scientific developments to a whole new level. Even his tritest pronouncements made headlines in the scientific circle.

Dr. Ramanov was a physicist and cosmologist, one of the most eminent professors of quantum physics and science in the University of Moscow. His disquisitions were world famous, and his seminal works were being researched by the top universities. Currently, he was working with the government in the space program. His works were popular amongst theoretical physicists as well as experimental physicists. His latest work on quantum mechanics had earned him awards and recognition in Europe and America.

It was during his visit to lecture a conference in New Delhi, India that he met Dr. Ramakrishna, a fellow physicist and renowned scientist from Kolkata in the Indian state of West Bengal, who had several patents for his inventions. Ramakrishna was a longtime friend of Mr. Shivraj. Ramakrishna had spoken with the Multimillionaire Shivraj to interest him in investing in a scientific research center and laboratory in India. Ramakrishna was confident that he and his group of scientists, which included Ramanov, would be able to use the facility to make tremendous progress in various fields of science, and through their contacts they would be able to get the necessary funds to run the center.

All Shivraj had to do was use his clout with the bank and arrange for a loan for the project with his existing assets as security. He would get forty percent from all projects that became viable business ventures through innovations and developments patented by the research center. In addition, Ramakrishna would be able to use his connections within the Indian government and ruling parties to connect the science universities in the country by providing them with a world class facility or laboratory for the students to experiment and develop ideas into sustainable projects.

With a leading physicist and pacesetter such as Ramanov as its head, it would attract a considerable media attention, and Ramanov had proposed to conduct projects where Indian and Russian scientists worked together with recommendations from the Russian government.

Shivraj was a shrewd businessman, and having saved a considerable amount of money, he was looking for stable ventures to invest in. Working with big names in the scientific arena, such as Ramanov and Ramakrishna was appealing to him. Therefore, when Mr. Shenoy introduced Amir, and his proliferating business, Shivraj became interested in coming up with a new concept and he wanted Amir to undertake the fosterage of the project.

At the restaurant, Amir ordered a lemon juice without sugar and a chicken cordon bleu. He scribbled some notes and as he waited for the food, recalling his conversation with Ramakrishna. They were looking to build a research center and laboratory that would attract the attention of universities across the world. They wanted a suitable island in the Maldives, which would not only house the laboratory, but also include a five-star resort complete with water bungalows and beach rooms. Oceanography was Ramakrishna's field of interest, and combined with Ramanov's expertise in cosmology, they were trying to build a state-of-the-art center for scientists from around the world to convene and discuss ideas, projects, and experiment within the facility.

Amir was shrewd enough to know that this project was backed by the Russian government. Under the pretext of educational research and leisure, they would have a perfect base in the midst of the Indian ocean. The Russian scientists who would form the majority in the project would be no less than trained experts of the KGB era.

Amir knew that finance was the last thing these people were worried about. It was getting the government approval that would be the challenge and that was why he was being roped in, in addition to his successful business campaigns. Amir knew that if things were done silently without creating a buzz in the media, it would be a smooth operation. Through his contacts in the ruling party, he could clear the path without much difficulty as the project would be bringing in millions of dollars in investment and creating jobs for the local population. Anyway, the government needed to pay back his favors, as he had financed many of their candidates in the last two parliamentary elections, the presidential election, and was a principal benefactor to the ruling party.

It was Aman who handled these politicians and their demagoguery. Amir was far too busy with his business. Aman seemed to be doing far better than Amir ever expected him to perform. His political acumen and predictions had been spot-on so far.

Ramanov was going to give Amir a summary of the project.

"I have three rules in life," Ramanov told Amir. "Don't try to take God away from people's lives, don't try to force people to have a medicine they are not ready to take, even if you know that it's what's right for them, and service to mankind is service to God. Apply these to anyone you know. Find out how their mind works. Of course, people change with experiences, education, and responsibilities. But deep inside there is something that will never change. That's why I say circumstances change, People don't. Therefore, don't waste your life trying to change a person."

"What is that which doesn't change?"

"I am not sure. But I think it's your first dreams. What you had decided to be in the very beginning. As you grow older you lose control of everything. Your parents, society, relatives, and friends dictate the terms and make you swerve. After that it is just a compromise."

"A compromise, that's all what becomes of us or our lives. Even the most valorous of us get conquered by our shattering dreams as life goes on, clinging to the things that let them survive the harsh world. You reach a point in life when you know the perfect life you dreamt of was never meant to be."

"But there are stories of success all around us. Fame, fortune, and glory."

"You mean people like Micheal Jackson?" They both laughed, "I tell you, he was a star, dancing on earth. But in the end, he was quarantined."

"But more seriously, like the footballers Ronaldo and Messi?"

"What would you call the famous gladiators of the roman era?" Ramanov responded. "Anyway, let me tell you about the chicken in the poultry farm. Almost all of them are in cages, waiting either to have their heads cut off or to lay eggs, but they are able to see a few free chickens on the ground moving freely and happily. In the hope of that freedom, the hens in the cages live and do not die of despair. It's a trick they use."

"Really? Interesting," Amir said.

"Amir, the rich, the elites, the film stars are not basking in glory, they are the ones who suffer from depression and mental diseases the most. If what you are suggesting is fame and money as a measure of success, why is this so? Because they dreamt of a totally different world than the one that they have to live in? It's much harder today with all the libel, tabloids, technology and social media, where they have to face lewd comments and get trolled and criticized for every move of theirs's and every look. Not to mention the highbrow tastes of the colleagues. They must have the courage to face the flak."

"I know, but it's hardly as dystopian as many had forecasted and at least in the developed world people are living a very high-quality life supplemented with great technology. Racial stereotypes are disappearing. Despite all these conspiracy theories, the powers that be are trying to build a better world for everyone. Equality, abolishing the apartheid, eradicating poverty, democracy, and people power and making the best use of earth's resources and sustainable development is what this era will be defined as other than an era of technology.

"It depends on which angle you are looking from. However, we cannot garble on a subject like this. It looks like you are a supporter of this globalization."

Amir shook his head. "Not really, I just think maybe it's better to go with the flow."

"Yes, there's only so much a single man can do. But the thought of millions can make a difference. Mark my words," he said. "Hitler made himself heard, his harangues and words went into the mind of his followers, structured it so intrinsically to make them machines following his every order. I call it collective intelligence. We are now eight billion and counting, anything is possible. What we feed the kids in their initial years is very important. We can build a generation based on intelligence or one that is deeply spiritual. We have to examine essentialism. Yes, science and mathematics and the formulas do work, but to make the masses believe that spirituality is fake, hearsay will never get the job done. Those who hold power know it well enough, that is why they censor everything, including the texts that create magic for instance. Again, we are talking about formulas and adjoint codes," Ramanov said.

"I think a day may come where we can combine science and spirituality. As you say, its formulas either way," Amir said.

"Exactly, it's just how you perceive it, or the words you describe them with. Although it might obfuscate the common man," Ramanov agreed, thumping the table.

Amir was critically examining the mind of this eminent scientist. "But I like your idea. Collective intelligence."

"Yes, but we do not have empirical data and the reality isn't quantitative in nature. We can't assume that the majority of the population are intelligent. This puts us in a rabbit hole that we are experiencing today," the scientist shrugged.

The preponderance of the stupid amongst humanity was a scary thought if this theory was true. Amir reflected. "Yes, as I said, the universe has to have come out of thought. Someone had to have ordained it to exist if that even makes any sense. However, here we are. So, if the formulas work, there must be great mathematics at play, and how is that possible without it having already been thought about? So, whatever is being thought about by weak mortals is being absorbed by the great mind, like a sponge absorbs water. In my opinion, it's the thoughts that create energy and thus everything that exists. I may be wrong; it may be that some essence or energy created the thought. It's a curious juxtaposition, but in the second case it has to be Magic. Now for some, it's God, the creator, a singular being separate from creation, if you want the Hindu or naturalist philosophy, everything is God or there is a piece of God in every one of us as he is ubique. So, our thoughts too create energy."

Ramanov shrugged. "Either way I believe it's human thoughts that will either lead us to a heaven or utopia or to our destruction, things get complicated if we bring into this scenario other intelligent beings or Aliens."

"Yes. Actually, we Muslims believe in other beings who live in different dimension of time, called Jinns and afreets."

"All religions do, like angels and demons and spirits of the dead, etc."

"Yes, so aliens have to be intelligent beings from another planet we can physically meet and talk to in our own dimension." Amir stated

"Agreed, and with the millions of galaxies we are discovering, the possibility of their existence is very real, maybe with better technology we may be able to locate them in a few decades from now."

"That is where collective intelligence comes in. If all the billions of us collectively think of this scenario we might just make it happen. For example, let's say that everyone on earth wishes for the coming of the Christ or Maitreya, or a messiah, which actually is prescribed in every religion, that might just happen. So, you see the power is with us or was with us from the beginning until the end. The only paradox here is, if there is a creator, he has already calculated all these scenarios and the forecasts are found in fragments in different scriptures. This is a recondite subject. If I speak of this to my scientific colleagues, I will have to face derision."

"Maybe that's the source of everything or the force, the primordial thought. The Qi, in the yin yang in Chinese philosophy," said Amir.

"Let's take interconnectedness; in that case, it's all for one and one for all. I have been researching Idealism and Zeno's paradox."

"Interconnectedness is very limiting, like finitism, because then even if there are different personalities the source is one which means how much ever you divide and name individuals there is only so much you can cook up in your mind as the limit of your imagination resides in what the source has thought about already, nothing beyond that."

"Exactly, in religion that's God, but then according to them, God's imagination is without limit."

"See the contrasting nature of the situation? How can you imagine anything without developing a scenario from what you have witnessed or are witnessing."

"Strange, it's like a thought having sex with another thought and giving birth to thousands of other thoughts. Something like nuclear fission. But the idea of thoughts generating energy lacks scientific substantiation."

"Precisely."

"But if there is a being that came out of nothing, just imagined to be, and was, that supernatural being should not need to multiply any thoughts to think of a new idea or a new concept. Once it does so, the sense is diffused throughout his creation with different people coming up with fragments and through centuries our minds evolve to understand the matter, thanks to great thinkers, innovators, scientists, and prophets etc."

The conversation was efficacious. "Prophets seem to be the strangest in that group, because they are assuming success in the next life. The problem is that this species is ominous in nature," Amir added with a chuckle.

"Well, in that case shouldn't everyone desire to be one?" I mean if you have a sure shot formula for success in this life and the next, then everybody should be taught that discipline, not just be a follower. Be like the Shakyamuni. However, it is audacious to become mendicant. The truth is there is no guarantee. No one alive has died and spoken to those who are alive to confirm to us that the afterlife exists. So, it maybe we just return to dust just as we expect to happen to animals. At present, this is an inscrutable topic," Ramanov said.

"So do we live the life the way we choose or follow codes of what is right and what is wrong propagated by people spiritually advanced than us?" Amir asked.

Ramanov took a bite of his Bacalao. "That's one way, but I think it's time to find out the truth. There should be a cohesion of the available knowledge. In terms of population, we have got the numbers now. If we can collectively use our intelligence, we can do great things. We need to have a direction which knowledge should correlate. But, you see, if everything becomes uniform, there would not be any fun, right? It's our differences with all the contradictions and idiosyncrasies that make life so colorful, so diverse.

"The truth will prevail in the end. Which means we should all aspire for the truth. The data available is Boolean in nature. We must use all our energies to find it, wherever it is, however it is, whatever it is. That day, humanity will win. What I am saying is that we should stop hiding the truth, the people in power have to let go of their fear and join hands with everyone by disseminating the available knowledge and all the truths that have been buried under the sands of time by history written by only those who won. Many a people laid their lives on the line fighting for the truth. Will their sacrifices go down in vain? I do not think so. We will build a wise generation, humanity will. Someday." Ramanov said.

"Cool, I hope we are part of it, or at least maybe our generation can lay the foundation for it."

"We are far from it. But science has come far. It has shown through the mighty telescopes how small we are and all those worm holes and black holes and stuff. I still believe in the anthropic principle because the existence of human life is a fact."

"Maybe the truth is in science?" Amir proposed.

"It is the thought. Are we using science to find the truth? Or are we using it control fellow human beings? That's where humanity fails me. At least this generation of ours will not escape this trap. There is too much at stake. The turpitude of those in power will amaze you. Science must not be used to stymie spiritual growth."

Amir was enjoying this conversation. "I think humanity will come together and use your concept of collective intelligence when they are threatened or they fear destruction."

"Exactly. Fear will unite us."

"Maybe a superior race or intelligent beings from another planet trying to invade us?" Amir said.

"Well, in such a scenario there is maybe more to gain than lose, because we can learn much truth if we meet another race of physical beings. If they are intelligent, they will cooperate, in my opinion."

Amir nodded. "I think this fear that will unite us will be caused by something we ourselves will create."

"Artificial intelligence"

"Yes, a Terminator-like scenario is becoming more and more apt with every passing year."

"If they develop a language of their own and start communicating, we will not be able to make head or tail."

"We can always pull the plug," Amir laughed.

"Maybe not, energy is all around us. The real technology is still latent to the gullible common man."

"Feelings, as long as they don't have feelings, they may not be able to attract the energy that they need. Literally, they are insensible."

Ramanov raised an eyebrow. "Intelligence, artificial or not, is stored information that is processed."

"For humans it's with feelings." Amir added "I think we need feelings to process this stored information intelligently."

"You are answering your own question. AI does process information intelligently, to a large extent."

Amir nodded in agreement.

"It might well be divine destiny that we are building something and, in the end, create a free will kind of power that might even be used against the very system we have created if the machines start rebelling. Although at present it's a far-fetched idea but not one that can be discounted. What a world we are building for our children," he added.

Ramanov seemed pleased. "That's why I said in the beginning, don't take God out of people's lives, however crazy their beliefs maybe, we need to find an equipoise. My personal belief is that the different faiths are all tautologies. Because that belief is our trust in the divine truth. For generations we have taught our children this concept and we have survived. I am afraid that if we give up on this or at least if the vast majority does so, we may become a lost race. A vulnerable one or even extinct. It may even cause havoc. I am not exactly a theist though."

"Well, you're right, Greeks thought about city states, democracy, and the republic centuries ago, today it's the dominant system of the world," Amir said.

"Yes, they were the first to document that, but maybe the thought existed among the Red Indians living in America at that time. Half the world didn't even think they existed. Similar to what we believe of no other humans living on other planets."

"Meditations is a powerful practice. I have met some experts in that area during my travels in India and southeast Asia," Amir told him. "Some people who would definitely interest you."

"Yes, I have met a few eremites in my travels in Eastern Europe. We must foster learning of these concepts along with scientific developments. If I ever get time after these projects, maybe we can travel Asia together."

"It would be a pleasure. You can count on me to make it a special adventure," Amir said.

After this interesting conversation, they finished their lunch and spoke briefly about the project. Ramanov averred that it was a done and dusted deal, that it would be a pleasure to work with Amir.

After finishing his work in Munich, Amir called Jane to ask her what the arrangements were for the week. She told him that he needed to attend some meetings in Bombay. As he was about to end the call, Jane told him, "One more thing. Aleesha has been trying to reach you. I told her your appointments were full. She said to tell you that Aleesha called, and she gave me her number."

"Okay, text me the number," Amir said, keeping his excitement hidden.

The number was an Indian one, which meant that Aleesha was in Kumily with her mother.

Chapter 10

"I have always loved you, ever since I met you, and maybe my soul did even before that. I left you because I could not bear to hurt you. I don't know how to say it. 'The bodement'. I cannot afford to see you in pain." Aleesha's tone was contrite.

Aleesha looked tired and much older compared to the last time he saw her, eight years ago.

"Amir, the world you see is just like a mirage. There are forces controlling this dimension in which humanity exists. There is a superior race. I know it's hard for you to believe, but I have seen them and have spoken to them. These creatures can get inside our bodies in this dimension and totally control our thoughts. We think that the ideas and our moods are our own, but often it is not so. Of course, we do retain our imaginations, but they are being influenced.

"Once you learn of their existence, which is what they call the awakening of the pineal gland, it's a complete overhaul of life. You can see them and communicate with them. But once you enter that level, they are not merely inside your body and influencing your thoughts, they control your whole body. We basically become a robot to them. We become helpless! If we try to fight them, we will have to face their obloquy and they will make you do crazy stuff. Normal humans will think you are crazy and put you in a mental asylum."

"You mean, they control our free will?"

"It's more physical than that. They don't interfere unless you conspire against them. but the moment they realize that you are a proscribe, they are vindictive, and will stop at nothing to destroy you and impede your progress. It is in their interest that humanity remain ignorant of their existence. If we all rebel together, maybe we may find a solution. But those who have awakened number just a few hundred thousand on this planet. They include those selected by the others and those who ferret and divulged into the ineffable mysteries of life and accidentally fell into the rabbit hole, I would say."

Amir didn't know what to make of this. "Well, then consider yourself lucky. I believe in other forces, like different species of jinns, angels, and demons. But personally, I have never experienced any of these supernatural phenomena or paranormal activity, except one night maybe, with Samad."

"Well, that exactly is the problem! They see the ultimate rebel in you. They are highly specialized in astronomy and have an oracle that predicts future events. They are time worshippers. They believe that with planetary alignments and specific rituals performed during specific dates and positions of the sun and moon that they could alter future events that might destroy, or negatively affect, their control on the servile human race and the holy earth, and stop giving rise to an awakening of mankind. It is in their prophecies that a human shall be born who would overcome all other forces and creatures and make man the supreme dominant being of the universe."

"Maybe they are talking about Jesus."

"That's according to our scriptures, it also brings about the apocalypse and an end. The Others don't believe in heaven and hell. They believe we are to live forever in our dimension, in this physical world, forever."

"Okay, so why are they allowing you to tell me? Someone who doesn't even have any intuition about the existence of these creatures, who according to you, control our thoughts."

"And read our minds too," Aleesha added.

"So, you bring me my lettre de cachet?" He asked.

"They think you are ominous. It is actually in their interest for you to know of their existence because that will alter your way of thinking, your dreams. They believe bad things would happen if you were killed without your consent. They have witnessed many portents. The power of your dreams is so great that if you die without fulfilling them, you will not cease to exist. Your curses and imprecations will infect all the worlds with diseases, trials, and tribulations, so prophesizes their oracle, who has calculated your midheaven precisely."

"I see, so they want me to make a noble sacrifice? Isn't this some diabolism of sorts? All my life I have valued my freedom as the most priceless gift I have, but as I grew older, I found myself losing grip of it in stages. I didn't know it would come to this. And if I may ask, you said they can get into our bodies and control them. I have had such sensations when I am asleep, where I struggle to move my body and remain so until I open my eyes. It's called sleep paralysis. And then I am free again in a moment. So why can't they make me obey their orders?" Amir asked.

Aleesha looked at him with sincerity. "They are trying, have been trying now for two decades. For some people to 'fall' as they call it, it takes powerful rituals to be performed in conjunction with the alignment of the heavens. They are far advanced in science and technology too; the internet is their brainchild. It has been used to influence the thought process of humans. In essence, deleting all spiritual learning and replacing it with scientific facts and thoughts. That's how we are going to be programmed."

"It doesn't make proper sense. Why this obscurantism? Why don't they share all this knowledge with us. Like, I mean, grow together? What is it that they have got to lose?"

"Power. They fear humans because they know the power of our thoughts. If we collectedly joined hands and rebelled, even if only through our thoughts, it is likely that the human race would overpower them."

Amir was reminded of the collective intelligence proposed by Ramanov. Amir knew from experience that Aleesha was not a person who could be manipulated easily. Maybe she had mental issues, however, he knew she wouldn't come up to him with such an absurd theory without facts. Maybe she was inculcated over the years. Amir realized he had to read between the lines, as she may be trying to equivocate. However, she was speaking with intense sobriety. "What is the proof of their existence?" Amir asked. "I mean, to an ordinary human being who believes only in science and facts, this would be ridiculous."

"This knowledge is not for everyone. I was initiated at Kythera."

Amir shrugged, "All this is objective relativism. To me, they don't exist if I don't believe you. The truth is for everyone. In my opinion, all of creation will be illuminated and reach a promised land if we all joined together. The truth is such a powerful tool which cannot be underestimated. You have an opportunity, you need to preach this to the world," he added.

"The world will call me crazy, mentally disturbed, put me in an asylum. The 'others' will surely make that happen if I try to vilify them. Micheal Jackson said it right. They don't really care about us. They have nothing to gain from being benevolent."

"So, what is the solution?" he asked.

"It's danger prone, Amir. They interpret the lines on your head as an augury of an end of an age."

Amir sighed and looked down at his lap. "I have lived a full life, I have had material success, but spiritually, I feel lost. I lost you, the one I truly loved. I have done the best I can do for my family. I have understood the way the world functions and accepted it. And now you come to me with this knowledge. So, what do I do? If I can do something for the sake of humanity, it would be worth it. I can at least die knowing my life worth something."

"It's now been seven years since I entered this realm." Aleesha said. "All the elitists of the world are initiated, we have to abide by the rules set by them. It's what the secret societies are for. Most of the ceremonies are held in castles and mansions of the rich so it all goes unnoticed."

"Have you been part of these rituals?"

"Yes. In fact, they are making me a priestess. A priestess heads the congregations. We must learn to chant mantras and perform certain procedures, similar to what the wiccans used to do."

"Why you?"

"Because they think my mind has the power to withstand the energy generated from such rituals. I will soon be promoted to a high priestess when all my rituals are completed, so says the sage. This has a lot to do with you," she said.

"Why?"

"Because they need you." She was maladroit in her explanation. Maybe she wasn't allowed to tell the whole truth. "The current priests and priestesses who is also the foundress of our order, have performed numerous rituals and used the most powerful souls in order to control you. However, it so happens that there is an unseen force protecting you. A fourth dimension which neither we humans nor the 'others' can see. But in that realm, we can feel these people. They certainly are more powerful, and they guide and protect you everywhere."

"Really?" Amir tried to reflect on his life. Looking back, he realized that he was quite safe, despite venturing into the unknown and travelling by himself. Amir wondered why anyone should be protecting him. He looked at Aleesha. He wanted to believe the strange things she was saying, but she could have been hypnotized or imagining things. Maybe someone was controlling her, or even worse, it could be that some force was inside her body and talking while she sat there helpless. They were all possiblilites, but his soul knew it was Aleesha herself.

"There is only one way they can control you. It is with your consent and by the power of someone you love truly, unconditionally. This is what their oracle tells them, and they think that I am the one you have loved truly in your life, apart from your blood relations. Nevertheless, I will still not be able to do it if you disallow me, if you yourself are not ready to give in."

Amir noticed that she was wearing an amethyst ring. "But why would I want some strangers to control my mind and my body?"

"Look back at your life. You have such a great mind, yet your life is controlled by the system anyway. They can get you anytime they want. You have had success with your business, but you are still among the also rans, they will never let you reach the top unless they can control you totally. The level you have reached is because they want to use your mind, the resources you get are actually stimuli, to make you think and plan. Of course, this talent of yours help the elite, so it's a compromise. However, they need you out now. You are becoming a threat to the order of things. Because you don't submit to what everyone else falls to, it is giving rise to rebellion among the humans who do not trust the others and are tired of being slaves to a superior race. Now their oracle tells them that true love is the only way they can make you fall."

"Fall?" he tried to make sense of her cryptic words.

"Yes, that's what happens to most of us when we enter the realm of the others for the first time. You must have heard of people you know falling accidentally, many a time this happens when someone of the others suddenly crashes into you. When you wake up, the other is inside you, and you can see everything happening in their dimension when he or she is in you. The problem is, no one, not even the greatest and strongest amongst them could make you fall."

"I did fall, once," Amir replied. "But that was because I hadn't slept for days and was very high. Me and Khalid went for dinner, and I had a vanilla milkshake. Then I realized things were not right. I went to the washroom and I crashed before I could return to the table. When I woke up seconds later, Khalid was beside me, kneeling, trying to resuscitate me. I remembered that there was wonderful music in my head before I opened my eyes. It was a sort of near-death experience."

"I know about that too. Again, you just woke up and it was as if nothing happened. You returned back to your normal life."

"Except that I lost my front tooth." Amir said, smiling. "So, now they have given you the mission to make me submit to them? They seem to be misanthropes. Why are you cooperating with them?"

"Do you want me to be in a mental asylum and you in prison, or do you want us both to get married and lead a simple, happy life with our kids?"

The idea of having to go to prison had not crossed Amir's mind yet. However, when Aleesha mentioned it, he realized how very possible such a scenario would be, given that his businesses and boats were used for illegal activities. Despite the assurance Mr. Firaz had given him, if he was seen as a threat to the elite and cartelists who ruled the world, it was very likely that he could be framed.

"I know what you are trying to show me. I would do anything for you, but there is a problem here. It's about spirituality. You are talking about dimensions and other worlds like ours living in other dimensions of time. As for you, you can see at least two dimensions, and you are telling me of people from a third who seem to be protecting me."

"Yes, which probably means someone from this new dimension which we don't know is operating from within you and not letting anyone else take his place. Maybe since you were a kid. And that person maybe like a king of that dimension."

"Highly unlikely, as I know myself. I don't hear voices, nothing is in my head that I have not heard or read or seen anywhere. I don't even remember lyrics of songs."

"The languages, Amir. They don't have to speak English, or any language for that matter, it can be emotions. Plus, it's just a probability. No one knows what's happening with you and around you. Which is why your every move is watched and analyzed. I have told you everything I know. It's now up to you to decide. The others might be wrong, and you might be wrong also. It may be that I am not your true love. Maybe you even haven't met her yet."

"Oh, don't be so naïve, Aleesha," Amir said, irritated. This was no divine impulsion. He had to use his free will. What she was saying warranted further exploration.

"I am not sure how true all the things you are telling me are, but one truth I certainly know for sure is that I love you. Truly, you are my elixir of peace" Tears began to form in his eyes.

"They want you to participate in a ritual, with your consent." she said.

"After that we can be together?"

"Yes, they told me so. But your freedom is the price. They want to forestall you at any cost."

Amir realized she was desperate, as she emoted fear all over her body.

"Okay, you know that I would do anything for you."

Live in love,

Die in love,

Love you, my dear,

Till the last breath.

My life,

Your poem,

Recite your wish,

For my command.

Amir was tired of life. He knew deep inside that he no longer needed to be heroized. He no longer had any unrealistic expectations. His truculence had died the day Aleesha left him.

Amir needed to speak to Samad. He had to grasp this paradigm shift. He immediately called Jane and asked her to postpone all the meetings in Mumbai till the end of the month. After that, he called Samad, who asked him to come to his house. Amir went there immediately. In his nervousness, Amir began to festinate.

Before Amir could explain, Samad said, "I know everything. The tribal King had told me I would meet the "one". They practice animism and have a deep understanding of natural events. So, when I saw the lines on your head, I knew it was you."

"Well, I don't think I am fit to be the man of the hour."

"Aleesha loves you. She was confused because when she realized the presence of the 'others', they told her that what she was feeling was because there was another female entity within her who loved you. She is adamant to make you hers."

"Who exactly are these people?" Amir asked interrupting him.

"They are just like us, humans, maybe. Only different dimensions of time. They eat, drink, smoke, and other things." Samad said. "They believe in a spiritually superior master race or elite amongst the humans, and they have joined hands in collusion with this human race to control and enslave the rest of us."

"Are they Jinns?" Amir asked.

"No. No, Jinns I know, in fact Jinns are also scared of them. They are also looking for a savior. Maybe some of them protect you and keep you safe from incursions of the enemy, others are against you."

"And what about our doubles from the parallel universe?"

"They are our Jinn companions. Qareen, they call them in Islam. Through magic they have learned to remove our Qareen from our body and they keep interchanging to different bodies. Your one is different. He would not leave you. Even I tried, not possible."

"This is so confusing. So, what has to be done now?"

The imbroglio had reached the maximum.

"Amir, the others are powerful and number in billions, how can only one man stand against the system that has been in operation for centuries?"

"I cannot let them control my body and use me. It makes my flesh creep to even think of it. That is not going to change. If that is what they are suggesting, I shall rather die. But if I don't, they will not leave Aleesha alone. I have to save her."

"I know that. But you must fulfill your purpose of life. Maybe death is the answer. Your sacrifice may liberate us, prevent them from controlling the human race."

"Well, then that's what it's going to be." Amir said.

"Well, then, amor fati," Samad said with a look of a zombie.

"So, it's the end of my odyssey?" Amir looked into his eyes without remorse.

"No, just the beginning. You will be like the King of the dead, it's a sacrifice they want, and you are the goat. Human sacrifices are almost as old as time. Anyway, I will join you there soon. A meeting in Valhalla."

"I don't think I would have enjoyed senectitude anyway. With all this knowledge and no power to do anything about it, I will die a wretched and irascible old man."

"I know this life is not the end of our soul. So, if that's the way I can give meaning to my life I am ready for it," Amir said. "You keep saying that the purpose of life is to have a family, earn bread and butter, and build a home. Is that it?"

Samad remained silent for a long time and said, "When man is old, all he can do is look back."

In the end, and after all the struggles, the old man realizes that the purpose of life is to be a good human being. But then when he looks back, the faces of all those he had hurt haunt him. The opportunities to help family members and friends that he gave up selfishly because he was too busy chasing his dreams. He would wish he could go back and correct the wrongs he had done. To wipe away the tears of all those whom he had made cry. But pride wouldn't let him. Accepting his mistakes, yet refusing to bow down before others, slowly eats away his desire to live. He could do nothing but endure the pain. Dreams seemingly shattered and hope of repentance lost forever because he had aimed to defeat everyone and rule over them all with power and wealth.

He faces two alternatives. Either he becomes wealthy and powerful only to realize that the evils he had done to reach there will never let him sleep nor rest in peace. He may try to atone for it by helping those weaker souls around him, but he will realize that they did not see his help as an act of kindness, but as a show of superiority. His entire wealth would not recompense for the pain he had caused one single human being he had hurt who truly had considered him a true friend. He would not find expiation for his guilt.

The other option, which is the most common one, is the man ends up as a failure in the eyes of the world and his own opinion. The old man, year after year, loses grip of his ambition. This man ends with no wealth and no power and becomes weak and frail. Sometimes chronic diseases afflict him and the hope of a full recovery fades away. Paradoxically, this man, when he looks back, has more wonderful moments of life to reminisce about. Good times with friends and family with no ulterior intentions but the bonding and spreading of love. However, this man may breathe his last without knowing what the purpose of life was. To help the needy, to bring a smile on the face of a grieving person, to share the pain of a total stranger, to let an ailing family member know that he is not alone, having contributed a widow's mite to a just cause and all the forgotten and unmentioned acts of kindness done in his lifetime is the fulfillment of the purpose of existence.

"Peace on earth and mercy mild, God and sinners reconcile."

After having said this, Samad went into a sort of trance, uttering nonsense and chatting away in what appeared to

Amir as Tamil. After more than five minutes the vagary stopped, and he calmed down. "Hello Amir. Nice to talk to you again," the One speaking through Samad said.

Amir realized that this was the one whom he had encountered in Bangalore many years back. "Yes."

"So, you have made your decision?"

"Well, I guess. But I will think over and discuss it with Aleesha before finalizing."

"You cannot die alone; you have to take Aleesha with you."

"What? Why?"

"She is your soul mate. She will agree. You mean the world to her."

"And exactly for that reason, I want her to be happy and lead a happy life. I cannot ask her to get killed."

"It's not getting killed. It's a sacrifice. It won't be in vain. Although, it's a lachrymose tale. We have already spoken to Aleesha. She has agreed. She just wants assurance that you both will be together in the next stage of life's journey, and the oracle has prophesied that it will be so. Travel with Aleesha to Mt. Zion. Jerusalem. That will be the altar. May I ask you why such an ambitious and powerful person like you are ready to give up all the greatness and fade away from the earth?" The voice asked.

Amir was resolute. "Because no greatness I achieve is mentally comforting if I am controlled by some sinister forces and all I can do is do what they direct me to. See, at this moment, I am speaking to my loving friend Samad, but it's actually you who is inside him and talking to me. Would I want to feel so helpless? Absolutely not. Plus, I've known a secret since I was a kid. An angel has directed me never to ever think about it. So, I know my decision is the right one."

The secret of the Enigma was finally out. It was finally time for Amir to divulge, as it was his farewell. It was the denouement.

"We all know you are not normal. To not even think of something is an impossible or onerous task to a normal mind or brain. Anyway, the decision is yours. Aleesha will make all the arrangements. You will travel to Jerusalem and do your pilgrimage there and wash away your sins and prepare for death. This is almost regicide."

"Are you from the others or a jinni?"

"As I told before, we are from the order of OM. I am from the parallel universe, a Jinn companion, or Qareen as you call, of the caretaker King of Jerusalem."

That was all he could say and soon started uttering jumbled sentences and after a short trance, Samad was back. Samad looked at him helplessly. "You are like a son to me." Samad said.

"I am, inasmuch as you are a guru to me." Amir said. "But don't worry. Even though we don't have the numbers to beat these others, I know a secret, one I will die with. We will achieve salvation soon."

After the conversation they went for dinner and Johnny joined them. It was a solemn occasion. They even spoke in hushed voices. The parties were going to be curtailed. They knew that this was their last meeting in physical form. Tears filled all their eyes as they ate silently.

Amir left the next day to attend to his work in Bombay. He had to hand over all the responsibilities to his younger brother, who had been the vice president of the company for a couple of years. After he finished the meetings in his office, Raju drove him to his hotel. On the way, Amir asked Raju to stop at the Gateway of India.

He got out and went and sat there, as he did more than thirty years back as an innocent child. The child dreamt a dream. He had passed the test of vigilance. Every time he thought of the dream he had, he would bring his Shen into his thoughts and divert his mind. He had an abnormally quiescent mind at times, and that was when the language without words spoke.

Sitting in the very spot where he sat as a child, it was time to reflect. Things didn't go as he had planned, but it was not his fault. The human race was hypnotized. When he looked back, he had achieved much materialistically and spiritually. He had had wonderful family, friends, and lovers. Most importantly he found his soul mate, his twin flame. The adventure was worth it. Now he was entering a different stage with a secret he knew. His spirit won't die. He would be the intermediary between the human and spirit world. but the Angel in his dream had told him that the barriers would be broken, and veils lifted only after years of contemplation and worship in various spots and may take years for him to be visible to the humans and communicate with them. Until then, he would be alone in this realm with angels and demons. The demons would try to disrupt his mediations and prolong his journey, while angels would protect him and try to provide him peace in order to shorten the trials and ascend higher spiritually. Amir would be restless, as he would be separate from Aleesha, and thus would try to complete his mission and return to the realm of the dead as soon as possible, when he had learned the language without words.

In his hotel room in Mumbai, he wrote his will and made a bequest of all his personal wealth for his mother.

A month later, Aleesha and Amir met in Maldives. Aleesha came directly from Greece after meeting her dad and family.

They got married in a small ceremony with a quite party. Amir's mother was enraged when he told her that he was getting married in a week's time and didn't want a grand party. He said that he was in his middle age and didn't need the extravagance. Finally, she obliged as she was happy that he was finally agreeing to start a family.

After the marriage they spent a night in a luxury private island and left for the honeymoon vacation next day. They took a flight to Delhi via Colombo. From there, they drove to Agra and visited the Taj Mahal. The symbol of love on earth. Then they made love in Rome and Paris, after which they would be going to Jerusalem. The final destination.

Amir always longed to be in Jerusalem. The land of the prophets. Fate had decided that it would be his final fantasy.

Jerusalem, Jerusalem,

O' city of peace,

The final coda,

With blood, I write,

Thus, this union,

Fatal shall remain.

Amir prayed in the Al Aqsa Mosque housing the dome of the rock in the Temple Mount, while Aleesha prayed in the Church of the Holy Sepulcher and at the wailing wall.

For three days and three nights, Amir was engaged in deep contemplation and worship. All his material desires had been washed away. The serenity that this city gave was unimaginable. It was serendipity. This was a union highlighted in bold, in the book of fate. A suppliant sinner asking for succor, he was where he belonged. He had a unique opportunity. A chastisement to wipe away his sins. His vain desires drifted away and the profundity of his love for the creator knew no bounds. He would die a thousand deaths to get the feeling he was getting, and tears trickled from his eyes and he wept. He wept like a child. Sought repentance for his every mistake. Thanked God for the wonderful life, life that now would be cut short, not because he didn't want to live or didn't have the courage to continue, but the child he was saw a dream and an Angel had guided him to make the correct decision when the time came. Just as Abraham was ready to sacrifice his son on the command of God, Amir was ready to make the ultimate sacrifice. Be the ultimate slave.

At the dawn of their fourth day in the old city, which was a Friday, Aleesha and Amir walked hand in hand up to the Temple mount. Gunshots were heard, an exchange of artillery.

The news channel reported that two tourists, five Palestinians, and one Israeli were killed in an exchange of fire between Israel armed forces and Palestinian armed fighters.

About the Author

Omar Zemin

Omar Zemin writes to share his thoughts and imagination with as many people as possible through his books, as he believes that we all share a common ground, despite the cultural and religious differences, ideologies and psychological mindsets.

Milton Keynes UK
Ingram Content Group UK Ltd.
UKHW032005230824
447235UK00001B/14